D1086854

THE
HOUSEMAID'S
SECRET

FREIDA McFADDEN

Published by Bookouture in 2023

An imprint of Storyfire Ltd.
Carmelite House
50 Victoria Embankment
London EC4Y 0DZ

www.bookouture.com

Copyright © Freida McFadden, 2023

Freida McFadden has asserted her right to be identified
as the author of this work.

All rights reserved. No part of this publication may be reproduced, stored in
any retrieval system, or transmitted, in any form or by any means, electronic,
mechanical, photocopying, recording or otherwise, without the prior written
permission of the publishers.

ISBN: 978-1-83790-132-6
eBook ISBN: 978-1-83790-131-9

This book is a work of fiction. Names, characters, businesses, organizations,
places and events other than those clearly in the public domain, are either the
product of the author's imagination or are used fictitiously. Any resemblance
to actual persons, living or dead, events or locales is entirely coincidental.

PROLOGUE

Tonight, I will be murdered.

Lightning flashes around me, illuminating the living room of the small cabin where I'm spending the night, and where my life will soon reach an abrupt end. I can just barely make out the wooden floorboards below, and for a split second, I imagine my body splayed out on those floorboards, a pool of red spreading beneath me in an uneven circle, seeping into the wood. My eyes open, staring into nothing. My mouth slightly ajar, a trickle of blood running down my chin.

No. *No.*

Not tonight.

Once the cabin goes dark again, I grope blindly in front of me, moving away from the comfort of the sofa. The storm is bad, but not bad enough to cut off the electricity. No, somebody else is responsible for that. Somebody who has already taken one life tonight and expects that I will be next.

It all started with a simple cleaning job. And now it might end with my blood being mopped off the cabin floor.

I wait for another flash of lightning to show me the way, then I move carefully in the direction of the kitchen. I don't have a plan in mind, but the kitchen contains potential weapons. There's an entire block of knives in there—short of that, even a fork might come in handy. With my bare hands, I'm a goner. With a knife, my chances might be slightly better.

The kitchen contains large picture windows that bring in a bit more light than in the rest of the cabin. My pupils dilate, straining to absorb as much as possible. I stumble toward the kitchen counter, but after taking three steps on the linoleum, my feet slide out from under me and I fall hard on the floor, cracking my elbow bad enough to bring tears to my eyes.

Although to be fair, there were already tears in my eyes.

As I attempt to scramble back to my feet, I realize that the kitchen floor is wet. Lightning flashes again, and I look down at my palms. They are both stained crimson. I didn't slip on a puddle of water or some spilled milk.

I slipped on blood.

I sit there for a moment, taking inventory of my body. Nothing is hurting. I'm still intact. That means the blood isn't mine.

Not *yet*, anyway.

Move. Move now. It's your only chance.

This time I am more successful in getting to my feet. I reach the kitchen counter, breathing a sigh of relief as my fingers make contact with the cold hard surface. I grope around for the block of knives, but I can't seem to find it. Where *is* it?

And then I hear the footsteps, growing closer. It's hard to judge, especially since everything is so dark, but I'm pretty sure there is now somebody in the kitchen with me. All the hairs on my neck stand up as a pair of eyes bore into me.

I am no longer alone.

My heart sinks into my stomach. I have made an incredibly bad judgment call. I have underestimated an extremely dangerous person.

And now I will pay the ultimate price.

PART I

ONE

MILLIE

Three Months Earlier

After an hour of scrubbing, Amber Degraw's kitchen is just about spotless.

Considering that, as far as I can tell, Amber seems to eat almost all her meals from restaurants in the area, it feels like the effort isn't quite necessary. If I had to put down money, I'd bet she doesn't even know how to turn her fancy oven on. She has a beautiful, enormous kitchen filled with appliances that I'm fairly sure she has never used even once. She has an Instant Pot, a rice cooker, an air fryer, and even something called a *dehydrator*. It seems somewhat contradictory that somebody who has eight different kinds of moisturizer in her bathroom also owns a dehydrator, but who am I to judge?

Okay, I judge a *little*.

But I have carefully scrubbed down every single one of these unused appliances, cleaned the refrigerator, put away several dozen dishes, and mopped the floor until it's shiny enough to almost see my reflection. Now all I have to do is put away the last load of laundry and the Degraws' penthouse apartment will officially be clean as a whistle.

"Millie!" Amber's breathless voice floats into the kitchen, and I wipe a bit of sweat off my forehead with the back of my hand. "Millie, where *are* you?"

"In here!" I call out. Even though it's fairly obvious where I am. The apartment—which has merged two adjacent apartments into one uber-apartment—is large, but it's not *that* large. If I'm not in the living room, I'm almost certainly in the kitchen.

Amber floats into the kitchen, looking her usual impeccably sleek self in one of her many, *many* designer dresses. This one is zebra printed with a plunging V-neck and sleeves that taper at her slender wrists. She's paired the dress with matching zebra-printed boots, and while she does look achingly beautiful as always, part of me is not sure if I should compliment her on her outfit or hunt her on safari.

"There you are!" she says with a hint of accusation in her voice, as if I'm not exactly where I'm supposed to be.

"I'm just finishing up," I tell her. "I'll just grab the laundry and—"

"Actually," Amber interrupts me, "I'm going to need you to stay."

I cringe internally. I clean for Amber twice a week, but I also do other errands for her, including babysitting for her nine-month-old daughter, Olive. I try to be flexible because the pay is fantastic, but she's not great at asking in advance. It feels like all my babysitting jobs here are on a strictly need-to-know basis. And apparently, I don't need to know until about twenty minutes before.

"I've got a pedicure," she says with all the gravity of somebody informing me that she will be heading to the hospital to perform heart surgery. "I need you to keep an eye on Olive while I'm gone."

Olive is a sweet little girl. I absolutely don't mind keeping an eye on her—usually. In fact, there are times when I would jump at the chance to earn a little cash at the exorbitant per-hour rate Amber gives me, which allows me to keep a roof over my head and eat food that isn't scavenged from a garbage can. But right now, I can't do it. "I have class in an hour."

"Oh." Amber frowns, then quickly makes her face blank again. She told me the last time I was here that she read an article about how smiling and frowning are the leading causes of wrinkles, so she's trying to make her expression as neutral as possible at all times. "Can't you skip it? Don't they have the lectures recorded? Or some transcript you could get?"

They don't. Furthermore, I have skipped two classes in the last two weeks because of last-minute babysitting requests from Amber. I've been trying to get my college degree, and I need a decent grade in this class. And anyway, I like the course. Social psychology is fun and interesting. And a passing grade is crucial for my degree.

"I wouldn't ask you," Amber says, "if it wasn't important."

Her definition of "important" may differ from mine. For me, "important" is graduating from college and getting that social work degree. I'm not sure how a pedicure could be that impor-tant. I mean, it's still the tail end of winter. Who's even going to *see* her feet?

"Amber," I start to say.

As if on cue, a high-pitched wail comes from the living room. Even though I'm not officially babysitting Olive right now, I usually keep an eye on her whenever I'm here. Amber takes Olive to a playgroup three times a week with her friends, and the rest of the time, she seems to be scheming ways to get Olive off her hands. She has complained to me that Mr. Degraw will not allow her to hire a full-time nanny because she herself does not work, so she pieces childcare together through a series of babysitters—mostly me. In any case, Olive was in her playpen when I started cleaning, and I stayed in the living room with her until the vacuum lulled her to sleep.

"Millie," Amber says pointedly.

I sigh and put down the sponge I've been holding; it feels like it has been melded to my hand lately. I wash my hands off in the sink, then I wipe them dry on my blue jeans. "I'm coming, Olive!" I call out.

When I get back into the living room, Olive has pulled herself up on the edge of the playpen, and she is crying so desperately that her little round face has turned bright red. Olive is the sort of baby that you might see on the cover of a baby magazine. She's so perfectly cherubic and beautiful, right down to the soft blond curls that are now smushed against the left side of her head from her nap. At the moment, she's not quite so cherubic, but when she sees me, she instantly lifts her arms and her sobs subside.

I reach into the playpen and heft her into my arms. She buries her little wet face in my shoulder, and I don't feel quite so bad about missing class if I have to. I don't know what it is, but the second I turned thirty, it was like some switch flipped on inside me that made me think babies are the most adorable thing in the entire universe. I love spending time with Olive, even though she's not *my* baby.

"I appreciate this, Millie." Amber is already tugging on her coat and grabbing her Gucci purse from the coat rack beside the door. "And believe me, my toes thank you."

Yeah, yeah. "When will you be back?"

"I won't be gone too long," she assures me, which we both know is a bald-faced lie. "After all, I know my little princess will miss me!"

"Of course," I murmur.

As Amber digs around in her purse for her keys or her phone or her compact, Olive nuzzles closer to me. She lifts her little round face and smiles up at me with her four tiny white teeth. "Ma-ma," she declares.

Amber freezes, her hand still inside her purse. All time seems to stand still. "*What* did she say?"

Oh no. "She said... Millie?"

Olive, oblivious to the trouble she is causing, grins up at me again and babbles louder this time, "Mama!"

Amber's face turns pink under her foundation. "Did she just call you *mama*?"

"No..."

"Mama!" Olive cries gleefully. *Oh my God, will you stop it, kid?*

Amber throws her purse onto the coffee table, her face twisted in a mask of anger that will almost certainly cause wrinkles. "Are you telling Olive that you're her mother?"

"No!" I cry. "I tell her I'm Millie. *Millie.* I'm sure she just gets confused, especially because I'm the one who..."

Her eyes widen. "Because you're around her more than I am? Is that what you were going to say?"

"No! Of course not!"

"Are you saying that I'm a *bad mother*?" Amber takes a step toward me, and Olive looks alarmed. "You think you're more of a mother to my little girl than I am?"

"No! Never..."

"*Then why are you telling her that you are her mother?*"

"I'm not!" My exorbitant babysitter pay is circling the drain. "I swear. *Millie.* That's all I'm saying. It sounds like mama, that's all. Same first letter."

Amber takes a deep, calming breath. Then she takes another step toward me. "Give me my baby."

"Of course..."

But Olive isn't making it easy. When she sees her mother coming toward her with outstretched arms, she clings to my neck tighter. "Mama!" she sobs into my neck.

"Olive," I mumble. "I'm not your mama. *That's* your mama." *Who is about to fire me if you don't let go of me.*

"This is so unfair!" Amber cries. "I breastfed her for over a week! Isn't that worth anything?"

"I'm so sorry..."

Amber finally wrenches Olive out of my arms, while Olive bawls her little head off. "Mama!" she screams as she reaches for me with her chubby arms.

"She's not your mama!" Amber scolds the baby. "I am. Do you want to see the stretch marks? That woman is *not* your mother."

"Mama!" she wails.

"Millie," I correct her. "*Millie.*"

But what's the difference? She doesn't need to know my name. Because after today, I'll never be allowed in this house ever again. I am *so* fired.

TWO

During my walk from the train station to my one-bedroom apartment in the South Bronx, I keep one arm firmly clutched around my purse, and the other holding the can of mace stuffed into my pocket, even when it's broad daylight. You can never be too careful in this neighborhood.

Today I feel lucky to even have my little apartment in the middle of one of the most dangerous neighborhoods in New York. If I don't find another job soon to replace the income I just lost after Amber Degraw let me go (with no offer of a reference), the best I could hope for is a cardboard box on the street outside the decrepit brick building where I currently live.

If I hadn't decided to go to college, I might have saved some money by now. But stupid me, I chose to try to better myself.

As I walk the final block to my building, my sneakers squishing against some slush on the pavement, I get the sensation that there's somebody behind me, following me. Of course, I'm always on high alert around here. But there are times when I strongly feel like I have attracted the wrong sort of attention.

For example, right now, in addition to a prickly feeling in the back of my neck, there are footsteps behind me. Footsteps that seem to be getting louder as I walk. Whoever is behind me is getting closer.

But I don't turn around. I just hug my sensible black coat tighter around my body and I walk faster, past a black Mazda with a cracked right headlight, past a red fire hydrant leaking water all over the street, and up the five uneven concrete steps to the door of my building.

I have my keys ready. Unlike in the Degraws' swanky Upper West Side apartment building, there is no doorman here. There is an intercom and there is a key to open the door. When the landlady, Mrs. Randall, rented me the apartment, she gave me a stern lecture about not letting anyone in behind me. *It's a good way to get robbed or raped.*

As I fit the key into the lock that always seems to stick, the footsteps grow louder again. A second later, there's a shadow looming over me that I can't ignore. I lift my eyes and identify a man in his mid-twenties, wearing a black trench coat, his dark hair mildly damp. He looks vaguely familiar—especially the scar over his left eyebrow.

"I live on the second floor," he reminds me when he sees the hesitation on my face. "Two-C."

"Oh," I say, although I'm still not thrilled about allowing him inside.

The man pulls a set of keys out of his pocket and jiggles them in my face. One of them has the same etchings as my own. "Two-C," he repeats. "Right below you."

I finally give in and step inside to allow the man with the scar over his left eyebrow to enter my building, considering he could easily push his way in if he wanted. I lead the way, trudging up the stairs one by one as I wonder to myself how the hell I am going to pay the rent next month. I need a new job—now. I had a part-time gig bartending for a little while, and I stupidly gave it up because babysitting for Olive paid so much better and the last-minute scheduling made juggling the second job difficult. And it's not like it's easy for somebody like me to find another job. Not with my history.

"Nice weather we're having," the man with the scar above his left eyebrow comments, following a step behind me on the stairs.

"Uh-huh," I say. The last thing I want is to talk about the weather right now.

"I heard it's going to snow again next week," he adds.

"Oh?"

"Yes. Eight inches are forecasted. One last hurrah before the spring."

I can't even attempt to feign interest anymore. When we get to the second floor, the man smiles at me. "Have a good day then," he says.

"You too," I mumble.

As he walks down the hall to his own apartment, I can't help but think about what he said to me when I let him in. *Two-C. Right below you.*

How did he know I live in Three-C?

I grimace and walk a little faster up the stairs to my own apartment. I've got the keys ready once again, and the second I'm inside, I slam the door shut behind me, turn the lock, and then throw the deadbolt. I'm probably making too much of his comment, but you can never be too careful. Especially when you live in the South Bronx.

My stomach is growling, but even more than food, I'm craving a hot shower. I make sure the blinds are drawn before I strip down and jump into the shower. I know from experience that there's a tiny range between the water shooting out boiling hot or ice-cold. In the time I've lived here, I've become an expert at adjusting the temperature. But it can drop or rise twenty degrees in a split second, so I don't linger too long. I just need to wash some of the grime off my body. After a day of walking around in the city, my body is always covered in a layer of black dust. I hate to think about what my lungs look like.

I can't believe I lost that job. Amber relied on me so heavily, I thought I'd be good at least until Olive was in kindergarten, maybe longer. I was almost starting to feel comfortable, like I had a steady job and an income I could rely on.

Now I have to search for something else. Maybe multiple other jobs to replace that one. And it's not as easy for me as most people. I can't exactly put an ad up on the popular childcare apps, because they all require a background check. And as soon as that happens, any job prospects are off the table. Nobody wants somebody like me working in their home.

At the moment, I'm a bit short on references. Because for a while, the cleaning jobs I took weren't exactly cleaning only. I used to do another service for several of the families I cleaned for. But I don't do that anymore. I haven't in years.

Well, no point in dwelling on the past. Not when the future looks so bleak.

Stop feeling sorry for yourself, Millie. You've been in worse situations than this and come out of it.

The temperature in the shower abruptly plummets, and I let out an involuntary shriek. I reach for the faucet and shut the water off. I got in a good ten minutes. Better than I even expected.

I wrap my terrycloth bathrobe around me, not bothering with a pair of slippers. I track little wet footprints into the kitchen, which is just an offshoot of the living room. In the Degraws' uber-apartment, their kitchen and living room and dining room were all separate spaces. But in this apartment, they have all merged into one single multipurpose room, which is ironically much smaller than any of the rooms at the Degraws'. Even the bathroom there is bigger than my entire living space.

I put a pot of water on the stove to boil. I don't know what

I'm going to make for dinner, but it's probably going to involve some sort of noodle being boiled in water, be it of the ramen or spaghetti or spiral noodle variety. I am examining my options when I hear pounding at the door.

I hesitate, tightening the belt of my robe around my waist. I pull a box of spaghetti out of the cabinet.

"Millie!" The voice sounds muffled behind the door. "Let me in, Millie!"

I wince. Oh no.

Then: "I know you're in there!"

THREE

I can't ignore the man banging on the door.

My feet leave a trail of wet footprints behind as I cross the few yards to my door. I bring my eye close to the peephole. A man is standing in front of my door, his arms folded across the breast pockets of his Brooks Brothers business suit.

"Millie." The voice has become a low growl. "Let me in. *Now*."

I take a step back from the door. For a moment, I press my fingertips against my temples. But this is inevitable—I have to let him in. So I reach out, open the deadlock, turn the lock, and carefully crack open the door.

"Millie." He pushes the door the rest of the way open and slides into my home. His fingers encircle my arm. "What the hell?"

My shoulders sag. "Sorry, Brock. "

Brock Cunningham, who I have been dating for the last six months, shoots me a look. "We had dinner plans tonight. You didn't show up. And you haven't been answering your messages or picking up your phone."

He is correct on all counts. I am pretty much the worst girlfriend ever. Brock and I were supposed to meet at a restaurant in Chelsea after I finished my classes for today, but after Amber fired me, I could barely focus on my class—and I definitely didn't feel like having dinner out—so I just went straight home. But I knew if I called Brock and told him I didn't want to go, he would have felt compelled to talk me into it—and as a lawyer, he is super convincing. So I had this plan to send him a text message to cancel, but I kept postponing it, and I was so busy feeling sorry for myself, I then completely forgot.

Like I said, worst girlfriend ever.

"I'm sorry," I say again.

"I was *worried* about you," he says. "I thought something terrible might have happened to you."

"Why?"

A deafening siren goes off right outside the window, and Brock gives me a look like I've asked a very stupid question. I feel a jab of guilt. Brock probably had a ton to do tonight, and not only did I make him wait at the restaurant for me like an idiot, but now he has wasted the rest of his night coming all the way out to the South Bronx to make sure I'm okay.

At the very least, I owe him an explanation.

"Amber Degraw fired me," I say. "So basically, I'm screwed."

"Really?" His eyebrows shoot up. Brock has the most perfect eyebrows I have ever seen on a man, and I'm convinced he must get them professionally shaped, but he won't admit to such a thing. "Why did she fire you? I thought you said she couldn't function without you. You said you're basically raising her child."

"Exactly," I say. "Her kid wouldn't quit calling me mama and Amber freaked out."

Brock stares at me for a moment, and then unexpectedly, he bursts out laughing. At first, I'm offended. I just lost my job. Doesn't he get how crappy this is?

But then a second later, I find myself joining in. I throw my head back and laugh at how ridiculous the whole thing was. I remember Olive reaching for me and sobbing "mama" while Amber got madder and madder. By the end, I seriously thought Amber was going to pop an aneurysm in her brain.

After a minute, the two of us are both wiping tears from our eyes. Brock puts his arms around me and pulls me closer to him, no longer angry about me standing him up. Brock doesn't get angry easily. Most people would count that among his good qualities, although there are times when I wish he would show a little more passion.

In general, though, we are in the sweet spot for our relationship. Six months. Is there any better time in a relationship than six months? I genuinely don't know because this is only the second time I have reached that landmark. But it seems like six months is that perfect time when you shed the early relationship awkwardness, but you're still showing each other your best side.

For example, Brock is a handsome thirty-two-year-old lawyer from a well-to-do family. He seems just about perfect. I'm sure Brock has bad habits, but I don't know what they are. Maybe he cleans the earwax out of his ear canal with his finger and then wipes it on the kitchen counter or the sofa. Or maybe he *eats* the earwax. I'm just saying, there are a lot of bad habits he might have that I don't know about, some of them not even involving earwax at all.

Well, he does have *one* imperfection. Despite the fact that he's a strapping young man whose face is flushed with good health, he actually has a heart condition that he developed as a child. But it doesn't seem to affect him at all. He takes a pill every day and that seems to be the extent of it. But the pill is important enough that he keeps a spare bottle in my medicine cabinet. And his illness and uncertainty about his life expectancy have made him a little more eager to settle down than most guys.

"Let me take you out to dinner," Brock says. "I want to cheer you up."

I shake my head. "I just want to stay home and feel sorry for myself. And then maybe look online for jobs."

"Now? You only just lost your job a few hours ago. You can't wait at least until tomorrow?"

I raise my eyes to glare at him. "Some of us need money to pay the rent."

He nods slowly. "Okay, but what if you didn't need to worry about the rent?"

I have a bad feeling I know where this is going. "Brock..."

"Come on, why don't you want to move in with me, Millie?" He frowns. "I've got a two-bedroom apartment overlooking Central Park, in a building where you won't get your throat slit during the night. And you come over all the time anyway..."

It's not the first time he has suggested moving in with him, and I can't say he doesn't make a persuasive argument. If I moved in with Brock, I would be living in the lap of luxury and I wouldn't have to pay a dime for it. He wouldn't even let me contribute if I wanted to. I could focus on getting my college degree so I could become a social worker and do some good in the world. It seems like a no-brainer.

But every time I consider telling him yes, a voice in the back of my head screams: *Don't do it!*

The voice in my head is just as persuasive as Brock's. There are a lot of good reasons to move in with him. But there's one good reason not to. He has no idea who I really am. Even if he really is eating his own earwax, my secrets are much worse.

So here I am, in the most normal and healthy relationship of my adult life, and it seems like I am determined to screw it all up. But I am in a bit of a bind. If I tell him the truth about my past, he might leave me, and I don't want that. But if I don't tell him...

One way or another, he's going to find out everything. I'm just not ready for that.

"I'm sorry," I say. "Like I said, I need my own space right now."

Brock opens his mouth to protest, but then he thinks better of it. He knows me well enough to know how stubborn I can be. See? He's already learning some of my worst qualities. "At least tell me you'll think about it."

"I'll think about it," I lie.

FOUR

I've got my tenth job interview in the last three weeks, and I'm starting to get nervous.

I don't even have enough money in my bank account to cover one month's rent. I know you're supposed to have a six-month buffer in the bank, just in case, but that works better in theory than in practice. I'd love to have a six-month buffer in the bank. Hell, I'd love to have a *two*-month buffer. Instead, I've got less than two hundred dollars.

I don't know what I did wrong in the other nine interviews for cleaning or babysitting positions. One of the women outright assured me that she was planning to hire me, but it's been a week and I haven't heard a peep from her. Or any of the others. I'm assuming she did a background check and that was the end of it.

If I were any other person, I could simply join some sort of cleaning service, and I wouldn't have to go through this process. But none of them will hire me. I've tried. The background checks make it impossible—nobody wants someone with a criminal record inside their home. That's why I put up ads online and hope for the best.

I don't have much hope for today's interview either. I'm meeting a man named Douglas Garrick, who lives in an apartment building on the Upper West Side, just west of Central Park. It's one of those Gothic buildings with mini towers rising out of the skyline. It vaguely looks like it should be surrounded by a moat and guarded by a dragon, instead of being a place that you can just walk into right off the street.

A doorman with white hair holds the front door open for me with a tip of his black cap. As I smile up at him, once again I get that prickling sensation in the back of my neck. Like somebody is watching me.

Ever since that night I came home after getting fired, I've gotten that sensation several times. It made sense in my neighborhood in the South Bronx, where there are probably muggers on every corner waiting to jump out if I looked like I had any money at all, but not here. Not in one of the swankiest neighborhoods in Manhattan.

Before I step into the apartment building, I whirl around to look behind me. There are dozens of people milling about on the street, but none of them are paying attention to me. There are plenty of unique and interesting people walking around the streets of Manhattan, and I'm not one of them. There's no reason for anyone to be staring at me.

Then I see the car.

It's a black Mazda sedan. There are probably thousands of cars just like it in the city, but when I look at it, I get this weird sense of déjà vu. It takes me a second to realize why. The car has a cracked right headlight. I'm certain that I saw a black Mazda with a right cracked headlight parked near my apartment building in the South Bronx.

Didn't I?

I peer through the windshield. The car is empty. I lower my gaze to look down at the license plate. It's a New York plate—nothing exciting there. I take a moment to memorize the number: 58F321. The plate number means nothing to me, but if I see it again, I'll remember it.

"Miss?" the doorman asks me, jerking me out of my trance. "Will you be coming inside?"

"Oh." I cough into my hand. "Yes. Yes, sorry about that."

I step into the lobby of the building. Instead of overhead lights, the lobby is lit by chandeliers and lamps on the sides of the walls that are meant to resemble torches. The low ceiling curves into a dome, which makes me feel slightly like I'm entering a tunnel. Works of art adorn the walls, all of which are likely priceless.

"Who are you here to see, Miss?" the doorman asks me.

"The Garricks. Twenty-A."

"Ah." He winks at me. "The penthouse."

Oh great—a penthouse family. Why do I even bother?

After the doorman calls upstairs to confirm my appointment, he has to go into the elevator and insert a special key so that I can get up to the penthouse. After the elevator doors swing shut, I do a quick inventory of my appearance. I smooth out my blond hair that I have pulled back into a simple bun. I'm wearing my nicest pair of black slacks and a sweater vest. I start to adjust my boobs, but then I notice that there's a camera in the elevator, and I'd rather not give the doorman a show.

The doors to the elevator open directly into the foyer of the Garricks' penthouse apartment. As I step out of the elevator, I take a deep breath, and I can almost *smell* the wealth in the air. It's some combination of expensive cologne and crisp hundred-dollar bills. I stand in the foyer for a moment, not sure if I should venture out without being formally welcomed, so instead, I focus my attention on a white podium displaying a gray statue that is essentially just a large smooth vertical stone—one that you could find in any park in the city. Despite that, it's probably worth more than everything I've ever owned in the entire world.

"Millie?" I hear the voice seconds before a man materializes in the foyer. "Millie Calloway?"

It was Mr. Garrick who invited me to the interview today. It's unusual to be called by the man of the house. Almost 100 percent of my primary employers in the cleaning business have been female. But Mr. Garrick seems eager to greet me. He rushes into the foyer, a smile on his lips, his hand already extended.

"Mr. Garrick?" I say.

"Please," he says as his strong hand slides into mine, "call me Douglas."

Douglas Garrick looks exactly like the sort of man who would be living in a penthouse on the Upper West Side. He's in his early forties and handsome in that classic, chiseled sort of way. He's wearing a suit that looks extremely expensive, and his dark brown hair is glossy and expertly cut and styled. His deep-set brown eyes are shrewd and make just the right amount of eye contact with mine.

"Nice to meet you... Douglas," I say.

"Thank you so much for coming today." Douglas Garrick flashes me a grateful smile as he leads me into the expansive living room. "My wife Wendy usually does the housework—she takes pride in trying to do it all herself—but she hasn't been feeling well, so I insisted on getting some help."

His last statement strikes me as strange. Women who live in huge penthouse apartments like this generally don't "try to do it all" themselves. Usually, women like this have maids for their maids.

"Of course," I say. "You mentioned you're looking for cooking and cleaning...?"

He nods. "General housekeeping stuff, like dusting, tidying, and laundry, of course. And meal preparation a few nights a week. Do you think that would be a problem?"

"Not at all." I'm willing to agree to just about anything.

"I've been cleaning apartments and houses for many years. I can bring my own cleaning supplies and—"

"No, that won't be necessary," Douglas interrupts me. "My wife... Wendy is very particular about cleaning supplies. She's sensitive to smells, you see. It triggers her symptoms. You need to use our special cleaning products, or else..."

"Absolutely," I say. "Whatever you'd like."

"Wonderful." His shoulders relax. "And we would need you to start right away."

"That's not a problem."

"Good, good." Douglas smiles apologetically. "Because, as you can see, this place is a bit of a mess."

As I step into the living room, I take in my surroundings. Much like the rest of the building, this penthouse makes me feel like I've been transported into the past. Aside from the gorgeous leather sofa, most of the furniture looks like it was constructed hundreds of years ago and then frozen in time to be specially transported to this living room. If I knew more about home décor, I might be able to pinpoint that the coffee table was hand carved in the early twentieth century or that the bookcase with the glass doors came from, I don't know, the French neoclassical revival period or something like that. All I can say for sure is that every item cost a small fortune.

And another thing I know is that this apartment is not a mess. It's the opposite of a mess. If I were to start cleaning, I'm not even sure what I would do. I would need a microscope to find a speck of dust.

"I'm happy to start whenever you want," I say carefully.

"Fantastic." Douglas nods in approval. "I'm so pleased to hear that. Why don't you have a seat so we can chat further?"

I sit down beside Douglas on the sectional, sinking deep into the soft leather. Oh my God, this is the nicest thing I've ever felt against my skin. I could leave Brock and just marry this sofa instead, and all my needs would be met.

Douglas stares at me intently with his deep-set eyes beneath a pair of thick dark brown eyebrows. "So tell me about yourself, Millie."

I appreciate from the start that there's no hint of flirtation in his voice. His eyes stay respectfully pinned on mine and don't drift down to my boobs or my legs. I've gotten involved with my employer only one time before, and I will never, ever go down *that* road again. I'd rather yank my own tooth out with a pair of pliers.

"Well." I clear my throat. "I'm currently a student at the community college. I'm planning to become a social worker, but in the meantime, I'm paying my way through school."

"That's admirable." He smiles, showing off a row of straight, white teeth. "And you have experience with cooking?"

I nod. "I've cooked for a lot of the families I work for. I'm not a professional, but I've taken a couple of classes. I also..." I glance around, unable to see any toys or signs of a child living here. "I babysit?"

Douglas flinches. "No need for that."

I wince, cursing my big mouth. He never mentioned babysitting. I probably reminded him of some horrible infertility problems. "Sorry," I say.

He shrugs. "No worries. How about a tour?"

The Garricks' penthouse puts Amber's uber-apartment to shame. This penthouse is an entirely different *species* of apartment. The living room is at least the size of an Olympic swimming pool. The corner contains a bar with half a dozen vintage barstools set up around it. Despite the antiquated theme of the living room, the kitchen has all of the latest appliances, including, I'm sure, the best dehydrator on the market.

"This should have everything you need," Douglas tells me as he sweeps a hand across the vast expanse of the kitchen.

"Looks perfect," I say, crossing my fingers that the oven

comes with some sort of manual to explain what each of the two dozen buttons on the display is supposed to do.

"Excellent," he says. "Now let me show you the second floor."

Second floor?

Apartments in Manhattan do *not* have two floors. But apparently, this one does. Douglas takes me on a tour of the upstairs, leading me to at least half a dozen bedrooms. The master bedroom is so large that I need a pair of binoculars to see the king-size bed at the other end of the room. There's one room that is entirely books, and I am vaguely reminded of that scene in *Beauty and the Beast* when Belle is taken into the book room. Another room seems to include a wall full of pillows. I guess that's the pillow room.

After he takes me into a room that contains what must be an artificial fireplace, and one entire wall is a huge window with a breathtaking view of the New York City skyline, we come to one final door. He hesitates, his fist poised to knock.

"This is our guest bedroom," he tells me. "Wendy has been in here recovering. I probably should let her rest."

"I'm sorry to hear your wife is ill," I say.

"She's been sick for most of our marriage," he explains. "She suffers from a... a chronic illness. She has good days and bad days. Sometimes she's her usual self, and then other days she can barely get out of bed. And other days..."

"What?"

"Nothing." He offers a weak smile. "Anyway, if the door is closed, just leave her alone. She needs her rest."

"I completely understand."

Douglas stares at the door for a moment, a troubled expression on his face. He touches the door with his fingertips, then he shakes his head.

"So, Millie," he says, "when can you start?"

FIVE

In 1964, a woman named Kitty Genovese was murdered.

Kitty was a twenty-eight-year-old bartender. She was raped and stabbed at approximately three in the morning about a hundred feet from her Queens apartment. She screamed for help, but while several neighbors heard her cry, nobody came to her aid. Her attacker, Winston Moseley, left her briefly and returned ten minutes later, at which point he stabbed her several more times and stole fifty dollars from her. She died from her knife wounds.

"Kitty Genovese was attacked, raped, and murdered in front of thirty-eight witnesses," Professor Kindred announces to the lecture hall. "Thirty-eight people saw her attack, and not one person came to her aid or called the police."

Our professor, a man in his sixties with hair that always seems to be sticking up, looks at each and every one of us, accusation in his eyes like we were the thirty-eight people who left that woman to die. "This," he says, "is the bystander effect. It's a social psychology phenomenon in which individuals are less likely to offer help to a victim when there are other people present."

The students in the room are scribbling in their notes or typing on their laptops. I just stare at the professor.

"Think about it," Professor Kindred says. "Over three dozen people allowed a woman to be raped and murdered, and they just watched and did nothing. This perfectly demonstrates diffusion of responsibility in a group."

I squirm in my seat, imagining what I would do in that situation—if I looked out my window and saw a man attacking a woman. I wouldn't sit back and do nothing, that's for damn sure. I would jump right out the window if I had to.

No. I wouldn't do that. I have learned to control myself better than that. But I would call 911. I would go outside and bring a knife with me. I wouldn't do anything with it, but it might be enough to scare off an attacker.

I still feel shaken thinking about that poor girl who was killed over half a century ago when I emerge from the lecture hall. When I get out onto the street, I almost walk right past Brock. He has to chase after me and grab my arm.

Of course. We made dinner plans.

"Hey." He grins at me with the whitest teeth I have ever seen. I've never asked him if he gets them professionally whitened, but he must. Teeth can't naturally be that white—it's inhuman. "We're celebrating tonight, right? Your new job."

"Right." I manage a smile. "Sorry."

"Are you okay?"

"I'm just... I'm shaken from the lecture I just had. We were learning about this woman in the '60s who was raped in front of thirty-eight bystanders, who did nothing. How could something like that happen?"

"Kitty Genovese, right?" Brock snaps his fingers. "I remember it from my own college psychology class."

"Right. And it's awful."

"It's bullshit though." He slides his hand into mine. His palm feels warm. "The story was sensationalized by the *New*

York Times. There were way fewer witnesses than the *Times* reported. And based on where the apartments were, most of them couldn't see what was really happening and thought it was just a lovers' quarrel. And a bunch of them *did* call the police. I think she was being cradled by one of her neighbors when the ambulance came."

"Oh." I feel slightly inadequate, the way I often do when Brock knows more about something than I do. Which happens a lot, actually. As far as I can tell, the guy knows just about everything. It's one of the many things that makes him so perfect.

"It's not as sensational a story though, is it?" Brock lets go of my hand and throws an arm around my shoulders. I catch a glimpse of our reflection in a store window, and I can't help but think we look good together as a couple. We look like the kind of couple that would invite five hundred guests to our wedding and then get a house with a white picket fence out in the suburbs and then proceed to fill it with children. "Either way, you shouldn't feel bad about something that happened decades ago. You're just... You're just a little too nice, you know?"

I've always had this itch to help people who are in trouble. Unfortunately, it gets *me* into trouble sometimes. If only I were as nice as Brock thinks I am—he has no idea. "Sorry, I can't help it."

"I guess that's why you want to become a social worker." He winks at me. "Unless I can talk you into a more lucrative career."

My last boyfriend was the one who convinced me to follow the career path to social work—so I could help people in need while staying within the confines of the law. *You need to help everyone, Millie. It is what I love about you.* He really understood me. Unfortunately, he's not around anymore.

"Anyway." Brock squeezes my shoulders. "Let's not think about women who were murdered in the '6os. Tell me about your new job."

I fill him in on the details of the impressive Garrick pent-house. When I tell him about the view, the location, and the second floor, he lets out a low whistle.

"That apartment must've cost a fortune," he says, as we step into the street, narrowly avoiding being sideswiped by a bike. As far as I can tell, bikers in the city have absolutely no regard for traffic lights or pedestrians. "I bet they paid like twenty million. At least."

"Wow. You think?"

"Definitely. They better be paying you well."

"They are." When Douglas discussed the hourly rate, I almost felt dollar signs popping up in my eyeballs.

"What did you say the guy who hired you was called?"

"Douglas Garrick."

"Hey, he's the CEO of Coinstock." Brock snaps his fingers. "I met him once when he hired my firm to help with a patent. Genuinely nice guy."

"Yeah. He seemed nice."

He did seem nice. But I can't stop thinking about that closed door on the second floor. The wife who couldn't even come out to meet me. As excited as I am about this job, some-thing about that makes me uneasy.

"And you know what else?" Brock pulls me into a crosswalk —the light is flashing, about to turn red, and we make it across just in time. "The building is only like five blocks away from where I live."

Hint, hint.

I knew about the proximity of the penthouse to Brock's apartment, of course. I squirm, feeling just as uncomfortable as I did in the classroom. Brock has become a dog with a bone. He wants me to move in with him, and he won't seem to let it go. I just can't seem to shake the feeling that if he really knew me, he wouldn't want that. I love being with Brock, and I don't want to ruin it.

"Brock..." I say.

"Okay, okay." He rolls his eyes. "Look, I don't mean to pressure you. If you're not ready to move in, that's fine. But for the record, I think we make a good team. And you spend half your nights at my place anyway, right?"

"Uh-huh," I say in the most noncommittal way possible.

"Also..." He flashes those pearly whites at me. "My parents would like to meet you."

Okay, now I'm going to throw up. Even though he's been bugging me to move in with him, it still didn't occur to me that he would have told his parents about me. But of course he did. He probably calls them once a week, on Sunday at 8pm, and fills them in on all the pertinent details of his perfect life.

"Oh," I say weakly.

"And I'd like to meet your parents as well," he adds.

This might be a great time to tell him I'm estranged from my parents. But the words don't come.

This is so hard. That last guy I dated knew everything about me from the start, so I never had to reveal my complicated past —there was never a terrifying moment where I laid everything out on the table. And like I said, Brock is so... perfect. The only things about him that aren't perfect are little insignificant details, like once he left the toilet seat up at my apartment. And even that is something he's only done once.

The problem with Brock is that he's ready to settle down. And even though I'm the same age, I'm not there yet. He doesn't want to wait either. He's got a great job at the top law firm, and he makes more than enough to support a family. Even though his last cardiology visit gave him a clean bill of health, he worries that he's not going to live out the expected lifespan for a Caucasian man in this country. He wants to get married and have kids while he can still enjoy it.

Meanwhile, I feel like I'm still in the process of growing up.

I'm still in school, after all. I'm not ready to get married. I just...
I can't.

"It's okay." He stops walking for a moment to look at me—a
man walking behind us almost collides with us, and he curses as
he goes on his way. "I don't want to rush you. But you need to
know, I'm crazy about you, Millie."

"I'm crazy about you, too," I say.

He takes both my hands in his as he stares into my eyes.
"Actually, I kind of love you."

My heart speeds up a bit. He's told me before that he's crazy
about me, but he's never told me he loved me before. Even with
a "kind of" modifier.

I open my mouth, not entirely sure what I'm going to say.
But before any words can come out, I get that prickling sensation in the back of my neck.

Why do I feel like somebody's watching me? Am I losing
my mind?

"Well," I finally say, "that's kind of sweet."

I'm not ready to say it back. I can't take that next step in our
relationship when there's so much about me that Brock still
doesn't know. Thankfully, he doesn't push the issue.

"Come on," he says. "Let's go get some sushi."

At some point, I probably also need to tell him that I don't
like sushi.

SIX

It's my first day working for the Garricks.

Douglas has already told the doorman to let me in, and left me a copy of the key so I'm able to insert it into the slot in the elevator. The elevator creaks and groans as it makes its way up twenty stories. Well, nineteen stories. Even though the apartment is Twenty-A, the building is missing the thirteenth floor. No bad luck here.

The gears in the elevator grind to a screeching halt as I reach my destination. Once again, the doors swing open to the Garricks' impressive apartment. Despite the fact that Douglas says they'll require my services several times a week, the apartment hardly seems to need it. It's dusty, like every apartment in the city gets, but other than that, it's relatively tidy.

"Hello?" I call out. "Douglas?"

No answer.

I try again: "Mrs. Garrick?"

I venture into the living room, which once again makes me feel like I've wandered into a home from a century or two ago. I would never be able to afford even one piece of this antique furniture, even if I spent my life's savings. Most of my own furniture came from the curb outside my apartment building.

I walk to the mantle that is positioned over what must be a faux fireplace. There are about half a dozen photographs lined up. Each of them features Douglas Garrick and a stick-thin woman with long auburn hair. There is one of them on a ski slope, another post in formal clothing, and another in front of what looks like a cave. I study the woman, presumably Wendy Garrick. I wonder if I'll meet her anytime soon or if she'll stay locked up in that room every time I come over. I have no problem with that though—I have had plenty of clients that I never laid eyes on the entire time I was cleaning for them.

A loud thump echoes from upstairs and I jump away from the mantle. I don't want anyone to think I've been snooping. That would definitely not be a good introduction to Wendy Garrick.

I back away from the mantle, looking over at the foot of the stairs. Nobody is on the stairwell, and I don't hear any footsteps. It doesn't look like anyone is coming.

I decide to get started on the laundry. Douglas pointed out the wicker basket where they keep their dirty laundry in the master bedroom. Once the washer is going, I can start tackling some of the other chores.

I head up the polished wooden stairs to the massive master bedroom. In the walk-in closet, I locate the large wicker basket Douglas showed me the other day. But when I open up the laundry hamper, I am stunned.

In my time doing other people's laundry, I've seen a lot of crazy things. I've seen laundry that didn't quite make it into the hamper and instead was scattered in a circle surrounding the hamper. I've seen every kind of stain from chocolate to oil to a few stains I'm pretty sure were blood. But I've never seen this before.

All the dirty laundry is *folded*.

I stare at it for a moment, trying to figure out if I got it wrong. Maybe this is laundry that has already been done and needs to be put away. Because why would dirty laundry be folded?

But this is the laundry hamper Douglas showed me. So I have to assume it must be dirty laundry.

I grab the hamper and haul it out of the master bedroom. Just as I'm heading down the hallway to the washer and dryer units, I notice that the guest bedroom door is cracked open.

"Mrs. Garrick?" I call out.

I squint at the crack in the door. I can just barely make out a green eye. Staring at me.

"I'm Millie." I start to raise my hand and then realize it's not going to be possible while holding the laundry hamper, so I put it down. "I'm your new cleaner."

I start to walk toward the door, my hand outstretched, but before I can even get halfway there, the open crack vanishes. The door has snapped shut.

Okay...

I understand some people aren't terribly social, and *especially* don't like to be social with the cleaning staff. But couldn't she at least have said hi? Just so I'm not standing here in the middle of the hallway awkwardly?

Then again, it's her house. And Douglas told me she has an illness. So I'm not going to bully her into meeting me.

Although would it really be terrible if I knocked on the door and just told her my name?

But no—Douglas told me not to bother her. So I won't. I'll finish up the laundry, make them dinner, and then I'll be on my way.

SEVEN

After I get the laundry going and tidy up a bit upstairs (although admittedly, there's not much to do), I go down to the kitchen to tackle dinner.

Thankfully, there is a list on the refrigerator door that has been left for me. It's a printed menu for the week, including recipes and specific instructions on how to get groceries. Some of the writing is by hand—it looks to be more feminine handwriting, but it's hard to say. As I read the instructions, I start to become less and less enthusiastic about my job:

> *Pate must be purchased on Tuesday from Oliver's Delicatessen prior to 4pm.*
>
> *If only terrine is available, do not purchase. In this case, purchase pate from Francois.*
>
> *Pate should be served on peasant bread obtained from the London Market. Take one slab and spread gently. Top with cornichon, obtained from Mr. Royal.*

All I can think is, what the hell is pate? And what's *cornichon*? At least I know what bread is. Except why do I have to go to four stores to buy these three items? And is Mr. Royal a person or a place?

On the plus side, little is left to the imagination. The recipes are sorted by date, so I simply find today's date and I get started on tonight's dinner of...

Cornish game hen. Okay, this will be interesting.

Two hours later, I have put away the laundry. The Cornish game hen is cooking in the oven, and it smells quite nice if I do say so myself. I have already put out two place settings in the dining room, so now I'm just standing in the kitchen, twiddling my thumbs and waiting for the food to be ready. Hopefully, that will coincide with mealtime, which is a strict 7pm.

Just as I'm opening the oven to look in on the hen, the elevator doors grind open—you can hear them a mile away. Heavy footsteps come down the hallway, growing louder. "Wendy!" It's Douglas's voice echoing through the apartment. "Wendy, I'm home!"

I step over to the entrance of the kitchen and look out at the stairwell to the second floor. I wait for a moment, listening for the sounds of the door to the guest bedroom opening, hopeful I'll finally get to catch a glimpse of the infamous Mrs. Garrick, but I hear nothing.

"Hello." I wipe my hands on my jeans as I come out of the kitchen. "Your dinner is just about ready—I promise."

Douglas is standing in the living room, his eyes on the stairwell. "Excellent. Thank you very much, Millie."

"You're welcome." I follow his gaze up the stairs. "Do you want me to fetch Mrs. Garrick?"

"Hmm." He looks down at the two place settings on the Victorian style oak dining table, which looks like where the queen herself might have been served dinner. "I have a feeling she won't be joining me tonight."

"Should I bring a plate upstairs for her?"

"No need. I'll bring it to her." He flashes a lopsided smile. "She's still feeling under the weather, I'm sure."

"Of course," I murmur. "Let me get the food out of the oven."

I hurry back into the kitchen to check on the food. I pull a Cornish game hen out of the oven, and it looks pretty amazing. I mean, considering I've never cooked it before and haven't even heard of it before except in a completely theoretical way.

It takes me another ten minutes to cut the stupid thing according to the specific instructions, but finally, I've got two beautiful plates of food. I carry them out to the dining room, just in time to see Douglas descending the flight of stairs.

"How is she doing?" I ask him as I set the plates down on the dining table.

He's quiet for a moment as if considering my answer. "It's not a good day. "

"I'm so sorry."

He lifts a shoulder. "It is what it is. But thank you for your help today, Millie."

"No problem. Would you like me to bring Mrs. Garrick's plate up to her?"

I don't know if it's my imagination, but Douglas's lips tighten at my suggestion. "You already offered, and I said I would do it, didn't I?"

"Yes, but..." I stop myself before I say anything stupid. He thinks I'm being nosy, and he's not entirely wrong. "Anyway, have a good evening."

"Yes," he says vaguely. "Good night, Millie. Thanks again."

I grab my coat and head over to the elevators. I hold my breath, waiting for the elevator doors to slam shut, then my shoulders sag. I don't know what it is, but there's something about that apartment that makes me uneasy.

EIGHT

"Maybe," Brock says, "she's a vampire. And she can't come out of her room during the daylight hours or else she will turn to dust."

I have told Brock all about the Garrick family, and over a post-dinner cocktail at his apartment, he is offering some very *un*helpful explanations for why I have been over there half a dozen times, and Wendy Garrick has not once come out of that guest bedroom even though I'm certain she's inside. That one time the door cracked open is the closest I've ever come to seeing her.

"She's not a vampire," I say, shifting my legs under me on Brock's sofa.

"You don't know that."

"I do. Because vampires aren't real."

"A werewolf then?"

I smack Brock in the arm which almost makes him spill the glass of wine he's holding. "That doesn't even make sense. Why would she need to stay in her bedroom if she's a werewolf?"

"Okay, then maybe..." he says thoughtfully. "Maybe she's

got a little green ribbon around her neck, and if someone unties it, her head will fall off?"

I take a sip of the expensive wine Brock poured for me. The expensive bottles are by far better than the cheap ones, but I can never detect all the subtle notes of honeydew or lavender or whatever. He keeps asking me, and now I'm lying and telling him that I can tell, but I really can't. I'm *faking* wine.

"I just get a weird vibe," I say. "That's all."

"Well, I've told you all of my best ideas." He puts his arm around me, bringing me closer to him. "So if it's not a vampire, a werewolf, or a severed head, what do *you* think is going on?"

"I..." I set my wine glass on the coffee table and chew on my lower lip. "Honestly, I have no idea. It's just a bad feeling."

Brock seems distracted for a moment, looking at my mostly full glass sitting on the table. "You're not finishing that?"

"I don't know. I guess not."

"But that's a Giuseppe Quintarelli," he says, as if that explains absolutely anything.

"I guess I'm not thirsty."

"Thirsty?" He looks traumatized by my statement. "Millie, you don't drink wine because you're thirsty."

"Okay." I pick up the glass and take another sip. Sometimes I wonder why he's even dating me, other than because he says he thinks I'm pretty. He acts like he's so lucky to be with me. But that's crazy. I'm not the catch—he is. "You're right. This is really good."

I finish the rest of the glass of wine, but the truth is, the whole time I'm thinking about the Garricks.

NINE

I have gotten into the habit of listening every time I pass the guest bedroom door.

It's snooping. I know it is—I won't deny it—but I can't help myself. I have been working for the Garricks for one month, and I still have not officially met Wendy Garrick. But I have heard noises coming from that room. And on at least three occasions, I have noticed the door cracked open. But each time, it swung shut before I could manage to introduce myself.

It would not be an understatement to say my imagination is running wild. I have seen a lot of strange things in my years cleaning houses. A lot of bad things too. For a while, I used to try to fix some of those bad things. But I haven't done that in a long time.

Not since Enzo took off.

This time as I'm walking down the hall, I definitely hear something coming from the guest bedroom. Usually, it's pretty quiet in there, so this is something different. I pause, vacuum in my hand, and press my ear against the door. And this time I can hear the sound much more clearly.

It's crying.

Someone is sobbing in there.

I promised Douglas that I wouldn't knock on the door. But for some reason, Kitty Genovese pops into my head. Even if Brock says the whole story was an over-exaggeration, I do know that bad things happen when normal people walk on by.

So I rap my knuckles against the door.

Instantly, the crying ceases.

"Hello?" I call out. "Mrs. Garrick? Are you all right?"

There's no answer.

"Mrs. Garrick?" I say again. "You okay?"

Nothing.

I try a different tactic: "I'm not leaving until I see you're all right. I'll stay here all day if I have to."

And then I stand there and wait.

After a few seconds, I hear soft footsteps behind the door. I take a step back as the door cracks open about two inches until I can see that green eye staring out at me. Sure enough, the white of the eye is marred by red veins and the eyelid is puffy.

"What. Do. You. Want?" the owner of the eye hisses at me.

"I'm Millie," I speak up. "Your cleaner."

She doesn't respond to that.

"And I heard crying," I add.

"I'm fine," she says tightly.

"Are you sure? Because I—"

"I'm sure my husband told you I'm not feeling well." Her tone is clipped. "I just want to rest."

"Yes, but—"

Before I can say another word, Wendy Garrick shuts the door in my face. So much for reaching out to her. At least I tried.

I trudge back down the stairs, lugging the vacuum with me. I'm wasting my time even trying to get involved. Every time I bring it up to Brock these days, he tells me I need to mind my own business.

I'm busy putting away the vacuum cleaner when the elevator doors grind open. Douglas comes into the living room, whistling under his breath, wearing another one of his painfully expensive suits. He's holding a bouquet of roses in one hand and a blue rectangular box in the other.

"Hi, Millie." He seems strangely chipper, considering his wife is sobbing upstairs. "What's going on? Almost finished?"

"Yes..." I'm not sure if I should tell him what I heard upstairs. But if his wife is crying, he would want to know, right? "Your wife seems a little down. I heard her crying in the bedroom."

Splotches of red appear on his cheekbone. "You didn't... talk to her, did you?"

I'm not inclined to lie, but at the same time, he did explicitly tell me not to bother Wendy. "No, of course not."

"Good." His shoulders relax. "You should just leave her alone. As I said, she's not well."

"Yes, you did say that..."

"And..." He holds up the blue rectangular box. "I've got a gift for her." He puts down the flowers so he can open the velvet box, and he holds it up to me so that I can take a peek inside. "I think she's going to love this."

I look down at the contents of the box. It is the most beautiful bracelet I've ever seen, studded with flawless diamonds.

"It's inscribed," he says proudly.

"I'm sure she'll love it."

Douglas snatches up the flowers and heads up the stairs. I watch him disappear down the hallway, then the sound of a door opening and closing.

I can't quite figure this one out. Douglas seems like a wonderful and devoted husband. Wendy, on the other hand, never leaves her bedroom. She may come out when I'm not around, but I've never even seen her entire face, except in the photographs.

There's something abnormal about this situation, and I don't know what it is.

But like Brock says, it's none of my business. I should just leave it alone.

TEN

Will you be over tonight?

Even though I already arranged with Douglas to come over to the penthouse tonight to bring groceries and clean, he always confirms with a text message. He's extremely organized. Considering what they're paying me, I always respond right away.

Yes, I'll be there!

I don't have any class today, so my afternoon will consist of going shopping for the Garricks, then heading over to their house to clean their invisible dirt and cook dinner. I've been working for their household for well over a month now, and I know the routine. I've got the shopping list in my hand, but I need to head into Manhattan to get everything they want.

Brock asked me to stay over last night, and I have been spending a lot of nights there, because he does live so close to the penthouse and fairly close to the college, but that's all the more reason to say no. If I'm at his apartment any more frequently, I'll basically be living with him. And that's something I can't do.

Not yet, anyway. Not until I tell him the truth. He deserves that much.

But I'm scared. I'm scared Brock will freak out and dump me on the spot if he knows everything about me. And I'm even more scared that when his wealthy, upper-class parents find out, they'll talk him into dumping me. Brock is perfect, and his family is perfect, and I am so far from perfect, it's not even funny.

My last relationship was the opposite of perfect. And somehow that felt better suited for me. I'm not sure what it says about me that my perfect match was a guy like Enzo Accardi.

Enzo and I started four years ago as friends, after a job of mine ended extremely unexpectedly. I didn't have a lot of friends, so I was obscenely grateful for the support he gave me. We got to the point where we were spending almost all our free time together, and on top of that, we helped about a dozen women escape from their abusive relationships. A lot of the time, it would just involve getting the proper resources for them, but other times we had to be creative. Enzo made connections that allowed him to obtain new identification, burner phones that couldn't be traced, and plane tickets to places far away. We got women out of their toxic relationships without having to resort to violence.

Well, no, that's not true. If I'm being entirely honest, there were a few times when things got a little... messy. Enzo and I agreed never to speak of those times ever again. We did what we had to do.

It was Enzo who talked me into going back to college to get a social work degree. Little did I know, he was putting me on the path to a normal life that I never dreamed was possible for me. Even with my prison record, I could still get a social work job. I could do what I loved within the confines of the law.

Brock likes to say he and I are a good team. Maybe that's true. But Enzo and I really *were* a good team: we *worked* together. We had a mission. On top of that, he was kind, passionate, and hot as hell. Especially that last one—as much as I tried to be his friend, it was hard not to be acutely aware of his more superficial attributes. At the time, I hated the fact that I was developing a frustrating crush on the man.

Then one night, I was at his apartment, sharing a box of pizza delivered from our favorite restaurant (also coincidentally the cheapest). We got our favorite toppings on the pizza: pepperoni and extra cheese. I remember Enzo taking a long swig from his bottle of beer and smiling in my direction. *This is nice,* he said.

Yes, I agreed. *It is nice.*

He plopped his beer down on the coffee table. After all the houses I cleaned, I felt a little bit of giddiness whenever somebody didn't use a coaster. *I like spending time with you, Millie.*

I didn't have a lot of experience with men, but the way he was looking at me was unmistakable. And if I had any doubts, they were abolished when he leaned in and gave me a long, lingering kiss that I knew I would dream about for years to come. And when our lips finally separated, he whispered, *Maybe we spend more time together?*

What else could I say but yes? No woman could refuse a request like that from Enzo Accardi.

It's funny because I always thought of Enzo as a bit of a player, but after that first kiss, he only had eyes for me. Our relationship moved fast, but it all felt very right. Within a few weeks, we were spending every night together, and soon after, we decided to live together. The two of us just clicked. Between school and my relationship with Enzo, I was the happiest I had ever been in my life.

I still remember the day it all fell apart.

We were sitting on our sofa, which Enzo had hauled in from

the curb in front of our apartment building, but it was still very nice and usable (with only one stain that we couldn't identify, but it was fine because we just turned that cushion over). He had one muscular arm slung around my shoulders and we were watching *The Godfather II*, because Enzo was recently horrified to discover I hadn't watched the trilogy. *Is classic, Millie!* I remember cuddling up against him, thinking how happy I felt and also that my boyfriend was way hotter than Robert DeNiro.

And then his phone rang.

The conversation that ensued was entirely in Italian, and I strained my ears, trying to pick up a word or two. *Malata*, he kept saying over and over. I finally typed it into my phone, which translated the word for me:

Sick.

After he hung up, he explained the situation to me with the heavy accent he sometimes got when he was stressed or angry. His mother had had a stroke. She was in the hospital. He had to go back to Sicily to see her, especially since his father and sister were both gone, and he was the only one she had left. I was confused because he always told me he could never go back home. Before he left, he had beaten a very powerful man half to death with his bare hands, and now there was a price on his head.

You told me you couldn't go back, I reminded him. *You said there were bad people who would kill you if you went back. Isn't that what you said?*

Yes, yes, he said. *But that is not a problem anymore. Those bad people... they were taken care of by other bad people.*

What could I say? I couldn't tell my boyfriend that he wasn't allowed to see his own mother after she'd just had a stroke. So I gave him my blessing, and he flew out to see her a day later. After I accompanied him to the airport and he kissed me for like five straight minutes before going through security, he promised he'd be back "very soon."

I hadn't counted on him never coming back.

I'm sure he meant to come back—he wouldn't have lied to me intentionally. In the early days, we talked on the phone every night, and it got pretty steamy at times. He would whisper into the phone how much he missed me and how we would be together again soon. But as his mother's illness dragged on, it became more and more obvious that he could not leave. And she could not come here.

I hadn't touched him or seen his face in an entire year when I finally asked him outright: *Tell me the truth. When are you coming back?*

He let out a long sigh. *I do not know. I can't leave her, Millie.*

And I can't wait forever, I told him.

I know, he said sadly. And then: *I understand what you must do.*

And that was it. That was the end. Just like that, we were over. So when a couple of months later, Brock asked me out, there was no reason to say no.

With Enzo, my life was some sort of exciting adventure, but now I'm on my way to the perfect, normal life I had never thought was possible for me. Brock doesn't know any guys who could dig up a fake passport in twenty-four hours—I imagine if I asked something like that of him, he would look at me in utter shock.

Enzo knew a guy for *everything*. That was practically his catch phrase when I asked him for help. *I know a guy.*

And now I am performing the most normal task there is. Going grocery shopping. Although to be fair, there's nothing normal about the list of items that Douglas has tasked me to obtain. As I check out the first few items on the list Douglas Garrick texted me this morning, I cringe at the scavenger hunt he is sending me on:

Buddha's hand

Fiddleheads

Cucamelon

Poha berries

I swear to God, he must be making these names up off the top of his head. *Cucamelon*? That's not a real thing, is it? Definitely sounds made up.

Clutching the grocery list, I grab my jacket and head down the stairwell. I have no idea how long it's going to take me to find a cucamelon, or even figure out what a cucamelon is, so I'd better give myself some time.

Just as I reach the landing for the ground floor, I almost run smack into that man who lives right below me. *Directly* below me. The one with the scar over his left eyebrow. I cringe when I see him.

"Hey." He grins at me. He's got a gold tooth for his left second incisor that makes me think of Joe Pesci in *Home Alone* —my favorite movie as a kid. "In a hurry?"

"Yes." I smile apologetically. "Sorry."

"No worries." His smile widens. "I'm Xavier, by the way."

"Nice to meet you," I say, pointedly avoiding giving him my own first name.

"Millie, is it?"

Well, that strategy failed. I get an uneasy feeling in my stomach—this man both knows exactly where I live and somehow knows my first name. Probably my last name too. Of course, he could have easily figured it out from our mailboxes.

I'm still intermittently getting the feeling that I'm being watched. There are times when I think it might be all in my head, but at this moment, I'm not so sure. Xavier knows just a little bit too much about me. Is it possible that he's...?

God, I can't think about this possibility right now. It's scary enough walking down the streets of the South Bronx without worrying that the guy who lives below me is stalking me. Maybe I should take Brock up on his offer to move in with him. Xavier will probably leave me alone if I relocate to the Upper West Side. And if he doesn't, he'll have to contend with the doorman in a little suit and hat. You don't get past one of those doormen. I think they can use those hats as boomerangs if they need to.

"What are you up to today?" Xavier asks me.

I move in the direction of the exit. "Just some grocery shopping."

"Oh yeah? Want some company?"

"No, thanks."

Xavier looks like he has more to say, but I don't give him a chance to say it. I push past him and out the door. Whether I end up with Brock or not, I might have to move in the near future. I don't feel comfortable around this man. I have a bad feeling he's the kind of guy who doesn't know how to take no for an answer.

ELEVEN

When I reach the Garricks' penthouse, I've got four overflowing grocery bags in my arms. I was doing fine juggling them until the last block, when I came close to dropping everything. But through the grace of God, I am here, cucamelon and all. (They are a real thing and I was able to find them at a Spanish produce store.)

Thankfully, I don't have to fiddle with the doorknob because the elevator doors swing open and I'm able to walk right inside. I was hoping to make it to the kitchen in one straight shot, but halfway there, I have to drop all the bags on the floor and take a break. If I dropped the cucamelon and it broke, I think I would have to sit down on the floor and cry.

While I'm standing in the living room, trying to figure out the best strategy for getting the groceries to the kitchen, I hear it.

Shouting.

Well, muffled shouting. I can't hear any actual words, but it sounds like somebody in the upstairs bedroom is really going at it. Leaving the groceries behind, I creep closer to the stairwell to see if I can hear what's going on. And that's when I hear the crash.

It sounds like shattering glass.

I put my hand on the banister of the stairwell, ready to climb the stairs and make sure everything is okay. But before I can take even a single step, a door slams upstairs. Then footsteps grow louder on the stairwell, and I take a step back.

"Millie." Douglas stops short at the bottom of the stairs. He's wearing a dress shirt and his face is pink like his tie is tied a bit too tightly, even though it's loose around his neck. He's holding a gift bag in his right hand. "What are you doing here?"

"I..." I look over at the four bags of groceries. "I bought groceries. I was going to put them away."

He narrows his eyes. "Then why aren't you in the kitchen?"

I offer a sheepish smile. "I heard a crash. I was worried that..."

As I say the words, I notice a rip in the fabric of his fancy dress shirt. And not a rip like a seam came loose. He has an angry tear right above the breast pocket.

"Everything's fine," he says shortly. "I'll take care of the groceries. You can leave."

"Okay..."

I can't take my eyes off the tear in his shirt. How did that happen? The man works as a CEO—no heavy labor involved. Could it have happened just now, up in the guestroom?

"Also..." He holds out the gift bag in his right hand. "I need you to return this for me. Wendy didn't want it."

I accept the small pink gift bag. I catch a glimpse inside of silky fabric. "Okay, sure. Is the receipt in here?"

"No, it was a *gift*."

"I... I don't think I can return it without a receipt. Where did it come from?"

Douglas grits his teeth. "I don't know—my assistant picked it out. I'll email you a copy of the receipt."

"If your assistant picked it out, wouldn't it be easier if she returns it?"

He cocks his head at me. "Excuse me, but isn't your *job* to run errands for me?"

I jerk my head back. This is the first time since I started working here that Douglas has spoken to me with such disrespect. I always thought he seemed like a nice enough man, albeit stressed and distracted. Now I realize there's another side to him.

Although isn't there another side to everyone?

Douglas Garrick is staring at me. He expects me to leave, but every fiber of my being is telling me that I should stay. That I should check upstairs and make sure everything is all right.

But then Douglas steps between me and the stairwell. He folds his arms across his chest and raises his thick eyebrows at me. I am not getting past that man, and even if I did, I have a feeling if I knocked on the door of the guest bedroom, Wendy Garrick would assure me that she's fine.

So in the end, there's nothing I can do except leave.

TWELVE

As I make the five-block journey from the subway station to my apartment building, I get that prickly feeling in the back of my neck once again.

When I feel it in Manhattan, in the swanky area where I am employed and where my boyfriend lives, it feels like I'm being paranoid. But now, in the South Bronx, when the sun has already dropped in the sky, paranoia is good common sense. I don't dress for attention. I'm wearing a pair of blue jeans that are at least a size too big, a pair of gray Nikes that once used to be white, and a coat that is more bulky than stylish—a dark color meant to blend into the night—but at the same time, I am clearly a woman. Even with the beanie stuffed on my blond hair and my ugly puffy coat, most people would peg me as a woman from all the way down the block.

So I pick up my pace. Also, I've got a can of mace in my pocket. My fingers are wrapped around it. But the feeling doesn't go away until I have entered the building and closed the door behind me.

That's the thing. I *never* get that prickly feeling when I am in my apartment. I don't get it when I am cleaning at the penthouse. I only get it when I'm outdoors, at a time when someone really could be watching me. It makes me think that the sensation is real.

Or I'm going crazy. That's a possibility too.

Brock texted me to ask if I wanted to come over to his house tonight, and I told him no. I'm too tired.

I push thoughts of Brock out of my mind as I pull a few letters out of my mailbox—all bills. How is it possible that I have so many bills? It feels like I subsist on practically nothing. In any case, I'm stuffing the letters into my purse when the lock turns on the door to the building. A second later, there's a burst of cold air and that man with the scar over his left eyebrow pushes his way inside.

Xavier. That's what he said his name is.

"Hi, Millie," he says, too cheerfully. "How are you doing?"

"Fine," I say stiffly.

I turn on my heel and head for the stairwell, hoping he'll lag behind and check his own mail. No such luck. Xavier hurries after me, trying to stay and step next to me.

"Any plans for tonight?" he asks me.

"Nope," I say, as I sprint up the steps to the second floor. That's when I'll be able to say goodbye to Xavier.

"You could come over," he says. "Watch a movie."

"I'm busy."

"No, you're not. You just said you had no plans for tonight."

I grit my teeth. "I'm tired. I'm just going to take a shower and go to bed."

Xavier grins at me so that his one gold tooth shines in the dim overhead lights of the stairwell. "Want some company with that?"

I turn away from him. "No, thank you."

We reached the landing for the second floor, and I expect Xavier to go on his way. But instead, he continues climbing the stairs next to me. My stomach turns and I reach into my pocket to feel for my can of mace.

"Why not?" he presses me. "Come on. You can't really like that preppy rich kid who always visits you here. You need a real man."

This time, I ignore him. In one minute, I will be at my apartment. I just have to make it that far.

"Millie?"

Five more steps. Five more steps to climb, and I'll be rid of this asshole. Four, three, two...

But then a hand grabs my arm, fingers biting into me.

I'm not going to make it.

THIRTEEN

"Hey." Xavier's meaty hand is wrapped tightly around my arm. "Hey!"

I squirm, but his grip is like a vise—he's stronger than he looks. I open my mouth, ready to scream, but he presses his palm against my lips before any sound can come out. The back of my head slams against the wall, rattling my teeth.

"So now you got something to say?" He smirks at me. "Before you thought you were too good for me though. Isn't that right?"

I try to shake him off, but he's pressing his body against me so that I can feel the bulge in his pants. He licks his cracked lips. "Let's go inside and have some fun, okay?"

He made the mistake of grabbing the wrong arm though. I pull out the can of mace and close my eyes as I empty it right in his face. He screams, and then the second I let go of the nozzle, I shove him as hard as I can.

I've always complained about how steep the stairs are in this building, but for once, it works to my advantage as Xavier tumbles down the flight of stairs. At one point, I hear a sickening crack, then a thud as he lands at the bottom. And then silence.

For a moment, I stand at the top of the stairs, staring down at the body sprawled out at the next landing. Is he dead? Did I kill him?

I sprint down the steps, skidding to a halt at the bottom. The can of mace is still in my right hand as I bend down to get a closer look. His chest looks like it's still rising and falling, and then he lets out a low groan. He's still alive. I didn't even knock him entirely unconscious.

Too bad. If anyone deserved a broken neck, it's this guy.

No. It's probably better he's not dead.

Impulsively, I pull back my foot and then kick him as hard as I can in the ribs. He moans louder this time. *Definitely* still alive. I kick him one more time for good measure. And then a third for the road. Every time my sneaker makes contact with his ribs, I smile to myself.

I look down at the next flight of steps. He survived the first flight. I wonder what would happen if he fell down a second flight of stairs. Or maybe a third. He doesn't even look that heavy. I bet I could roll him over and...

No. God, what am I thinking?

I can't do this. I spent ten years in prison. I'm not going back there.

I take out my phone and dial 911. I'm going to get my justice, and it won't be by killing this man.

FOURTEEN

An hour later, the police and an ambulance are parked outside our apartment building. It's not incredibly unusual to see a police car parked on our street, but this time the lights are flashing.

I had hoped they would take Xavier directly to jail, but he had a broken arm, a concussion, and possibly a few broken ribs. By the time the police got here he was starting to become more coherent and even trying to get up. Good thing they arrived, or else I would've had to find something else to knock him out with.

I was annoyed none of my neighbors came out to assist me. Whatever Brock said about that incident with Kitty Genovese, I can say with certainty that a man tried to rape me in the hallway of my apartment building, and not one person came to my assistance. What is wrong with people? Seriously.

A policewoman asked me a few questions when they first came, but then they asked me to go wait in my apartment while they took care of things. So that's what I've been doing. I called Brock and told him that a neighbor tried to attack me, although I was vague on the details of how I escaped. He's on his way, but

I'm not going anywhere until I make a formal statement that will get Xavier thrown in jail as soon as they take care of his broken arm. I hope the bastard needs surgery.

From the window, I get a good look at the ambulance driving away. I've been watching everything since they told me to go back upstairs. The police have been talking to a few of my neighbors out there, and they were talking to Xavier in the back of the ambulance a long time before they took him away. A few of the police officers are still talking out front. I can't even imagine what there is to talk about. A man attacked me seconds away from my own door. It feels pretty cut and dry.

And then one of the officers points up at my window.

A second later, one of the cops enters the building, and I back away from the window. I rub my sweaty hands on my jeans. There's still a red mark on my arm from where Xavier grabbed me, and the back of my head throbs slightly from where it banged against the wall, but he's in much worse shape than I am.

That's what he deserves.

A second after the pounding on my door starts, I yank it open. The officer standing there is in his thirties or so, with too much stubble on his chin and a slightly bored expression. Like this is the fifth guy he's dealt with tonight who tried to rape a woman on the stairs outside her front door.

"Hello," he says. "Are you Wilhelmina Calloway?"

I wince at the use of my full name. "That's right."

"I'm Officer Scavo. Can I come in?"

Back when I was in prison, all the women would say that if a policeman asks to come into your house, you have the right to say no. *Don't let those assholes inside.* But then again, they're not here to investigate me. I compromise—I let him inside, but we don't sit down.

This is a different cop than the one I talked to right after the incident. That one was a female, and she hugged me. I don't think this guy is going to hug me. I don't even want him to.

"So I gotta go over what happened tonight," Scavo says, "between you and Mr. Marin."

"Fine." I wrap my arms across my chest, suddenly cold, even though the heat is actually working for a change. "What do you want to know?"

Scavo looks me up and down. "Was that what you were wearing tonight during the incident?"

I don't know what he's talking about. He's saying it like I am dressed inappropriately. I'm wearing a T-shirt and the same blue jeans I had on earlier. The T-shirt is slightly snug, but not anything that would attract attention. As if that would even matter. "Yes, but I was wearing a coat over it."

"Uh-huh." Scavo makes a face like he doesn't quite believe me. Like I was seducing Xavier with my super sexy T-shirt and baggy blue jeans. "So tell me exactly what happened."

I repeat the story for the third time tonight. It's easier this time. My voice doesn't shake when I describe the way he grabbed me. I hold up my wrist as evidence to show Scavo the red marks, although he looks decidedly unimpressed.

"And that's it?" he says. "He just grabbed your arm?"

"No." I clench my fists in frustration. "I *told* you. He grabbed me and he pushed against me."

"Like, how?"

"Like he shoved his body against mine!"

He frowns. "Is it possible you misread the whole thing? Like maybe he was just being friendly?"

I stare at him.

"Because here's the thing, Miss Calloway." Scavo levels his gaze at me. "Mr. Marin is saying he was just making friendly conversation with you, and you freaked out. You sprayed him with mace and then pushed him down the stairs."

"Are you kidding me?" Right now I want to spray Officer

Scavo with mace and push him down the stairs. "That's not what happened at all! Do you seriously believe that? You're taking *his* side?"

"Well, one of your neighbors saw you standing over him, kicking him repeatedly in the ribs. She was afraid to come out."

I open my mouth, but all that comes out is a squeak.

"We think Mr. Marin has a couple of broken ribs," the officer continues. "And we have a witness who saw you kicking him in the ribs while he was unconscious on the ground. So tell me what I'm supposed to think."

I really, really wish I hadn't kicked Xavier in the ribs. But it was so tempting. And I know how painful rib fractures can be. "I was just upset."

"Why were you upset? Mr. Marin thinks you were upset because you were flirting with him and he wasn't responding. He said that's why you attacked him."

I feel like somebody just sucker punched me in the gut. Or the ribs. "I attacked *him?*"

Scavo raises an eyebrow. "And you do have a prison record, don't you, Miss Calloway? A history of violent behavior?"

"This is bullshit," I gasp. "That man attacked me. If I hadn't defended myself..."

"So here's the thing," he says, "it's just your word against his that he attacked you, and a witness saw you kicking him while he was on the floor. And he's the one with all the broken bones."

My legs wobble underneath me. I suddenly wish we had decided to sit down for this conversation. "Am I under arrest?"

"Mr. Marin has not yet decided whether to press charges at this time." Scavo makes a face like he thinks my attacker absolutely should press charges. Like he wishes he could snap a pair of handcuffs on me right now. "So until he makes up his mind, I suggest you stay local."

I hate this man. What happened to the female officer? The

one who hugged me and told me that Xavier would never be able to hurt me again? Where did *she* go?

With those words, I lead Officer Scavo back to the door. When I open it up, Brock is standing there in his work clothes—a sky-blue dress shirt and tan slacks—his hand poised to knock. Scavo smirks when he sees him, but he doesn't comment. Brock looks like he wants to ask the officer something, but thankfully, Scavo seems in a hurry to leave.

I manage to keep it together until I have pulled Brock into the apartment and locked the door behind him. It's only then that the tears jump to my eyes. Except they're not tears of sadness. They are tears of *fury*. How *dare* he speak to me that way? I was attacked in my own building, and somehow my *attacker* is the victim?

"Millie." Brock wraps his arms around me. "Jesus Christ, are you okay? I got here as quickly as I could."

I nod wordlessly as I pull away. If I speak, I won't be able to hold back the tears. And for some reason, I don't want to cry in front of Brock.

"I hope that asshole goes to prison for a long time," he says.

I should tell him what happened. What that officer said to me. But if I do, I'll have to explain why. I have to explain my history of violence. About my prison record. About all the reasons why nobody believes me.

If Enzo were here, it would be different. I could tell him everything. And he would get it. There *would* be a small chance he would rip Xavier Marin limb from limb with his bare hands, but I'd be okay with that—more than okay. When I look at Brock, the thought of him doing something similar makes me almost laugh out loud. But on the plus side, if Xavier does get me charged with assault, Brock could defend me. Yes, that would be super good for our relationship.

"You can't possibly sleep here," Brock says. For once, I

completely agree with him. "I've got my car parked right outside. Let me take you back to my place."

My shoulders sag. "Okay."

"And you should stay with me," he says. When he sees the look on my face, he quickly adds, "I'm not saying you should move in. But take like a week's worth of clothing. Maybe start looking for another place to live."

I don't have it in me to argue with him right now, and he's right. If Xavier comes back to this building, I can't live here anymore. I'll have to find a new place. Although I can barely afford the rent on this apartment, even with the money the Garricks are paying me. Am I going to have to find an even worse neighborhood in the Bronx?

Anyway, I'll think about it later. Right now, I need to pack.

FIFTEEN

The master bedroom in the Garricks' house is so large; if I spoke, I swear there would be an echo.

I'm putting away a pile of laundry. I would have thought the two of them get most of their clothing dry cleaned, but given Wendy never seems to leave the bedroom, I don't suppose she dresses in things that require dry cleaning very often. Based on what I'm seeing go through the wash, she mostly wears nightgowns. Right now, I'm folding a delicate white nightgown with lacing at the collar, which looks like it would come down to Wendy's ankles, based on her height during the one almost conversation we had.

And that's when I see it.

At the collar of the nightgown, there's a stain. An irregular stain that is brown layered with red, now ground into the fabric. I've seen stains like that before while doing laundry. It's unmistakable.

It's blood.

Not only that, it's a fair bit of blood. Right at the neckline, bleeding into the fabric below. I close my eyes, unable to keep from thinking about what the cause of this blood could have been.

My eyes pop open again at the sound of my phone ringing. I take it out of the pocket of my jeans, and my heart sinks. The screen identifies the call as coming from the police station in the Bronx. It doesn't feel like this is going to be good news.

Well, they probably wouldn't arrest me by phone.

"Hello?" I say as I sit on the side of the Garricks' bed, which is roughly the size of an ocean liner.

"Wilhelmina Calloway? This is Officer Scavo."

My stomach turns—the sound of that policeman's name makes my skin crawl. "Yes?"

"I've got good news for you."

If this man is still on the case, there's no good news. But maybe I should try to be optimistic. At this point, I am owed a win. "What?"

"Mr. Marin decided not to press charges," he says.

That's the good news? I squeeze the phone so hard my fingers start to tingle. "What about me? I want to press charges."

"Miss Calloway, we have a witness that saw you attacking him." He clears his throat. "You're lucky this is the only outcome. If you were still on parole, you'd be going right back to prison right now. Of course, he could always bring civil charges against you."

I swallow a lump in my throat. "So where is he right now?"

"He was released this morning."

"You released him from jail this morning?"

Scavo sighs. "No, he was never under arrest. He was released from the hospital this morning."

That means he'll be back at the apartment building tonight. Which means I can't ever go back there.

"Listen, lady," Scavo says, "you got lucky this time, but you need to be seeing some kind of shrink. Get your anger issues under control. Or else you're going to end up right back in prison."

"Thanks for the tip," I say through my teeth.

Just as I hang up, I look up and realize I'm not alone in the master bedroom. At the other end of the bedroom, standing in the doorway, is Douglas Garrick. Wearing an Armani suit with a red power tie, his dark brown hair slicked back as always.

I wonder how much of that conversation he heard. Of course, it would only be bad if he heard Scavo's end.

"Hello, Millie," he says.

I scramble back to my feet and shove my phone into my pocket. "Hi. Sorry, I... I was just doing laundry.

He doesn't challenge my assertion with the fact that I was talking on the phone. Instead, he wanders into the room, loosening his red tie with his thumb. He pulls off his jacket and tosses it onto the top of the dresser.

"Well?" he says.

I look at him blankly.

"Are you going to leave my jacket just lying there on the dresser?"

It takes me a second to realize what he wants me to do. His closet is about six feet away from us, and it would have been easy enough for him to hang up his own jacket, but instead, he is leaving it for me. Fair enough, since it's my job, but there's an edge to his voice that makes me uneasy. I've been noticing it more and more during my interactions with him.

"I'm so sorry," I mumble. "I'll hang that up for you."

Douglas Garrick watches me fiddling with his jacket, studying me carefully. I googled him the other day, but there isn't much about him—not even a decent photo. He's apparently an extremely private person. All I could figure out is that he's the CEO of a very large company called Coinstock, like Brock said. He's some kind of tech genius who invented a piece of software used by practically every bank in the country. Brock had told me he seemed like a nice guy, but you don't really know somebody just from a business interaction. Douglas seems like a man who is skilled at turning up the charm when he needs to.

"Are you married?" Douglas asks me.

I freeze at the question, his jacket halfway onto the hanger. "No..."

One corner of his lips quirks up. "Boyfriend?"

"Yes," I say tightly.

He doesn't comment on my answer, but his eyes rake over me until I start to squirm. It doesn't matter how handsome he is —I don't appreciate him looking at me that way. When we first met, I was impressed by how he kept his eyes to himself but I guess that was just for show. If he keeps looking at me like that...

Well, there's not much I can do about it, I guess. Not after a police officer just accused me of assaulting a man.

I'm about to verbally redirect his eyes to my face when his gaze finally comes to rest on the white nightgown still laid out on the king-size bed. He's staring at the blood stain on the collar. Maybe it's my imagination, but I'm certain I hear a sharp inhalation of breath.

"Well." I look down at the nightgown, then back at Douglas. "If you'll excuse me, I need to look up how to get tomato sauce stains out of fabric."

He stares at me for another moment, then thankfully nods in approval. "Good. You do that."

But I don't need to google anything. I already know how to get blood stains out of fabric.

SIXTEEN

Brock and I are having dinner together, but I can't focus on one word he is saying.

The weather has warmed up, and we got an outdoor table at a cute little Middle Eastern restaurant in the East Village. Brock looks devastatingly handsome in his suit from work, and I put on a new sundress. While we eat our entrees, Brock is telling me all about one of his clients, and usually I feel happy to be spending an afternoon with my amazing boyfriend. I'm always slightly amazed that somebody like Brock would take an interest in somebody like me, and ordinarily, I would be hanging on his every word (even though he's talking about patent law, which is honestly kind of boring). But today, my head isn't in the game.

Because I've got that prickling feeling in the back of my neck again. Like somebody is watching me.

I should have told Brock I wanted to eat inside. I don't feel safe anymore with Xavier out on the streets. I don't know why he has chosen to target me, but it's been a week since he attacked me, and I frequently feel those eyes boring into me. I'd like to think it's my imagination, but I'm not so sure. Even with a broken arm—even in another *borough*—Xavier could still be trailing me around.

"Don't you think so, Millie?" Brock says.

I look up at him blankly. I'm holding my fork in my right hand and I've stabbed a cube of lamb, but I don't think I've taken a bite in at least ten minutes. "Huh?" I say lamely.

Brock's eyebrows bunch together and the little patch of skin between them crinkles up in a way I usually find cute, but right now I find it annoying. "Are you okay?"

"Yes," I lie.

He accepts my answer without question. I've noticed that, especially for a lawyer, Brock is very trusting. Anyone else probably would have interrogated me about my past, but he isn't like that. It's a relief that I don't have to tell him everything, but sometimes I wish he would press me. Because I'm tired of keeping all the secrets from him.

Brock and I met during a brief period when I thought I might be interested in some sort of legal career, before I realized that my background would make it difficult, if not impossible. The community college set up an opportunity for me to shadow him, although on the first day, Brock admitted in a sheepish voice, *My job isn't very exciting.* I had imagined going to courtrooms, but instead, he mostly just did paperwork. While I watched.

I'm sorry, he told me at the end of our week together. *I'm sure you were expecting something different.*

That's okay, I told him. *I didn't want to be a lawyer anyway.*

Let me make it up to you. I'll treat you to dinner.

Later, Brock admitted he had been trying to think of a way to ask me out the entire week. The truth is, I almost said no. I was still feeling sorry for myself after Enzo told me he had no intention of coming back to the States, and I didn't feel like getting my heart broken a second time. But then I imagined the beautiful Italian women hitting on my ex-boyfriend, and I decided, what the hell. Why shouldn't I get to have a little fun, too?

Brock has been a good boyfriend. With every passing week, I am searching for his fatal flaw, but he remains frustratingly perfect. And when he found out they didn't charge Xavier with assault, he looked appropriately angry. He offered to come with me to the police station and speak to the officer in charge of the case. An offer I had to decline for obvious reasons.

And then he just let it go. I haven't been able to stop thinking about it all week, but Brock has moved on, although he has repeatedly stated the obvious: I need to find another place to live.

"You look a little pale," Brock notes.

I rub the back of my neck, then I turn around to look behind me. I'm certain that I'm going to come face to face with Xavier, but nobody is there. At least, I don't see him. But he's definitely out there.

"Let's move in together," I blurt out.

Brock pauses in the middle of a sentence. He's got a tiny blob of tahini sauce in the corner of his mouth. "What?"

"I think we're ready," I say. That's another lie. I don't feel ready to move in with Brock, but I also have absolutely no intention of ever going back to my apartment in the South Bronx while Xavier is still living there, and I don't know if I'm going to feel safer anywhere else in that neighborhood. I'm not even sure I feel safe here, but certainly not in the Bronx.

In any case, it's the right thing to say. A huge smile lights up my boyfriend's face. "Okay. Sounds good to me." He reaches for my hand across the table. "I love you, Millie."

I open my mouth, knowing that I have reached a critical point where I need to say it back to him. But at that moment, that creeping sensation in the back of my neck becomes unbearable. I whip my head around one more time, certain I'm going to see Xavier standing a few feet away from me, staring at me.

My eyes narrow as I scan the street behind me. Where is that asshole?

But I don't see Xavier anywhere. Either he ducked behind a mailbox, or he's not there. Except I do see one person I hadn't expected.

Douglas Garrick.

SEVENTEEN

Douglas Garrick is behind me.

More specifically, he's crossing the street. The light is red, and he darts into the crosswalk as a yellow taxi leans hard on its horn. I watch him for a moment, my heart pounding. I had somehow assumed it was Xavier who had been following me, but now I'm not so sure. Was it Douglas all along?

"Hang on a minute," I say to Brock. "I'll be right back."

"What the..."

I don't give Brock a chance to finish his thought before I dash after Douglas into the street, forcing a blue sedan to slam on its brakes. The driver curses at me, but I ignore him and keep walking.

What is Douglas doing in the East Village? He lives on the Upper West Side, and he works on Wall Street.

If he was watching me, he's not anymore. And the other interesting thing is that he's not alone. He appears to be walking with a woman who has blond hair and is clutching a utilitarian brown purse, slung over her right shoulder.

What's going on? Why was he watching me? And who is that woman? Even though I haven't gotten a good look at

Wendy Garrick in real life, I've seen photos of her, and that woman isn't Mrs. Garrick.

I follow him for another block. Maybe I'm deluding myself, but I don't think he has any idea I'm behind him as he and the woman walk along Second Avenue. She's raising her voice, but I can't quite hear what they're saying. And if I get any closer, they might see me.

I don't know how much longer I can follow him. Brock is still back at the restaurant, and he probably thinks I've lost my mind. I hope this little incident doesn't make it into his weekly phone call with mom and dad.

Thankfully, Douglas and the woman come to a halt in front of a small brownstone apartment building. Like my own building, this one doesn't have a doorman. She shuffles around in her purse for a key, unlocks the door, then pushes it open. I manage to get a good look at the woman just before they disappear inside.

It's painfully obvious what is going on. Douglas has a mistress on the side who lives in this building. It's still early enough that he could tell Wendy that he's been working late tonight when he gets home.

But why were they arguing?

Of course, it isn't hard to imagine. If she's his girlfriend and he's married, maybe she is angry that he hasn't left his wife. The woman was at least in her thirties and didn't look like a floozy who is just out for a good time. Maybe she is hoping that Douglas will dump Wendy and marry her instead.

I'm still staring at the brownstone, trying to figure out my next move, when my phone starts ringing in my pocket. I cringe when Brock's name flashes on the screen. I wish I had left my phone in my purse. But at this point, I have to take the call. The guy told me we could move in together, told me he *loved* me, and then I leaped out of my seat like a crazy person and ran off in the opposite direction.

"Millie?" He sounds baffled on the other line. "What happened? Where did you go?"

"I... I saw an old friend," I say. "I wanted to catch up with her. I haven't seen her in years."

"Okay..." He reluctantly seems to accept my ridiculous explanation, as I knew he would. "Are you coming back?"

I give the brownstone one last look. "Yes. I'll be back in a few minutes."

"A few *minutes*?"

Whatever Douglas Garrick is up to in that apartment building, I'm not going to figure it out from standing here and staring at the building. So I start walking back to the restaurant, already bracing myself for the third degree from Brock. He's going to want more of an answer as to why I ran off. But the truth will make me sound insane.

"I'm walking back right now," I tell him. "I promise."

"Do you want me to pay the bill?" he asks. "Are you okay? What's going on?"

"Nothing." I cross the street to get back to the restaurant, picking up my pace just a little bit. "Like I said, I saw an old friend."

"You didn't look okay."

"I am," I insist. "I..."

Right in the middle of insisting that I am completely fine, I stop talking. Because I am looking at something that makes my heart sink into my stomach.

It's a black Mazda with a cracked right front headlight. The same one I have seen parked near my apartment building and sometimes near where the Garricks live.

I drop my gaze to look down at the license plate. 58F321. I search my brain, trying to remember what the plate was the last time I saw it. Why didn't I write it down? I was so sure I would remember it.

But that right cracked headlight. It looks so familiar.

"Millie?" Brock's voice is coming out of my phone. "Millie? Are you there?"

I stare at this car. All along, I had assumed it was Xavier who was following me. But now I find this car parked close to Douglas's mistress's building. Even though I'm not 100 percent sure it's the same car that's been following me, I'd be willing to bet good money on it. It does look like a pretty crummy car to be driven by a multimillionaire, but maybe not if he's trying to be inconspicuous.

Except why would Douglas be following me? After all, I've been getting this sensation before I even started working for the Garrick family. That would mean that Douglas has been following me even before I started working for him.

A horrible cold sensation goes down my spine. What is going on here?

EIGHTEEN

Today I am packing up my stuff to move.

The truth is, I still don't feel great about moving in with Brock, but if Xavier Marin is living in that apartment building, then I will not be. And I have to admit, it won't be torture staying in Brock's two-bedroom Upper West Side apartment. It isn't exactly a penthouse, but it's gorgeous. It even has a porch that *doesn't* double as a fire escape. Also, when it gets hot during the summer, he has air-conditioning. Air-conditioning! It's the height of luxury.

Brock drives me to the Bronx in his Audi. It doesn't have a ton of trunk space, but fortunately, I don't have a ton of stuff. One of the bonuses of this apartment was that it came partially furnished, so most of the stuff in it isn't mine. Whatever doesn't fit in the trunk and back seat, I can leave behind.

"I'm so glad we're moving in together," Brock tells me as we navigate the streets to my apartment for the last time. "This is going to be great."

The smile on my face feels like plastic. "Yes."

How can I do this? How can I move in with Brock when he

doesn't know the truth about my past? It's not fair to him. And it won't be fair to me when he finds out and kicks me to the curb.

I am still working for the Garrick family—for now. The more I thought about it, the less certain I felt that Douglas had been watching me that day. After all, he was talking to his mistress, and he didn't seem focused on me at all. I jumped to conclusions. And learning my boss is having an affair is no reason to give up a lucrative job, especially since finding a new one is always difficult for me. I may be moving in with Brock, but it would be a mistake to become dependent on him. I need my own income—just in case he does kick me to the aforementioned curb.

At a red light, Brock reaches out and rests his hand on my knee. He smiles at me, and he looks oh so handsome—like movie-star handsome—and all I can think is that this is a bad idea. He's making a terrible mistake and he doesn't even know it. And part of me wishes he would take his damn hand off my knee.

He hasn't told me he loves me again since that day at the restaurant. I can tell he's itching to say it, but he's said it twice now, and I have said it zero times. If he says it again, I'll either have to say it back or... Well, I have to say it back if I want this relationship to continue. There's no question anymore.

"Hey." Brock pulls his hand away as we turn onto my street. "What's going on here?"

There is a police car with flashing lights parked in front of my building. I press my lips together to refrain from telling him that police cars are parked here all the time. My stomach turns as I wonder if there's a chance they could be here for me. Maybe Xavier changed his mind about pressing charges.

Oh God, are they going to take me away in handcuffs?

"Brock," I say urgently. "Maybe we should get out of here. Come back another time."

He crinkles his nose. "I'm not driving back to the Bronx again tomorrow. Come on, it'll be fine."

Just as I'm about to have a full-blown panic attack, the door to my building swings open, and an officer is leading a man onto the street, his hands cuffed behind his back. Looks like they aren't here for me after all. It's probably another drug bust.

And then I see the scar above the left eyebrow of the man in handcuffs. It's *Xavier*.

I roll down my window just in time to hear Xavier shout at the officer leading him to the police car: "You've got to believe me! Those drugs... I never even saw them before. They aren't mine!"

Even from where we're parked, I can see the officer roll his eyes. "Yeah, that's what everyone says when we find a shitload of heroin in their apartment."

A second before they get to the patrol car, Xavier's eyes fill with panic. Even though he has to realize it's a stupid move, he shakes off the cop and starts running down the block. Of course, he's got his hands cuffed behind his back, which means he isn't going to get far. The policeman catches up to him a few seconds later, and I watch as he gets thrown to the ground.

This is the best show I've seen in months.

Brock's eyes widen at the scene unfolding in front of us. "Jesus Christ. You're lucky you're moving out of here."

"That's him," I breathe. "That's the man who assaulted me."

"Wow. So he was on drugs too? I guess that's no surprise."

I didn't get the sense that Xavier was on drugs during our interactions. He always seemed completely sober. But if they found it in his apartment... better yet, if there were a lot of drugs found there—enough to imply he was dealing—he's not coming back anytime soon.

"I don't have to move," I blurt out.

Brock's mouth falls open. "What?"

"He won't be living in the building anymore," I point out. "So I don't have to leave."

Brock's lower lip juts out. "I don't understand. Don't you *want* to live with me?"

That is an incredibly tricky question. Yes, it would be nice to have the extra space and the air-conditioning and the doorman to keep out burglars. But that's not a good reason to move in with your boyfriend.

"I do," I say. "Someday. But... not yet."

"I see." His tone is icy.

"I'm so sorry." I reach out to squeeze his hand, but he doesn't squeeze mine back. "I'm just the sort of person who needs my own space. That's all."

His blue eyes meet mine. "Is that really all?"

I imagine Brock's parents are the kind of people who do a background check on any woman his son would move in with. Hell, they may have already done one. But I'm betting they looked up Millie Calloway, which was my only saving grace. It's only a matter of time before they find out my first name is actually Wilhelmina, and then Brock will find out everything.

I've got to come clean before that happens.

But with that asshole Xavier in jail, I've given myself a short reprieve.

NINETEEN

The Garrick penthouse seems quiet today.

I heard a sound coming from the guest bedroom, but it wasn't crying or screaming or anything else suspicious. It just sounded like there's somebody in there—a woman who I'm not supposed to disturb.

After finding the blood on that nightgown, I genuinely thought Douglas would find an excuse to fire me, but he hasn't so far. It's a good thing, considering I need the money. (Brock is still hinting that I should move in with him, but I have managed to deflect him so far.)

And now that I've had a few days to think about it, I'm not convinced the crimson on the nightgown was as ominous as it seemed at the time. I'm still certain the stain was blood, but there are plenty of innocent reasons for blood stains on clothes. I've dealt with enough children with gushing nosebleeds to know it's a mistake to jump to conclusions. So I've managed to put it out of my head.

Well, mostly.

After I tidy up some of the other bedrooms, I head down the hallway to the main upstairs bathroom. In general, the bathrooms aren't very dirty. It makes sense, considering there are only two people living here, and it hardly seems like they need someone to clean so frequently, but I'm not going to argue with them. I get paid to clean, and if I have to clean something that is already fairly clean, then that's what I'll do.

Except when I walk into the bathroom now, there's something I've never seen before. Something that makes me feel like I just got punched in the gut.

It's a bloody handprint on the bathroom sink.

Well, to be fair, it's about half a handprint. Like somebody was gripping the sink with a hand caked in blood.

My eyes drop to the floor. I didn't see it when I first walked in, but now I notice little droplets of blood on the linoleum tiles. They seem to form a little trail.

I follow the trail of crimson droplets out of the bathroom. There are no lights in the hallway, so somehow I didn't notice it the first time, but now I can make out the specks of blood forming a pathway in the carpeting. And the trail ends at the door to the guest bedroom.

I'm not supposed to knock on the door. Douglas made it very clear when I first started working here. And the one time I did knock on the door, Wendy Garrick was *not* pleased to see me.

But I think of Kitty Genovese again. How can I not investigate when there is literally a trail of blood leading to the door?

So I raise my fist and knock on the door.

I had heard some sounds before, but it suddenly becomes silent on the other side of the door. Nobody tells me to come in or don't come in. So I knock again.

"Mrs. Garrick?" I call out. "Wendy?"

No answer.

I clench my teeth in frustration. I don't know what is going on in there, but I'm not leaving until I can verify that she isn't bleeding to death. I have a rule about not cleaning around dead bodies.

Even though I shouldn't, I put my hand on the doorknob. I try to turn it, but it doesn't budge. *Locked.*

"Mrs. Garrick," I say, "there's blood all over your bathroom."

Still no answer.

"Listen, if you don't open the door, I'm going to have to call the police."

That gets a response out of her. I hear some scrambling behind the door, and then a slightly choked voice. "I'm here. I'm fine. Don't call the police."

"Are you sure?"

"Yes. Please... go away. I'm trying to sleep."

I could walk away, but really, I can't. Not after seeing all the blood in the bathroom. It's not even that the blood was there, but the fact that whoever did it was too injured to be able to clean it up.

"I want to see you," I say. "Please open the door."

"I'm fine—I told you. I just had some bleeding from a cracked tooth."

"Open the door for two seconds and I'll leave you alone. But I promise you, I'm not leaving until you open the door."

There is another long silence behind the door. While I wait, my eyes stray to the trail of blood droplets from the bathroom. There are plenty of innocent explanations for it. Perhaps she was shaving and cut herself. Maybe it really was a cracked tooth.

And then there are some not-so-innocent explanations.

Finally, a click comes from the doorknob. The door has been unlocked. And very slowly, she cracks it open.

And I have to clap a hand over my mouth to keep from screaming.

TWENTY

"Wendy," I breathe. "Oh my God."

"I told you," she says, "I'm fine. It isn't as bad as it looks."

I have seen a lot of bad things in my lifetime, but Wendy Garrick's face is one of those things that will haunt me for years to come. That woman had been pummeled, and from the looks of her, it didn't happen all at once. The bruises covering her face are in various stages of healing. One on her left cheekbone looks fresh, but others have a yellow appearance that makes it look like they were formed from a blow that came much earlier.

Wendy told me that the bleeding came from one of her teeth, and I absolutely believe that whatever did this to her face was capable of knocking out one of her teeth.

"It's from my medications," she tells me. "I had a fall, and I take blood thinners. It makes me bruise easily."

Has this woman looked in a mirror? Is she really trying to tell me that this happened from a *fall*?

She's wearing a pink nightgown with flowers on it and, much like the bathroom, there is blood staining the front of it. And it's not even the first bloody nightgown I've seen since I've been here.

"You need to go to a hospital," I manage.

"A hospital?" She flinches. "And what would they do, exactly?"

"Check if you have any broken bones."

"I don't. I'm fine."

"And then you can report this," I add.

Wendy Garrick stares at me through eyes rimmed with bruises. She takes a breath and winces. I wonder if she has a broken rib. It wouldn't surprise me.

"Listen to me, *Millie*," she says in a low voice. "You have no idea what you're dealing with here. You do *not* want to get involved with this situation. You need to walk away and leave me be."

"Wendy..."

"I mean it." Her bruised eyes grow wider, and for the first time, I see real fear there. "If you know what's good for you, you need to close this door and get out of here."

"But—"

"You need to *walk away*, Millie." And now there is a terrible urgency in her voice. "You have no idea. Just *walk away*."

I open my mouth to protest, but before I can, she has slammed the door in my face.

The message is crystal clear. Whatever is going on in this house, Wendy does *not* want my help. She wants me to stay out of it. Mind my own business.

Unfortunately, I've never been very good at that.

TWENTY-ONE

In 2007, an acclaimed violinist named Josh Bell, who had recently sold out a concert with average ticket prices of a hundred dollars each, posed as a street musician. He stood in a subway station in Washington, DC wearing jeans and a baseball cap, where he played the exact same music as at his concert, on a handcrafted violin worth more than three and a half million dollars.

"Hardly anyone even stopped to listen," Dr. Kindred explains to the lecture hall filled with students. "In fact, when children would occasionally stop, their parents would grab them and usher them on their way. This man played a sold-out concert in Boston, and on that day, only about fifty people stopped long enough to put a dollar in his violin case. So how do you explain this?"

After a hesitation, a girl in the front row raises her hand. That one is always eager to answer questions. "I think part of it was that beauty is less easily perceived when it's in an unassuming setting."

I take the subway every day from the Bronx into the city,

and I often see people playing their instruments as I wait for the subway to arrive. The station right by my apartment building reeks of urine, for reasons I prefer not to think about, but if there's somebody playing music while I'm waiting, it's not so bad.

I would have stopped and listened to Josh Bell. I might have even put a dollar in his violin case, even though I need every dollar I have.

"Okay," Dr. Kindred says. "Any other possible factors at play?"

I hesitate for a moment before raising my hand. I don't usually participate in class because I'm about ten years older than the oldest person in the room (aside from the professor). But nobody else seems to be answering.

"Nobody wanted to help him," I say.

Dr. Kindred nods and strokes the stubble on his chin. "What do you mean by that?"

"Well," I say, "he had a violin case out with money in it. People assumed he was looking for help in the form of money. And because they didn't want to help him, they ignored him. They felt that stopping would have meant they had to help."

"Ah." He nods. "So that doesn't say much good about the human race, if nobody was willing to enjoy beautiful music because it meant they might have to help a person in need."

The professor is still looking at me, so I feel like I have to say something. "At least fifty people stopped. That's something."

"Very true," he says. "That *is* something."

I would have helped though. I always help. I can never, *ever* walk away, even when I should.

After the lecture ends, just as I'm getting out of the building, I spy a familiar face coming down the street. I am a little surprised to note that it's Amber Degraw, the woman who fired me after her baby daughter wouldn't stop calling me mama. I'm not as much surprised to see her as I am to see her pushing a stroller containing little Olive, who is playing with some sort of rattle that is pushed about as far into her mouth as she can get it. Her fingers are sticky with drool.

When I was working for Amber, she never seemed interested in taking Olive out for a walk. So this is a good thing for both of them.

I consider ducking around the corner to avoid an awkward encounter, but then Amber spots me and raises a hand in an enthusiastic greeting. Apparently, she's just plum forgotten about the way she fired me.

"Millie!" she calls out. "My goodness, how *lovely* to see you!"

Really? Because that isn't what she said last time we saw each other.

"Hi, Amber," I say, already resigned to making polite conversation.

She skids to a halt beside me, releasing the handle of the stroller long enough to smooth out her shiny strawberry blond hair. Today, Amber is all about leather. She's wearing a pair of leather pants, stuffed into knee-high leather boots, and a creamy brown leather trench coat.

"How are you doing?" She cocks her head to the side like I am a random friend who has come into a bit of bad luck, rather than a person who she fired. "Everything okay?"

"Sure," I say through my teeth. "Just great."

"Where are you working now?"

I'm reluctant to tell her anything about my present position. She's already fired me herself for the stupidest reason—I put nothing past this woman. "I'm between jobs."

"I saw you on the street the other day," she says. "You were going into that old building on 86th Street. Douglas Garrick lives there, doesn't he?"

I freeze, surprised that she's privy to that information. Then again, in rich people circles, everyone seems to know everyone. "Yes, I'm working for the Garricks now."

"Oh, is that what you were doing there?"

The smile curled across Amber's lips makes me uneasy. What is she implying exactly? "Yes..."

She winks at me. "I'm sure you're making the most of it."

I don't appreciate her tone, but I remind myself that I don't have to stand here and chat with Amber—one of the benefits of no longer being in her employment. But I do have to say hello to little Olive, whose chin is shiny with drool. I haven't seen her in a while, and a baby can change quickly at that age. She probably barely recognizes me.

"Hi there, Olive!" I chirp.

Olive extracts the rattle from her throat and raises her humongous blue eyes to stare up at me. "Mama!" she shrieks with delight.

The color drains out of Amber's face. "No! She's not your mama! I am!"

"Mama!" Olive stretches out her pudgy arms to reach for me. "Mama!"

When I don't scoop Olive into my arms, the little girl starts sobbing. Amber shoots me a dirty look. "Look how you've upset her!"

With that remark, Amber does an about-face and sprints down the street to get away from me, while Olive continues to wail, "Mama!" Despite everything, that encounter put a smile on my face. Turns out she remembered me after all.

While I'm watching Amber disappear into the distance, my phone starts ringing—instantly, my good mood evaporates. This is likely one of two people. It's either Douglas, telling me I'm fired for harassing his wife, or it's Brock, which would be even worse.

Things have been decidedly chilly between me and my boyfriend since I abruptly told him I didn't want to live with him. I repeatedly explained about needing my own space and feeling safer now that Xavier has been locked up for the foreseeable future, but he still doesn't get it. I have a bad feeling that we have to move forward in our relationship very, very soon, or else it's going to end.

Except when I look at my phone, it's not Douglas or Brock. It's a number I don't recognize.

"Hello?" I say.

"Is this Wilhelmina Calloway?"

I pause, wondering if the voice on the other line is going to tell me that my car warranty is about to expire, or else let loose with a string of some foreign language. "Yes..."

"Hi! This is Lisa from Jobmatch!"

My shoulders relax. Jobmatch was the service that I used to place my ad for the housekeeper jobs. "Hi, Lisa."

"Ms. Calloway," Lisa says in her chipper voice, "we didn't get any response to our emails, so this is the second call regarding your credit card."

"My credit card?"

"Yes," Lisa says. "Your American Express was declined."

I shake my head at my own stupidity. "I'm so sorry. I canceled that card. I meant to use my MasterCard. But I don't need the ad anymore."

"Well," Lisa says, "I just want to make sure you understand that the ad never went live because we never received payment."

I stop walking right in the middle of First Avenue. "Wait," I say. "My ad for the housekeeper position never went live?"

"I'm afraid not, since we never received payment. As I said, we've been trying to contact you..."

But I'm not listening. I don't know how it's possible that my ad for the housekeeper position never appeared online. "Are you sure?" I blurt out. "You're saying my ad was never online at all? Even for a day?"

"Not even for a day," Lisa confirms.

I think back to when I was looking for jobs a couple of months earlier. Most of the interviews took place with potential employers who I had contacted through their own ads. In fact, there was only one person who contacted me unsolicited.

Douglas Garrick.

TWENTY-TWO

All I know is that I am going to get to the bottom of this.

Douglas Garrick called *me*. I remember it so clearly. I picked up the phone and he told me that he was looking for a housekeeper who would do cleaning, laundry, light cooking, and random errands. He didn't mention the ad, or at least I don't think he did, but at the time, I just assumed that was why he was calling. After all, there was no other reason.

How did he get my number if it wasn't from the ad?

The whole thing gives me a sick feeling. I'm still getting that sensation that somebody is watching me, even though Xavier is allegedly in jail. And that black Mazda was parked outside the building that Douglas went into with his mistress. Douglas had my number somehow, even though the ad never went live.

He knew who I was.

I stand there on the street, in front of a pizza parlor. The tantalizing aroma of tomato sauce, grease, and melted cheese invades my nostrils but only makes me feel sick to my stomach. I scan the street in front of me, searching for anything suspicious.

I don't see Douglas. I don't see Xavier.

But somebody is out there. Somebody's watching me. I'm absolutely certain of it.

I pull out my phone again. There's a message there from Douglas confirming that I will be coming over tonight to clean, even though I was only there two days earlier and I'm sure the house is still nearly spotless. Usually, I text him back, but now I stare at the screen. Before I can second-guess myself, I click on his number to call him.

As the call connects and starts ringing, a phone rings right behind me. My stomach drops.

I whirl around, but the ringing phone seems to belong to a teenage girl. She takes the call and I can hear her screaming "Oh my God!" into the phone as she walks past me. Geez, I am jumpy.

"Hello? Millie?"

It's Douglas's voice on the other line. He's not standing two feet behind me. Wherever he is, it sounds a lot quieter than the busy street that I'm on. "Oh, hi."

"Everything okay? Are you still coming tonight to clean?"

"Yes..." I curse to myself for not preparing a story before calling. I was being impulsive. "I was just working on my résumé, and I had a quick question for you."

"You're not leaving us, are you?" There's a touch of humor in his voice, but also something dark lingering beneath the surface. "I sure hope not."

"No, definitely not. I just wanted to pick up some extra work, and I was wondering, how did you hear about me? Like, how did you get my number when you called me?"

He thinks for a moment. "Actually, it was Wendy who gave me your number."

"Wendy? Your wife?"

"Do you know another Wendy?" He chuckles. "She told me that a friend gave her your number and said that you were really good."

"Did she say what friend?"

"No." Now his voice has taken on a slightly defensive edge. "We've given you enough information here. Please don't bother Wendy about this."

"Of course not," I say. "Thank you very much for the information. And I'll certainly be coming tonight."

I will be coming tonight. But if he thinks I'm not going to ask Wendy about this, he's got another thing coming.

TWENTY-THREE

This evening, I show up at the penthouse with an arm full of dry cleaning. All of it belongs to Douglas Garrick. I'm picking up four suits, each of which probably cost more than I earn in a year. If I went rogue and tried to sell these on my own, I would probably clean up. But it's not worth it. I'm already terrified of Douglas, and the last thing I want to do is make him angry with me.

Although what I am about to do today may very well serve that purpose.

When I get into the living room with the dry cleaning slung over my arm, the house is silent. Wendy is likely upstairs, and presumably Douglas is working late—or with his mistress. I carry the dry cleaning up to the second floor, the pounding of my sneakers against each step echoing throughout the penthouse. I've cleaned in houses much larger than this one, but I've never been in one that seems to have such loud echoes. I wonder if it's related to the age of the building.

It's no surprise that the door to the guestroom is closed. I take the dry cleaning and bring it into the master bedroom. I hang up Douglas's suits, but my mind is on the woman shut in the guestroom. I'm determined to talk to her today.

So as soon as I put the suits away, I creep down the hallway to the guest bedroom.

For some reason, the lights in the hallway don't turn on. I asked Douglas about it once, and he mentioned some sort of wiring problem. He mumbled something about getting it fixed, but those lights have been nonfunctional the entire time I've been working here. In addition to the architecture being so ancient, the lack of lights on the second floor gives it a creepy feel.

I stop in front of the guest bedroom. The carpet beneath my feet is clean—I scrubbed off all the blood in the bathroom and removed the stains from the carpet using hydrogen peroxide. There's no sign that Wendy's blood was ever dripping all over the carpet. And Douglas does not know that I know.

I lift my hand, ready to knock on the door, and a chill goes through me. I can't help but remember Wendy's warning the last time I spoke to her:

If you know what's good for you, you need to close this door and get out of here.

I swallow down my doubts. No, I *never* walk away. With renewed resolve, I rap my fist on the door.

I am fully prepared to beg her to open up again, but this time, I hear footsteps behind the door. A moment later, the door cracks open. Once again, I am staring into Wendy's bruised face, although admittedly it looks better than it did a few days ago.

"What is it?" There is a tone of resignation in her voice. "I was trying to sleep."

My eyes drop to her pale yellow nightgown, which thankfully doesn't appear to have any blood on it this time. "That's a pretty nightgown. I always just sleep in my Mets T-shirt."

She folds her arms across her chest. "Is that what you woke me up to tell me?"

"No, it... it's not. The truth is, I need to ask you something."

Wendy shifts between her slippers. I hadn't realized before how thin she is. The woman is downright emaciated. I suppose it could be from her illness, but I don't know if I've ever seen a woman quite so skinny before. Her collar bones jut out painfully, and when she tugs at her nightgown, I can make out every single bone in her blue-veined hand. Her eyes look enormous on her thin face. "What do you want?"

"I want to know how you got my number."

She toys with a lock of her auburn hair, and I recognize the bracelet hanging off the wrist. It's the same one Douglas gave her as a gift recently. "What do you mean?"

"Douglas told me you gave him my number to call me for the cleaning job. But how did you get my number?"

"You placed an ad, didn't you? That must be how I got it." She lets out a long sigh. "Now if you don't mind, I'm going back to bed. It's been a long day."

"Actually, I found out the ad never went live. So, like I said, how did you get my number?"

I can almost see the gears turning in Wendy's brain. Before she can concoct another lie, I cut her off: "Tell me the truth."

Wendy drops her eyes. "Please. I don't want to do this. Just leave it alone."

"Tell me," I say through my teeth.

"Why won't you ever do what I ask?" She throws up her hands. "Fine. I got your number from Ginger Howell."

And now I feel like somebody just sucker-punched me. I know who Ginger Howell is, but I haven't seen her in years. Two years, to be exact. She was one of the last women I worked for before Enzo took off for Italy. We found her a lawyer who was willing to work on a contingency basis to help her get a divorce from her monster of a husband. He fought tooth and nail, and we were on the brink of trying to get her a new passport and ID, but he finally let her go.

I hope she's doing okay. Ginger seemed like a nice person. She didn't deserve what her husband was doing to her.

But if Wendy heard about me from Ginger, then...

"Why did you tell Douglas to call me, Wendy?" I say. She starts to open her mouth, and I add, "I need you to tell me the real reason."

She still won't look at me, instead staring down at the carpet. "I think you know why."

A dull ringing echoes in the back of my head. I suspected the moment I walked in here that something was strange about this house. But every time I tried to reach out to Wendy, she didn't seem interested in talking to me.

"I broke my wrist," she says bitterly. "He pushed me down and it broke, but when I saw the doctor, he wouldn't leave the room. I had to tell them I slipped on some ice and fell. That's the only reason he let me get some help for the house—he never allows anyone else to come in here otherwise."

My hands ball into fists. "Why didn't you say anything?"

"Because it was a stupid idea to bring you here." Her bloodshot eyes fill with tears. "I was desperate, but once I saw you, I knew I couldn't go through with it. You don't know Douglas. You don't know what he's like. Getting away from him is *not an option.*"

"You're wrong," I say.

She throws her head back and lets out an acid-tinged laugh. "You have no idea what you're talking about. Douglas is *everywhere.* He sees *everything.*"

I think back to all the times on the street when I felt like somebody was watching me. "Does he see us right now? Is he listening to this conversation?"

"I... I don't know." Her eyes dart around the hallway. "I haven't been able to find any cameras in the house, but that doesn't mean they're not there. Douglas has access to technology that we can't imagine. He's a genius, you know." Her laugh is sad this time. "I used to find that attractive about him."

"It's still worth trying."

Her bruised cheeks color slightly. "You don't understand. He would spend every penny he has to track me down."

She's right—and Douglas has a lot of pennies to spend. With a husband like Douglas, escaping would be difficult—I indeed have no idea what he is capable of. And I don't know if I can help her. Especially since I don't have the resources that Enzo had... I don't have "a guy" for everything. That's why I swore I would give up this life and focus on getting my college degree, so I could help women in a way that didn't involve bending the law. But every molecule in my body is crying out that I have to try to help this woman—now.

I would never walk by a man in a subway who needed help. Or a woman who was being stabbed to death outside my window. I can't allow this to happen under my nose.

"Do you have any money?" I ask. "Cash, I mean?"

She nods hesitantly. "I've been slowly selling off some of my jewelry. I've got so much of it—every time he hits me, he buys me something new and expensive. I've got some money tucked away in a place where I don't think he'll find it. It won't last long, but maybe long enough."

My mind is racing. "Do you have any friends who can help you? Friends that maybe he doesn't know about? From high school or college or...?"

"Please stop," she croaks. "You don't seem to understand what I'm trying to tell you. Douglas is extremely dangerous. You cannot underestimate this man. If you try to help me, it won't work and... and you'll be sorry. Trust me."

"But, Wendy—"

"I can't do it, okay?"

She looks down at the bracelet on her left wrist—I remember how proud Douglas was when he showed it to me. A wild look in her eyes, she fumbles with the clasp until it slips from her narrow wrist.

"I hate the gifts he gives me." Her voice is dripping with venom. "I can barely look at them, but he expects me to wear them."

She squeezes the bracelet in her fist, then reaches out and grabs my own hand. She presses the bracelet into my palm. "Get this out of my sight. I can't even look at it anymore. If he asks, I... I'll tell him I lost it."

I open my hand to look at the small bracelet. I wonder if it's stained with her blood. "I can't take this, Wendy."

"Then throw it out," she spits. "I don't want it in my house anymore. Especially after what he wrote on it."

I bring the bracelet closer to my face to examine the inscription. I read the tiny lettering:

To W, You are mine forever, Love D

"His forever," she says bitterly. "His property."

The message is unmistakable.

"Please let me help you." I grab her wrist, forgetting that it might be the broken one. She winces and I let go. "I'll do whatever it takes. I'm not scared of your husband. We can figure out a way out of this."

And then I see it in her eyes. A flicker of hesitation. Of *hope*. It only lasts a split second, but it's there. This woman is desperate.

"No," she says firmly. "And now you need to leave."

Before I get out another word, she slams the door in my face.

Wendy Garrick is absolutely terrified of her husband—and I'm afraid of the man, too. But after all these years, I've learned not to let fear control me. I took down Xavier. I've taken down men who are just as powerful as Douglas. I don't care what Wendy says. I can handle him.

TWENTY-FOUR

If I had a nickel for every time a biker nearly mowed me down in the bike lane while I was crossing the street, I wouldn't have to work for the Garrick family. As I'm crossing the street to get to the Garricks' apartment building, a biker with no helmet and holding a cell phone to his ear comes within millimeters of sending me to the hospital. Why is it always the bikers on cell phones who also don't have helmets? It's like a *rule*.

Just before I reach the entrance to the building, my phone rings inside my purse. I hesitate, considering letting it go to voicemail. Then I dig into my purse and pull it out. Brock's name is on the screen. Now I'm even more tempted to let it go to voicemail. I don't want to have yet another conversation with him about why I can't move in with him. Or as he likes to put it, I *won't* move in with him.

Finally, I sigh and press the green button on my phone to accept the call. "Hey," I say.

"Hi, Millie," he says. "Are you up for dinner tonight?"

"I'm probably going to be at the Garricks' late tonight," I tell him, which isn't entirely a lie.

"Oh."

I wonder how many dinner invitations I'll need to turn down before he stops asking. And I don't want that. I like Brock a lot, even though I might not quite love him yet. I don't want to lose him.

"Listen," I say, "Douglas is going away for a few days starting tomorrow, so they don't need me to cook. What if we have dinner tomorrow night?"

"Okay." His voice sounds a little strange. "Also, when we're having dinner, I think we need to have a talk."

I let out a strangled laugh. "That doesn't sound good."

"I just..." He clears his throat. "I like you a lot, Millie. We just need to discuss where I stand."

"You stand just fine."

"Do I?"

I don't know what to say. But he's right. Brock and I do need to have a talk. Sooner rather than later. I need to come clean to him about everything in my past, and then he can decide if he wants to move forward. I'd like to think he's a decent enough guy that he won't be scared off by a decade in prison, but I keep imagining the look on his face when I tell him. And it's not one of happiness.

"Fine," I say. "We can have a talk."

"Meet at my apartment at seven?"

"Sure."

There's a pause on the other line, and I'm almost scared he's going to tell me he loves me again, but instead, he says, "I'll see you tomorrow."

After we hang up, I stare down at the screen of my phone for a moment. What if I called him back right now and told him everything? Just rip the Band-Aid right off. And then I wouldn't have to wait and carry around that sick feeling in my stomach for another day.

No, I can't do it. It'll have to be tomorrow.

I continue to the apartment building, a heavy feeling in the pit of my stomach. The doorman rushes over to hold the door open for me, and as he does, he winks at me.

It strikes me as a little strange. The guy is at least thirty years my senior. Is he trying to hit on me? For a moment, I try to remember if I've noticed him winking at me before, but then I put it out of my head. A creepy doorman is the least of my problems.

When the gears grind to a halt on the twentieth floor and the doors open to the penthouse, I nearly jump out of my skin. In all the times I have come here in the last few months, this is something I have never seen before. And it is enough to make my jaw drop open.

Wendy is standing in front of the penthouse elevator door—she has emerged from the bedroom. And she is staring at me with her big green eyes.

"We need to talk," she says.

TWENTY-FIVE

Wendy grabs me by the arm and pulls me over to the sofa. Given how skinny she is, she is strong. Somehow, I'm not entirely surprised.

I sit down on the sofa and she sits beside me, smoothing her nightgown over her bony knees. The bruises on her face look much better, but her eyes are just as bloodshot as the last time I saw her.

"You said you were willing to help me," she says. "Did you mean it?"

"Of course I meant it!"

The tiniest of smiles touches her lips. I realize at this moment that Wendy is very pretty. Between how wasted her body looks and her bruises, I hadn't noticed it before. "I took your advice."

"My advice?"

"After you left," she says, "I thought about killing myself."

I suck in a breath. "That was *not* the advice I gave you."

"I know," she says quickly. "But it all felt so hopeless. When I had Douglas hire you, that was like my last life boat out of this terrible situation. And when I sent you away, it felt like there was no possibility of ever escaping him. So I went to the bathroom and I thought about slitting my wrists."

"Oh my God, Wendy..."

"But I didn't." She squares her jaw. "Because for once, I didn't feel entirely alone. And I remembered what you said about reaching out to somebody Douglas doesn't know. Somebody from my past that he's never met. And I remembered my old college friend Fiona. She was one of my best friends, and we haven't talked in ages, and I had no contact with her through social media."

I raise my eyebrows at her. "So are you going to try to find her?"

"I already did." Wendy's usually pale cheeks flush pink. "I tracked down her phone number by calling another friend from college—and I have of course sworn her to secrecy—and this morning Fiona and I talked for hours. She's got a farm right outside Potsdam in upstate New York. She's mostly off the grid except for her landline. I told her everything about my situation, and she told me I could stay with her as long as I need to."

While I applaud her initiative, this won't solve her problem. Even if he doesn't find her there, she can't stay hidden out in upstate New York forever. She won't even have a way to get a job without any kind of ID or social security number. That's what Enzo used to help with. With the kind of resources Douglas has, he will find her in a heartbeat when she uses her real name. I've also learned from experience that there's no point going to the cops when it comes to these incredibly rich and powerful men—they know how to grease the right palms.

"I know it's not a permanent solution," she acknowledges. "But that's okay. If I could just stay there for a little while and figure out my next move. Maybe I can find an attorney that can help me navigate the system while I'm hidden from him. Or maybe I can find somebody to help me start over." She takes a shaky breath. "The important thing is that I won't be with him anymore. And he won't be able to get to me."

"That's amazing, Wendy," I say. And I mean it, even though I'm about to lose a very lucrative job. I did save that bracelet she forced on me the other day, and I could probably hock it for a month's rent. Plus, I have a feeling after my conversation happens with Brock tomorrow, we might be moving in together after all. (Or breaking up forever. One or the other.)

"But here's the thing," Wendy says, "I need your help."

"Of course! Anything you need."

"It's something kind of big," she says. "But I'll compensate you."

"*Anything.*"

"I need a ride." Her hand is shaking slightly as she tugs at her collar. "My plan is that when Douglas goes out of town tomorrow, I'll take off then. He'll be all the way across the country, so even if he does get an inkling that I'm gone, there won't be anything he can do about it—not right away, anyway."

"Okay..."

"Fiona says she can pick me up if I can make it out to Albany," she says. "She can't leave her farm the whole day. So I need a ride out to Albany. I would rent a car, but I'll have to give them my ID and—"

"I'll do it," I interrupt her. "I'll rent the car. I'll drive you to Albany—no problem."

"Thank you, Millie." She clasps my hands in hers. "I promise, I'll give you the money in cash. You don't know how much I appreciate this."

"Don't worry about the money," I say, even though I am very worried about money in general. "You need it more than I do."

Wendy throws her arms around me, and it's only then that I feel how fragile her body truly is. I could crush her if I hugged her just a little too tightly.

When she pulls away, there are tears in her eyes. "You have to know, if you help me, you're putting yourself in danger."

"I understand that."

"No, you *don't*." She licks her slightly cracked lips. "Douglas is an extremely dangerous man, and I'm telling you, he will do whatever it takes to find me and bring me back to him. *Whatever it takes*."

"I'm not scared," I tell her.

But in the back of my head, there's a voice telling me that maybe I *should* be scared. That it would be a grave mistake to underestimate Douglas Garrick.

TWENTY-SIX

The next morning, I rent a car.

Even though I told her she didn't have to, Wendy gave me the cash value of the rental, but I'll be using my credit card to rent the car. I don't want this rental to be connected to her in any way.

Of course, there's a reasonable chance that Douglas Garrick will suspect that I have something to do with his wife's disappearance. But I will never, ever give her away. Even if he tortures me, which I honestly wouldn't put past him. A man who could do that to his wife's face is capable of anything.

"Hello, welcome to Happy Car Rental," a girl at the front desk chirps, who doesn't look old enough to rent a car herself. "How can I help you?"

"I reserved a gray Ford Focus," I tell her. "I put in the reservation online."

The girl types my information into the computer while I drum my fingers on the desk. As I stand at the counter, I can't help but notice a prickly feeling in the back of my neck. Like somebody's watching me. Again.

I turn around. The store front of the rental car place is all picture windows from ground to ceiling, so somebody could easily be looking in. I almost expect to see a man with his face pressed against the glass, staring at me. But there's nobody.

I shiver involuntarily. According to Mrs. Randall, Xavier Marin is in jail. No bail, she told me—she's evicted him. So why do I still get the sensation like somebody's watching me? And this isn't the first time. I have felt this way at least half a dozen times since Xavier was arrested.

The truth is, I don't know who has been watching me all this time. What if it really is Douglas Garrick who has been following me around town? It doesn't quite make sense, because I felt these eyes behind me even before I started working for him. But I can't discount the possibility. He's the one I saw when I was at that outdoor restaurant.

What if Douglas knows exactly what we're up to? What if he's out there, *watching*?

"So I've got your car," the girl says. "It's the red Hyundai."

"No," I say impatiently. "I put in a reservation for a gray Ford Focus." Being anonymous and not drawing attention to ourselves is key. I learned that from Enzo.

"I don't know what to tell you. It says red Hyundai here. We don't have a gray Ford Focus in our inventory right now."

"This is unbelievable. I put in a reservation, and you don't even have the thing I reserved?"

She shrugs helplessly. This isn't even the first time this has happened to me. What is the point of placing a reservation if they just give away the thing you reserved? "I don't want a red car," I say tightly. "How about a gray Hyundai?"

She shakes her head. "We're low on sedans. I can rent you a gray Honda CRV."

I spend a moment debating whether an SUV would stand out more than a red sedan. Finally, I agree to the red Hyundai.

Truthfully, I just want to get out of here. The purpose of this trip is to get Wendy out of town, but I don't think it would be so bad getting out of town myself.

TWENTY-SEVEN

It will be roughly a five-hour drive to our destination, taking traffic into account. Or at least, that's what my GPS tells me.

Our plan is to find a cheap motel off the side of the highway when we get close to Albany. I'll drop Wendy off there to spend the night, then Fiona will pick her up the next morning. She's bringing enough clothing to last a couple of weeks, and enough cash to last several months.

Douglas will never find her.

I park my painfully conspicuous red Hyundai a block away from the building, so the doorman who keeps winking at me will not report to Douglas that his wife got into a red sedan with his housekeeper. The car is so ridiculously red, it's like I'm driving a freaking fire engine. But there's nothing I can do about it now.

As I wait in the car for Wendy to materialize, a text message arrives from Douglas on my phone:

Will you be coming tonight?

Douglas asked me to clean while he's gone. I agreed to do it, and it doesn't surprise me that he is continuing to monitor and confirm my cleaning schedule, even though he's going out of town. It makes me a little uneasy, considering he is going to come home to find out his wife has disappeared. But in the interest of trying to pretend things are as normal as possible, I text back:

I'll be there.

Of course, I will not be there. I will be transporting his wife to a safe place.

Despite my annoyance about the mix-up at the car rental place and the long drive ahead of me, I have to smile to myself. Wendy is finally leaving Douglas. This is what I used to find so rewarding. And this is why I decided to get a degree in social work. What I want is to spend my life helping people like this.

In the rearview mirror, I can see Wendy coming down the street carrying two pieces of luggage. She's got her hair pinned back in a simple ponytail, a pair of dark sunglasses are perched on her nose, and she's dressed in a comfortable hoodie sweatshirt and blue jeans.

I come out of the car to help put her luggage in the trunk. She's absolutely beaming at me. "I forgot how comfortable jeans are," she comments.

"You don't wear jeans?"

"Douglas hates them." She scrunches up her nose. "That's why all I am bringing with me are jeans!"

I laugh as I throw her luggage into the trunk. We both climb into the car, I start up the GPS, and we get on the road. I haven't been behind the wheel in a couple of years now, and it feels good to be driving again. Of course, driving in the city is super stressful, but soon I'll get on the highway and that will be smooth sailing—at least until we hit rush hour traffic.

"So Douglas didn't suspect anything?" I ask Wendy.

She pushes her sunglasses up the bridge of her button nose. "I don't think so. He came in to say goodbye before he left, and I pretended to be asleep in bed." She looks down at her watch. "And right now, he's probably boarding a plane to Los Angeles."

"Good."

She raises her sunglasses to peer at me. "You didn't tell anyone about any of this, did you?"

"Absolutely not. Not a soul."

She looks relieved. "I can't wait to get out of here. I could hardly even sleep last night."

"Don't worry. I am a super-fast driver. We'll be at the motel before you know it."

As I say that, I come to a screeching halt at a red light, narrowly missing a pedestrian, who graciously gives me the finger. Okay, we need to get there fast, but more importantly, we need to get there in one piece.

As I wait for the light to change, I glance in the rearview mirror, and I can't help but notice a car behind me. It's a black sedan.

And it has a cracked right front headlight.

Or is it left? I crane my neck to look behind me, because I always get left and right confused in the mirror. No, it's definitely a cracked *right* front headlight.

I crane my neck further to get a look at the front grill, which has a little circle on it that is the Mazda logo. My heart sinks. It's a black Mazda with a cracked right front headlight. The same car I have been seeing multiple times in the last couple of months.

I try to catch a glimpse at the license plate, but before I can make out anything clearly, a blast of horns sounds off behind me. Okay, I need to start moving again before somebody gets out a gun and shoots me.

"Are you okay?" Wendy's forehead is bunched up above her sunglasses. "What's wrong?"

I debate how much I should tell her. There's no way I'm going to be able to get a good look at that license plate while I'm driving, but at the same time, she's already extremely nervous. I don't want to freak her out and tell her that I think somebody might be following me.

Especially if that someone is her husband.

It doesn't have to be Douglas. Despite what Mrs. Randall said, it's entirely possible that Xavier Marin got out of jail. And now he is tormenting me.

But that doesn't quite make sense. Whether or not he's in jail, Xavier surely has his own problems right now. He isn't going to be wasting his time following me into Manhattan, and certainly not all the way to Albany.

As I make my way to the highway, I try to drive creatively. I keep the Mazda in my sight as I change lanes, trying to see if it will change lanes with me. It doesn't always, but every time I look in my mirrors, it's behind me. And at one point I managed to catch the first three characters of the license plate: 58F.

The same characters of the car that's been following me around.

"Millie!" Wendy gasps, as I nearly sideswipe a green SUV. "Slow down, please! I don't want to get in an accident."

"Sorry," I mumble. "It's just been a little while since I've been behind the wheel."

We finally reach the FDR drive, and I've got one eye on my rearview mirror. That black Mazda has been behind me the entire time. And it's going to be so much easier for the car to continue following me when I'm on the highway. We haven't hit rush-hour traffic yet, so the lanes should be wide open.

But that also means I can go as fast as I want and avoid him.

As I get onto FDR, I put my foot on the gas, getting ready to gun it. *Let's see if that beat-up old Mazda can do eighty.* But then I check my rearview mirror.

The Mazda is gone. It didn't turn onto the highway with me.

I let out a breath, simultaneously relieved and confused. I was sure that the car was following me. I would've bet my life on it. But it turns out it was all just a coincidence. Nobody is following me.

Everything is going to be fine.

TWENTY-EIGHT

"Let's stop for McDonald's," Wendy suggests.

She is obscenely excited about the idea of getting fast food. About fifty percent of my diet consists of fast food, so I'm not nearly as excited. But Douglas is strict about what Wendy can and can't eat, even though I'm scared she's so skinny and deprived of fat products that if she eats even one McDonald's French fry, it might kill her.

Fortunately, a sign pops up on the side of the highway, with the McDonald's logo prominently displayed. So I get off at the next exit. I could use some gas anyway.

I pull into the McDonald's parking lot, and Wendy's eyes light up. When she opens her door, the odor of frying food invades my nostrils. I'm about to follow her out of the car when my phone rings. I grab for it, and my stomach sinks when Brock's name appears on the screen.

Oh *no*—I was so caught up in rescuing Wendy that I completely forgot to cancel our dinner. How could I have done that to him again? I'm so crazy about Brock. Why do I keep sabotaging our relationship?

Sometimes I wonder if I'm doing it on purpose. So that he'll dump me now, before I have to tell him the truth about me and he dumps me for a reason that will hurt much more.

"You go ahead," I croak out. "I'll meet you in there."

This is not going to be a quick conversation. Or maybe it will be *very* quick.

As soon as Wendy is out of the car, I take the call. Not surprisingly, Brock sounds just short of furious. "Where are you? I thought you were coming here at seven."

"Um," I say. "I had a change of plans."

"Okay, so when will you be here?"

I wish I could say that I'm right around the corner, but the reality is that I am hours away. And there's no easy way to tell him. "I don't think I'm going to make it tonight."

"Why not?"

More than anything, I wish I could tell him. It would be a relief to share this with somebody, but Wendy has sworn me to secrecy with good reason. "I've got work to do. Studying."

"Are you serious?" Brock has gone from just short of furious to full-on enraged. "Millie, we had plans for tonight. And not only did you not show up without telling me, but now you've got some bullshit excuse about studying?"

I don't know why that isn't a valid excuse. I could need to study tonight! "Listen, Brock..."

"No, you listen," he grunts. "I've been patient, but I'm running out of patience. I need to know how you feel about me and where this whole relationship is going. Because I'm ready for something more, and I'd like to know that I'm not wasting my time."

Brock is so ready to settle down. I know it's partly about his bum heart, and maybe some of it is just that indescribable craving for something more that so many people get in their thirties. He isn't messing around. I've got to either take him seriously or cut him loose. It's the right thing to do.

"You're not wasting your time," I murmur into the phone. "I

promise. Things are just a little crazy for me, but I swear, I really care about you."

"Do you? Because sometimes I'm not sure you do."

I know what he's looking for. And I know that I've got two choices. I either have to tell him what he wants to hear, or else I have to break it off.

And I don't want to break it off. Even if I don't mean what I'm about to say, Brock is a really, really good guy. The life I have imagined with him is what I've always wanted. And I don't want to lose him.

"I do care about you." I take a deep breath. "I... I love you."

I can almost hear the fight going out of my boyfriend. "I love you too, Millie. I really do."

"And we do need to have a talk." I've got to tell him everything about me—soon. I can't stand waiting for the other shoe to drop. I need to lay it all out and make sure he still wants to be with me. "As soon as things settle down, okay? Next week."

"Okay," Brock says, because I'm pretty sure he would agree to anything right now. "And if you finish your studying, maybe we could have dinner tomorrow? And spend the night at my place."

We *always* spend the night at his place. I don't even know why he bothered to leave a change of clothing and a bottle of his pills at my place. But admittedly, his place is nicer and a lot more convenient. "Sure."

"I love you, Millie."

Oh. We're apparently ending our conversations this way now. "I love you too."

I hang up the phone, still not feeling great about the conversation. I've still got my boyfriend, but for how long? He says he loves me, but sometimes I feel like he barely knows who I am.

But maybe it will all be okay. Maybe he'll find out the truth about me, and he'll still love me. And we can still be together, and get that house in the suburbs and fill it up with kids together. We can have a normal, perfect life together.

Except I strongly suspect that could never happen for me. I have never been normal or perfect, and there has only been one man in my life who has understood that.

TWENTY-NINE

Under the best circumstances, the drive would've taken three to four hours. With traffic, it ends up taking me close to five hours on the road, then an extra thirty minutes tacked on for when we stopped at that McDonald's—it was worth it to see Wendy scarf down a quarter pounder and a medium French fries. Now I still have to make the trip back, although it's after nine o'clock, so the roads should at least be clear. I'm sure I can make it in under three hours.

When we get close to Albany, I pull off the highway at a rest stop that advertises a motel. It turns out to be exactly what we were looking for—a cheap-looking place with a flickering light advertising vacancies. The rooms open to the outside, so Wendy won't have to go through a lobby to get to them. I pull into the sparsely occupied parking lot.

"Well," I say, "here we are."

"Yes..." Wendy and I have not talked much during the trip, mostly listening to music, and now the panic mounts in her eyes. "Millie, maybe this is a mistake."

"It's not a mistake. You're absolutely doing the right thing."

"He's smarter than me." She squeezes her hands together.

"Douglas is a genius and he has a fortune at his disposal. He's going to find me. He's going to check every motel, and the guy at the desk will probably tell him everything about me."

"No, he won't," I say firmly. "Because I'm going to reserve the room for you, remember? Nobody will see you."

Wendy still looks almost on the brink of a panic attack, but she takes a couple of deep breaths and finally nods. "Okay, maybe you're right."

Wendy hands me some cash from her purse, and I get out of the car to go to the main office of the motel. The guy manning the front desk is in his early twenties with a bushy beard and a phone in his right hand, and he couldn't look less excited to be working the graveyard shift.

"Hi," I say. "I'd like to reserve a room please."

He doesn't look up from his phone. "Photo ID please."

I was ready for this demand, which is why I didn't allow Wendy to make her own reservation. But I still feel safe handing over my driver's license. It won't be entered in the system—probably just the hard drive of this one computer. Not that Douglas would necessarily be searching for *me*, but you never know. If he is as smart as Wendy thinks, he might put it together.

And if that's true, I might be in serious danger.

Thankfully, he accepts the cash without argument and doesn't ask for my credit card. I would have had to hand over my credit card if he needed it, but it seems like we can get through this without leaving an electronic trail.

"Room 207." The man takes a key off the rack behind him. This is super old-school. "It's around the back."

"Great," I say.

He winks at me. "I knew that's what you wanted."

I groan inwardly. Of course, I knew there was no chance this guy wasn't going to remember me—a single woman asking for a room late at night—but hopefully, he doesn't make too much of it. Maybe he will think I'm turning tricks there. That's the goal.

I go back out to the car with the key to the motel room. Wendy climbs out of the passenger seat, and she has shifted the baseball cap that she's wearing to be low on her forehead. I imagine at some point in the near future, she's probably going to cut and color her hair, probably using kitchen shears and some cheap dye from the drugstore. But for now, the baseball cap will do.

"Thank you so much for this," Wendy says tearfully. "You saved my life, Millie."

"It was the least I could do."

She gives me a look. "I think we both know that's not true."

I help her grab her bags out of the trunk, and for a moment, we just stand there in the deserted parking lot, staring at each other. I'm not sure if I'll ever see Wendy again. I hope I don't, because if I do, it means this mission has failed.

"Thank you," she says one more time. And before I entirely know what's happening, she has thrown her arms around me. Once again, I marvel at how fragile her body seems to be. I hope she eats a lot of McDonald's in the next few years.

"Good luck," I tell her.

"Be careful," she says in a hoarse voice. "*Please* be careful. Douglas is going to come looking for me, and he is not going to leave anything unturned."

"I can handle him. I promise you."

Wendy doesn't look like she quite believes me, but she grabs her bags from my trunk. I watch her walk in the direction of room 207, which is all the way around the back of the motel. I keep watching until she disappears from sight, then I get back in the car and drive home.

THIRTY

It's nearly midnight by the time I get back to the city.

In stark contrast to the bumper-to-bumper traffic when I first left, the streets are deserted, and even when I'm slow to go through a green light, nobody honks at me. Nobody is out at midnight on a Wednesday night.

Happy Car Rental will charge me for an extra day if I return the car after midnight, so I've got to get to the rental location in time. When I pull into their lot, it's five minutes to midnight. They better not give me a hard time.

There is a boy at the counter at the car rental place who looks about as alert and enthusiastic as the boy at the motel three hours earlier. I drop the keys to the Hyundai on the counter and push them toward him.

"It's before midnight," I inform him. "So it's just one day."

I brace myself for an argument, but the boy just shrugs and accepts the keys. "Okay," he says.

I let out a yawn. I've been driving for nearly eight straight hours, and it hits me how tired I am. I can't wait to crawl into my bed. Fortunately, I don't have class tomorrow so I can sleep in. And my cleaning job obviously no longer exists.

Except the second I step back out on the streets, I question the wisdom of returning the car at midnight. Now I have to get back to the South Bronx, and I have no car. Even though I feel confident I can protect myself, I'm still not sure the subway is a good idea at this hour. Maybe on a weekend, but on Wednesday night, it's going to be just me and the muggers and rapists.

But I can't afford an Uber right now. I don't even have a job anymore.

As I stand at the street corner down the block from Happy Car Rental, weighing my options, a set of headlights illuminate the street. I swivel my head, just in time to catch sight of a car drawing closer to me. A black sedan with the Mazda logo on the front grill.

And a cracked right headlight.

Before I even get a good look at the license plate, I know it's the same car that's been following me the last couple of months. The same one that was behind me this afternoon when I was driving with Wendy. And now they have caught me alone. On a deserted street corner. In the middle of the night.

The Mazda pulls over to the side of the road. I can just barely make out the silhouette of a man in the driver's seat. The engine shuts off, but he leaves the headlights shining in my direction, bright enough that I need to turn away.

And then the door to the car swings open.

THIRTY-ONE

I will not go down without a fight.

I frantically rifle around in my purse, searching for my can of mace. I've still got some left after spraying Xavier that first time. If it's Douglas, I am not letting him squeeze any information out of me. And if it's Xavier, I took him out once, and I can do it again. I'm not afraid.

Although my heart is pounding pretty hard as he gets out of the car.

My fingers make contact with the can of mace. I pull it out, my finger on the nozzle. "Don't come any closer!" I hiss at the dark shadow.

Slowly, the shadow raises his hands in the air. A familiar voice speaks up, "Do not shoot, Millie."

It takes me a split second to recognize the voice. All at once, a warm feeling comes over me, and my face involuntarily breaks out in a smile. I lower the can of mace and propel myself at the man still standing with his hands up in the air.

"Enzo!" I cry as I throw my arms around him. "Oh my God!"

He hugs me back, and for a moment, I feel nothing but pure

joy, wrapped in my former boyfriend's warm embrace. I always used to feel so safe when he hugged me like that, and I wasn't sure I would ever be in his arms ever again. And now, here he is. His broad shoulders, his thick black hair, his penetrating eyes. And my favorite thing about him—the smile that makes me feel like he thinks I'm the most amazing person he's ever met.

"Millie," he whispers into my hair, "I am so happy to be back."

"When did you get back?"

He hesitates briefly. "A little over three months ago."

If there were a record playing beautiful reunion music, this is the moment when the record would have screeched to a halt. I pull away from Enzo, my jaw hanging open. "Three *months* ago?"

His sheepish expression tells me everything I needed to know—and unfortunately, it all makes terrible, perfect sense. For the last few months, I have had this feeling like somebody was following me—watching me. I blamed it on Xavier or Douglas, but neither of them had anything to do with it. It was *Enzo* all along. *Enzo* is the owner of the black Mazda with the cracked right headlight. I was so excited to see him, I was ignoring what was staring me right in the face.

"You were stalking me!" I smack him in the arm. "I can't believe you! Why would you do that?"

"Not stalking." His jaw tightens—God, I'd forgotten how sexy he is. It's distracting, and I can't let myself get distracted, because I am rightfully furious with this man. "Not stalking—I am bodyguard."

"Bodyguard?" I fold my arms across my chest. "That's a pretty weak excuse. Why didn't you just come up to me and say hello instead of following me around for three months?"

"Because..." He lowers his dark, dark eyes. "I thought you were mad at me because I did not come back when you wanted me to."

"Right. I *was* mad. I asked you when you were coming back, and you wouldn't even give me an answer."

"But, Millie, I couldn't. My mother... I was all she had and she was so sick. How could I leave her?"

"You left her now," I point out.

"Yes." He frowns. "That is because she is dead."

Well, now I feel like a huge jerk. "I'm really sorry, Enzo."

He's quiet for a moment. "Yes."

"I would have..." I swallow a tiny lump that has formed in my throat. "If you had told me, I could've been there for you. But you just... you blew me off. You know that."

"I *could not* come back." He grits his teeth. "That is all I told you. I never told you that I did not love you anymore." He shoots me a look. "*You* are the one who wanted to end what we have. You are the one who started dating this Broccoli."

I roll my eyes. "His name is *Brock*."

"I am just saying, you are the one who wanted to move on. Not me. I still... I never stopped feeling love for you."

I snort. "Okay, right. You expect me to believe that you have not been with any other women since me."

"No. No other woman."

His eyes meet mine—he means it. One thing Enzo doesn't do is lie. Not to me, anyway. Then again, I could be wrong. I didn't take him for a stalker either.

"You shouldn't have started following me like that," I say sternly. "It was creepy. You should have told me you were back."

"So you can tell me to get lost?" His black eyebrows shoot up. "Anyway, like I say, I am bodyguard. You need bodyguard."

"I really don't. I can take care of myself."

Now it's Enzo's turn to snort. "Oh, *really*? You live in this terrible neighborhood in South Bronx. You think you do not need me to look out for you? Let me promise you, there was at least one day when you would not have made it from the train station to your apartment building if I had not been behind you, being bodyguard."

All the hairs on the back of my neck stand up. Is he telling the truth? Was there danger lurking in the shadows behind me that he vanquished before I even knew about it?

"Like you said, I have a boyfriend," I say quietly. "And if I need it, he can protect me, thank you very much."

"Like he protected you from Xavier Marin?"

Hearing that man's name on Enzo's lips is like a punch in the face. "What do you mean?"

Even in the dark, I can see Enzo's hands balling into fists. "That man... he attacked you. I could not do anything to stop him because it was in your own building. And then they just *let him free*. And this Broccoli of yours—"

My face burns. "Brock."

"Sorry, *Brock*." His voice is tinged with fury. "He does nothing. *Nothing*. He does not care that the man who attacked his girlfriend is *still out there*. No punishment! He has gotten away with it! But I—I care." He pounds on his chest with a fist. "So I make sure that he gets what he deserves, that he will never bother you again."

My head is suddenly spinning. I remember Xavier being led out of my building in handcuffs, shouting about how the drugs they found didn't belong to him. Mrs. Randall said everyone was surprised to learn he was dealing drugs. "*You* were the one who..."

He lifts a shoulder. "I know a guy."

It's because of Enzo that Xavier is in prison. If not for him, that man would still be walking around the streets. Enzo is right—Brock did nothing.

Suddenly, I'm not sure what to think anymore.

"Come on." He waves a hand in the direction of his Mazda. "I give you ride home. You think over whether you hate me or not."

Fair enough.

I climb into the car next to Enzo, who sits in the driver's seat. The car smells like him. That woodsy scent he always has. I close my eyes, lost in the past. Why did he have to leave? Now things are so complicated. He's done too many things wrong. I can't just forgive him.

Can I?

"So," he says as we start driving uptown. "Where were you driving in so much big rush today?"

I tug at a loose thread on my jeans. "As if you don't know."

"I do not know everything, Millie." He glances over at me, his face partially obscured by shadows. "Tell me."

So I do.

THIRTY-TWO

I tell him everything. Every last detail of Douglas's abuse and Wendy's escape.

I promised Wendy I wouldn't tell anyone, but Enzo isn't anyone. He gets it. He and I worked side by side helping women like Wendy. If there is any human being in the entire world I can trust to tell the story to, it is him.

It takes me nearly to my front door before I get to the end of the story. Enzo hasn't said much. That's typical for him though. I've never met such an intense listener. I often appreciate how he makes me feel so heard. But at the same time, it drives me nuts when I can't tell what he's thinking.

"So," I finally say after I describe dropping Wendy off at the motel and driving back to the city, "that's that. She's safe now."

Enzo is still quiet. "Maybe," he finally says.

"Not maybe. She *is*."

"This man, Douglas Garrick," he says. "He is a powerful and dangerous man. I don't think it will be this easy."

"You're just saying that because I did it without you. You don't believe I can do this without you."

He pulls up onto the street in front of my apartment building. The street is completely quiet and dark except for a lone man on the corner who is smoking something that probably isn't a cigarette. When I look at this street, I can see why Enzo felt compelled to protect me, even though I still don't believe I needed it.

He turns to look me in the eyes. "I believe you can do anything," he says quietly. "But, Millie, I am just saying... be careful."

"Wendy is very careful."

"No." His dark eyes bore into me. "*You* be careful. She is gone, but you are still here."

I understand what he is saying. If Douglas gets an inkling that I was involved with his wife's disappearance, he could make things very difficult for me. But I'm ready for him. I've dealt with worse men than him and come out ahead.

"I'll be careful," I tell him. "It's not your responsibility to worry about me anymore. So you don't need to protect me."

"So who will? Broccoli?"

My face burns. "Actually, I don't need *either* of you to protect me. When that asshole attacked me in my building, I took care of myself very nicely. So don't worry about me. If you're worried about anyone, you should worry about Douglas Garrick's safety—from *me*."

"Well," he says, "that too."

We stare at each other for a moment. I wish he hadn't left me and gone back to Italy. If that hadn't happened, he could've helped me with Wendy. He could have told me his reservations earlier so we could have addressed them. He could've helped her to get a new ID so that she could have more options.

And I'd be going home with him tonight, instead of Broccoli. I mean, *Brock*.

"I better go," I say.

He nods slowly. "Okay."

I unbuckle my seatbelt, although I feel reluctant to get out of the car. "You need to stop following me."

"Okay."

"I mean it." I glare at him. "I'm dating someone else right now. You're *stalking* me. It's creepy, and it's unnecessary. You need to stop. Or else... I'll have to call the police or something."

"I said okay." He places a hand on his chest. He's wearing a T-shirt under his light jacket, and I can sadly still make out all the muscles underneath. "I give you my word. No more watching."

"Good."

I won't be getting that creepy sensation anymore that somebody is watching me. I have officially solved the mystery of the black Mazda with the cracked headlight, and this car will not be bothering me ever again. I should feel relieved, but I don't. If anything, I feel even more uneasy. I had a guardian angel, and I didn't even know it.

"Anyway..." I open up the passenger's side door. "I guess this is goodbye."

I start to get out of the car, but then Enzo's hand encircles my forearm. I turn to look at him, and his dark eyebrows are bunched together. "I still have the same phone number," he tells me. "You need me, you call. I will be there."

I try to force a smile, but it doesn't quite materialize. "I won't need you. You should... like, find another girlfriend. I mean it."

He releases my arm, but that frown is still on his lips. "You call. I will wait."

It's maddening how certain he seems that I will call him. If there's one thing he should know about me, it's that I am capable of taking care of myself. Sometimes a bit *too* well.

But as I'm walking up the steps to the third floor of my building, a terrible feeling mounts in the pit of my stomach. What if Enzo is right? What if I did underestimate Douglas

Garrick? After all, he is a truly terrible man based on everything I have seen. And on top of that, he is incredibly rich.

It can't possibly be that easy for Wendy to get away from him, can it? When Enzo and I used to help women get away from their abusive spouses, we planned it out so meticulously, and even then, we would sometimes be found out. I have a feeling Douglas is smarter than many of the other men we've dealt with. Even though I know now he wasn't the one in the car following me, he may have other ways of keeping tabs on his wife.

What if he knew exactly what we were planning tonight?

The thought hits me like a ton of bricks as I reach that landing for the third floor. Much like the street, the third floor of my building is completely silent. And even if Enzo is lingering outside—even though I made him promise not to—he can't help me in here.

I stare at the closed door to my apartment. There's a deadbolt inside, but I can't lock that when I am leaving for the day. The lock on the door is almost pathetically easy to pick. Even I could probably do it. But I was never bothered by it, because I have nothing worth stealing.

If someone wanted to get into my apartment, it would be far too easy.

The keys to my door are in my right hand, but I hesitate before fitting them into the lock. What if Douglas really is one step ahead of me? What if he is waiting inside my apartment, ready to persuade me to give Wendy's location away by any means necessary?

Wherever Enzo is, he could not have gotten far. I have his number programmed into my phone—I never deleted it. I could call him and ask him to come into the apartment with me, just to make sure it's safe.

Of course, after that speech I made about how I don't need

him, it would involve swallowing my pride. But I've done plenty of that in my lifetime. What's one more time?

I clench the keys in my fist. I need to make a decision.

I push away my nagging doubts and fit the key into the lock. As it turns, my heart thuds in my chest, but I push the door open.

For a second, I almost expect something to jump out at me. I curse myself for not having my mace ready to go. But when I get inside, everything is quiet. Nobody is waiting for me. Nobody jumps out at me. Nobody is here at all.

"Hello?" I call out. As if the intruder is sitting around, waiting for a proper greeting.

There's no answer. I'm alone in this apartment. Maybe Douglas will put it all together, but it hasn't happened yet.

So I close the door to the apartment behind me and I lock the deadbolt.

THIRTY-THREE

"You know," Brock tells me as he shoves a forkful of pad Thai noodles into his mouth, "a part-time receptionist position opened up at my law firm. Are you interested?"

The two of us are eating dinner at Brock's apartment, in his tiny dining room. The Garricks have a legit dining room, but most apartments in New York just have a tiny little area off the living room with a table that can be manually extended to accommodate more than four people. And Brock's apartment is considered *large* by Manhattan standards. In a *small* apartment, there wouldn't be a dining area at all, and the kitchen and the living room and the bedroom and the bathroom would all be one room, like at my place.

That said, he could afford better if he wanted. His parents are wealthy—not insanely rich like Douglas Garrick, but definitively upper class—but he doesn't want to take any of their money, as much as they try to offer it to him. *They taught me to fish*, he's fond of saying. He feels like it's enough that they paid for his Ivy League college degree and law degree, and now it's up to him to earn his own living, i.e. fish.

I respect that about him. He really is a great guy. And I

appreciate that he hasn't pressured me to set another specific date to have The Talk, although now it feels like I could just postpone it indefinitely—even though I know I shouldn't.

I mix a little bit more of my red curry with the white rice. I love the food from this restaurant, because the curries are always super spicy. "A secretarial job, huh?"

Brock nods. "You're looking, right?"

It's been three days since I dropped Wendy off in Albany. I told Brock something vague about them not requiring my services anymore, and he had no reason to suspect anything else was going on. Douglas Garrick is supposed to return from his business trip tomorrow, and when I think about it, I get a sick feeling in my stomach. But I still believe it's all going to work out.

Either way, I'll have to find a way to leave that cleaning position. Maybe I'll send Douglas a text message in the next week to let him know my schedule has filled up and I can't work for him anymore. That will leave me woefully unemployed, and the idea of a job with regular hours and *oh my God benefits* is amazing.

"That sounds great," I say. "But would a receptionist job work with my school schedule?"

"Like I said, it's part-time," he says. "They're actually hoping for somebody who could do weekends, so that would be perfect for you."

It would be perfect. Absolutely perfect. And Brock has told me that everybody at his company is well paid. And then I wouldn't have to deal with working for all these neurotic Manhattan couples.

Of course, if Brock's company is considering hiring me, they're going to do a background check. And when they find out about my past, so will he. I can just imagine someone at his firm ribbing him about it. *Hey, Brock, heard your girlfriend has a prison record.*

I can almost imagine his reaction. His usual easy smile sliding off his face. *What? What do you mean?* And then the conversation when he gets home from work... oh God...

This is getting crazy. I have kept this from him long enough. And if I told Enzo that this guy is The Guy, then that means I'm serious about him. That means being completely honest.

"Also," Brock says, "my parents are coming into town for a wedding next month. And I..." He flashes me a crooked smile. "I'd like us all to have dinner together."

"Your parents?" I gulp.

"I want them to meet you." He reaches across the tiny dining table and places his hand on top of mine. "I want them to get to know the woman I love."

If we were in an "I love you" competition, Brock would be clobbering me by a ratio of like ten to one.

This is getting out of control. I can't postpone The Talk any longer. I have to tell him everything. Now.

"Hey, Brock." I put down my fork. "There's something I need to talk to you about."

He arches an eyebrow. "Oh?"

"Yes..."

"That doesn't sound good."

"No, it's..." I try to swallow, but my throat is too dry. I reach for my glass, but I drank all of my water while eating my spicy curry. "Let me get some more water."

Brock is staring at me as I grab my water glass and hurry to the kitchen. I stick the glass under the water filter, wishing for once that the water poured out a little slower. While I'm filling up my water, my phone buzzes inside my pocket. Someone is calling me.

Wendy's name is on my phone screen. I took down her number, in case something went wrong with our escape plan and she needed me to intervene. But she left that phone behind in the penthouse. So why is she calling now?

I take the call, lowering my voice so Brock can't hear. I'm sure he wouldn't approve of any of this, and it's especially important not to say a word to him since he apparently knows Douglas Garrick and thinks he's a nice guy. "Wendy," I whisper. "What's going on?"

For a second, there's only silence on the other line. Then the sound of quiet sobbing. "I'm back. He brought me back."

"Oh God..."

"Millie." Her voice cracks. "Can you please come here?"

Brock's apartment is only about a fifteen-minute walk from the penthouse. I could be there in twenty minutes. But how can I? I just initiated a serious discussion with my boyfriend that will probably take up the rest of the night.

But he doesn't need me as badly as Wendy does.

"I'll be there soon," I promise her.

I leave my glass of water in the kitchen and march back out to the dining area. Brock looks like he has barely touched his pad Thai noodles since I left the kitchen. "So?" he says.

"Listen," I say, "I had an emergency come up. I... I have to go."

"*Now?*"

"I'm so sorry," I say. "We'll talk tomorrow night—I promise."

Brock's lower lip juts out. "Millie..."

"I *promise*." I plead with him with my eyes. "And... I'd love to meet your parents. I think it will be great."

That last statement seems to placate him. "I know you're nervous about meeting my parents," he says, "but you'll love my mom. She's from Brooklyn too. She went to Brooklyn College, and she's got the same accent as you."

"I don't have an accent!"

"You do." He grins at me. "A slight one. It's cute."

"Yeah, yeah..."

He stands up from the table and reaches for me. Even though I'm itching to run over to the penthouse, I let him take me in his arms. "I just want you to know," he says, "that whatever terrible thing you feel like you need to tell me about yourself, it's okay. I love you no matter what."

I look into his blue eyes, and I can tell that he means it. "We'll talk about this soon," I promise. "And... I love you too."

It gets easier every time I say it.

He kisses me deeply on the lips, and for a moment, I truly wish I did not have to leave. But I don't have a choice.

THIRTY-FOUR

The gears in the elevator are grinding more than usual.

I wonder how old this elevator is. I read somewhere that elevators were first used in homes in the late 1920s. So even if this elevator is one of the very first elevators in history, it's still less than a century old. So that's comforting, I guess?

Still, one of these days, I'm certain that all the ancient gears are going to rust mid-turn and I will just be trapped in this elevator for the rest of my life.

I glance down at my watch. It is just under twenty minutes since Wendy called me. I tried calling again to let her know I was on my way, but she didn't pick up. I'm scared about what I'm going to find when I get up to the twentieth floor.

My God, can this elevator go any slower?

Finally, the elevator grinds to a halt and the doors swing open. The sun has dropped in the sky, and the penthouse is dark. Why hasn't somebody turned on the lights? What's going on here?

"Hello?" I call out.

Then a terrible thought occurs to me.

What if Douglas is here? What if he forced Wendy to call

me and asked me to come over, so he could punish me for helping her? That seems like the sort of thing he is capable of.

I feel around in my purse for my mace. I locate it next to my compact, and I pull it out, gripping it in my right hand.

"Wendy?" I squeak.

With my left hand, I reach into my jeans pocket, where I stuffed my phone. I don't want to call the police, but at the same time, I have a terrible feeling about what I'm going to find in this penthouse.

I step into the living room, my footsteps on the floor as loud as gunshots in this quiet, vacuous apartment. My heart stops when I spot the red staining the carpet. And then the body lying strewn across the sectional sofa.

"Wendy!" I cry out.

This is so much worse than I thought. Douglas isn't searching for his wife or trying to exact revenge. He already found her, and now she is lying dead on the sofa. I run over to her, expecting to see a gaping knife wound on her chest and crimson staining the front of her dark blue dress. But I don't see any of that.

And then she opens her eyes.

"Wendy!" I feel like I'm about to fall over from a heart attack. I wish I had some of Brock's medication available, because my heart has gone into some crazy irregular rhythm. "Oh my God! I thought you were—"

"Dead?" She sits up on the sofa, and that's when I realize the crimson on the floor is red wine that's spilled from a glass tipped over on the coffee table—Douglas will go crazy if I don't get it cleaned up. She laughs bitterly. "Oh, I wish."

I was so focused on searching her body for wounds or blood, I didn't notice the fresh bruise blossoming on her left cheek, where the last one had almost faded. I wince at the sight of it—I can only imagine what caused such a thing.

"Your face," I breathe.

"That's not the worst of it." Wendy props herself up on the sofa, and she flinches and grabs her rib cage. "He definitely broke my ribs."

"You need to go to the hospital!"

"Not a chance." She shoots me a look. "But I could use an ice pack."

I run into the kitchen and find an ice pack sitting in the freezer. I cover it in a dish towel, then I bring it out to her. She takes it gratefully, debates for a moment where she wants to put it, then finally rests it on her chest.

"He was waiting for me," she says in a voice that is not much louder than a whisper. "When we got to Fiona's farm in Potsdam. He was already there. He *knew*."

I shake my head. I don't understand how this happened. I had expected he might find her eventually, but so fast?

"I don't know how he found me so quickly." She shuts her eyes as if trying to ward off a headache. "I thought there was a chance he might find me eventually, but not so quickly. I thought I had more time..."

"I know..."

"Millie." She shifts so that the ice pack slides out of place briefly. "Did you tell anyone where we went?"

"Absolutely not!"

Well, that's not entirely true. I did tell one person. I told Enzo.

But telling Enzo is as good as telling nobody. Enzo would never breathe a word about something like this. If anything, he would try to protect her.

"I was stupid to think I could ever get away from him." She adjusts the ice pack. "This is my life. It's easier if I just... accept it."

"You shouldn't accept it." I reach out and squeeze her hand. "Wendy, I'm going to help you. You do not have to spend the rest of your life putting up with him."

"I know you mean well..."

"No." My jaw twitches. "Listen to me. I'm going to help you. I promise."

Wendy doesn't say anything. She doesn't believe me anymore. But I'm going to make this right somehow.

I won't let Douglas Garrick get away with hurting her like this.

THIRTY-FIVE

I am still working for the Garrick family.

I couldn't tell Brock the real reason why I decided to stay with them and turned down the interview at his firm, only that they decided they needed me after all. He didn't ask any further questions, but mostly because I've been avoiding him.

The next time I see him, I have to come clean about my past. It's time. But that doesn't mean I'm not dreading it, so I've been conveniently "busy" the last couple of days. Even though I promised to explain it all to him "soon," there is literally never a good time. Maybe there never will be.

But I have to tell him. He has to know the truth before he goes through introducing me to his parents, for God's sake.

Tonight I'm preparing dinner for the Garricks. I've got chicken breasts roasting in the oven and I'm boiling potatoes on the stove, which I will be running through the food processor to make a perfectly silky potato purée, exactly the way Douglas likes it. I'd be tempted to spit in it if I didn't know that Wendy was eating it too.

While I'm checking the oven, Wendy peeks into the

kitchen. Her bruised face looks a lot better and she doesn't flinch when she walks anymore, so I assume she's healing.

"Dinner is almost ready," I tell her.

She lingers in the doorway to the kitchen for a moment. Finally, she says, "I need to talk to you for a moment, Millie. Can you come into the living room?"

The food should be okay to leave for a few minutes, so I immediately follow Wendy into her living room and over to a desk in the corner of the room. She has a strange expression on her face, and I feel a flash of worry. A couple of days ago, I promised her that I would figure out a way out of her situation, and I have not yet delivered on that promise. But I *will*.

I'm just trying to figure out a way to do it without involving Enzo.

"I discovered something the other day in Douglas's bookcase," she tells me. "Something I'd like you to see."

I follow her with a mixture of curiosity and anxiety as she limps up the stairs to a bookcase in the hallway. She pulls what appears to be a dictionary out of the bookcase and lowers it down onto an empty shelf. She flips it open and that's when I realize that the dictionary has been completely hollowed out.

And inside is a gun.

I clasp a hand over my mouth. "Oh my God. That belongs to Douglas?"

She nods. "I knew he had a gun somewhere in the house, but I never knew where he kept it."

"He doesn't even lock it up?"

"I guess he wants to be able to get to it quickly if he needs to." Wendy lifts the gun out of the hollowed book. She holds it like somebody who has never held a gun before. "This is a way out."

"No. *No.*" I push back a swell of panic in my chest. "Trust me, no matter how desperate you are, you do *not* want to do this."

I don't have much experience with guns, but I have a *lot* of experience with doing something drastic out of desperation. I am never, *ever* going down that road again. And neither should she.

But Wendy isn't listening. She holds the gun clasped in both hands and points it across the room. Her finger isn't on the trigger, but her intention is obvious.

"Please don't do that," I beg her.

"It's loaded too," she says. "I looked up how to check. It's got five bullets in it."

I can't stop shaking my head. "Wendy, you don't want to do this. I promise you."

She turns to look at me, her left cheekbone still purple from her husband's fist, although it's fading to yellow. "What choice do I have?"

"Do you want to spend the rest of your life in prison?"

"I'm already there."

"Listen to me." As gently as I can, I tug the gun out of her hands. I lay it back down on the desk. "You don't want to do this. There's another way."

"I don't believe you anymore."

I imagine Wendy pointing the gun at Douglas's face. With the way she was holding the gun just now and how much she was trembling, she would probably miss even at close range. "Do you even have any idea how to fire this thing?"

She shrugs. "You point it at whoever you want to kill, then you pull the trigger. It's not rocket science."

"There's a little more to it than that."

Her eyes widen. "Have *you* ever shot a gun before, Millie?"

I hesitate a bit too long. Yes, I do have a little bit of experience shooting a gun. Enzo was convinced it was a good skill to know, so the two of us went to the firing range a few times. We took a gun safety course and we got certificates. But I've never shot one except at the firing range. I'm hardly an expert. "Sort of."

She gives me a meaningful look. "Millie..."

"No." I pick up the gun and place it back in the fake dictionary. I close it with a snap. "That's not going to happen."

"But—"

Whatever Wendy was about to say gets cut off by the sound of the elevator doors grinding open. I quickly pick up the dictionary and shove it back on the shelf where I found it, while Wendy dashes back into the guest bedroom with shocking speed. I hurry down the stairs, so Douglas won't realize what I was doing.

Douglas wanders into the living room and looks slightly taken aback to see me coming down the stairs. His thick black eyebrows creep up his forehead. "I thought you would be preparing dinner?"

"I am," I assure him. "It's in the oven right now."

"I see..." His deep-set eyes study my face, carefully enough to make me squirm. "What's for dinner then?"

"Roasted chicken breast, potato purée, and glazed carrots," I reply, even though today's menu was carefully arranged by Douglas himself.

Douglas thinks it over for a moment. "Don't put any potatoes on my wife's plate. They upset her stomach."

"Okay..."

"And just a half portion of chicken for her," he adds. "She hasn't been well, and I doubt she'll be able to eat much."

As I drain the potatoes that Wendy will not be able to partake in, I finally understand why Wendy is so painfully thin. Douglas is the one who brings her food every night. He controls every bite that goes into her mouth.

On top of everything else, he's systematically starving her. Yet another way to control her, keep her weak, and kill her spirit.

Wendy is right. This needs to come to an end.

On the plus side, now I can safely spit in the potato purée.

THIRTY-SIX

I'm still thinking about that gun hidden in the dictionary as I crawl into bed.

The look in Wendy's eyes when she showed it to me was unmistakable. She means business. She has reached a point of desperation in which she's thinking to herself, *him or me.* And that's a bad place to be. That's when you start making stupid mistakes.

Sooner rather than later, I need to give Enzo a call. He will help her better than I can. But I can't call him now. It's close to midnight, and if he sees me calling him at this hour, he will definitely think this is a booty call. I do not want him to get the wrong idea.

Although there is a small part of me that hasn't stopped thinking about him since that night I went to Albany.

I'm still mad at him for disappearing like he did, but I can't deny the pure joy I felt when he came out of that car. It hits me now that I have never felt that way for Brock, and I'm not sure I ever will.

But that's not fair to Brock. My boyfriend has so many good

qualities. Most of all, he is a solid guy who would never abandon me in a time of need. I'm sure of that much.

Then again, I haven't been able to tell him any of the stuff going on with Wendy. His response would be to call the police immediately and not get involved. Typical lawyer thinking.

As if his ears are burning in the next borough, a text message from Brock pops up on my phone:

Love you.

I grit my teeth. Oh my God, how many times does this man have to tell me he loves me? He's expecting me to write it back, but I just can't make myself do it right now. These "I love you's" are holding me hostage. So instead, I take a selfie of myself making a kissy face and I text it back to him. That's kind of like saying I love you, right? He writes back instantly.

You look cute. I wish you were here.

Oh my God, does literally everything he says to me have to be some sort of guilt trip about the fact that I didn't move in with him?

I toss my phone aside, frustrated. I start to get up to brush my teeth when the phone starts ringing. It's probably Brock, considering I didn't answer his text. He's probably going to ask if he can come over. And I'm going to have to nicely tell him no.

Except when I look down at the screen of my phone, it's not Brock. It's *Douglas.*

Why is *Douglas* calling me at midnight?

I stare down at my phone for a minute, my heart pounding. There's no good reason my boss would be calling me at midnight. I'm tempted to let it go to voicemail, but instead, I swipe to take the call.

"Millie." His voice sounds slightly clipped. "I didn't wake you, did I?"

"No..."

"Good," he says. "I'm sorry to call you so late, but I thought it's better if you hear this now. After this week, we will no longer be requiring your services."

"You... you're firing me?"

"Well," he says, "not firing, exactly. More like letting you go. Wendy seems to be feeling better, and she would like to have some privacy in our own house again."

"Oh..."

"It's not that you didn't do an adequate job." Gee, thanks. "It's just that a married couple needs their privacy. Do you understand what I'm saying?"

I'm getting the message loud and clear. He doesn't want me to talk to Wendy or attempt to help her.

"You understand, don't you, Millie?" he presses me.

"Sure," I say through clenched teeth. "Of course I do."

"Good." His tone lightens. "And just to thank you for everything you have done for us, I'd like to give you a pair of tickets to a Mets game. You'd like that, wouldn't you?"

"Yes," I say slowly. "I do like the Mets..."

"Great! It's all settled then."

"Uh-huh."

"Good night, Millie. Sleep tight."

As I hang up the phone, I still have an uneasy feeling. Something was bothering me about that conversation—something I can't quite put my finger on. I plop back down on my bed, and that's when I look down at the oversized T-shirt that I'm wearing to sleep in.

It's a Mets T-shirt.

I raise my eyes to look at the window across from me. The blinds are closed like they always are. I run over to the window and crack my fingers between the blinds to look outside at the street. It's completely dark. I don't see any ominous men standing outside. Nobody is staring at my window with a pair of binoculars.

Maybe it was just a coincidence. I mean, I'm from New York. Who doesn't like the Mets?

But I don't think it was. There was something in his tone when he mentioned getting me Mets tickets. *I'd like to give you a pair of tickets to a Mets game. You'd like that, wouldn't you?*

Oh my God, what if he can see me in here?

But it's not like it's some huge secret I wear a Mets shirt to sleep in. I may have opened the door wearing it at some point. And all the boyfriends I've had know about it, even if that list only includes Brock and Enzo.

Still—I've got a few other shirts I sleep in too. Douglas knew what I was wearing *tonight*.

I swore to Wendy that I would never give up on her, but I have to admit, I am thoroughly freaked out. The blinds are closed. I never open them in the evening, especially when I'm changing into my nightshirt.

My hands are shaking as I pick up my phone and send a message to Brock:

Do you want to come over?

As always, he answers right away:

I'll be there as soon as I can.

THIRTY-SEVEN

As soon as I finish folding this laundry, I am going to meet Brock for dinner.

Douglas texted me and arranged a time for my final cleaning session. After this, I will have to look for a new job, so I'm hoping he gives me an enormous tip. Although I'm not holding my breath.

I'm glad this will be my last time working for the Garricks. I haven't given up on Wendy, but I don't want to be in this house anymore. Douglas Garrick gives me the creeps, and the further away from him I can get, the better. I'll do whatever I can to help Wendy on the outside.

There's something else weighing heavily on my mind tonight: As soon as I'm done here, Brock and I are going to have The Talk. We have carefully avoided any serious discussions the last few times I've seen him, but that's gone on long enough. I am meeting him at his apartment, and I am going to tell him everything. A Complete Guide to Millie. And maybe it will be over, but maybe he'll be fine with everything. There's only one way to find out.

Most of the Garricks' clothing goes to the dry cleaner, so it's just a small load of undershirts, underwear, and socks, most of which barely even seemed dirty when I threw them in the washing machine. As I sort them and place them in the appropriate drawers, I can't stop thinking about the gun hidden in the bookcase.

I made Wendy swear she wouldn't do anything stupid, and although she did promise me, I don't entirely believe her. She has reached the end of her rope. I could see the desperation in her bruised face as she held that gun in her hands. The next time Douglas pisses her off, she very well might kill him.

Not that I have a problem with that asshole getting 86'd. But if she does it, she's going to prison. She never went to any doctors or hospitals to document the way he was abusing her, and although I would swear to what I know in a courtroom, it might not be enough.

I've officially decided I'm going to call Enzo tomorrow. The best thing might be for me to step away from this situation entirely—especially since I won't even be working here anymore—and I'll let him handle it. After all, he's the one who knows all "the guys." It made sense to be a team when we were dating, but the truth is, it's hard to be around him now.

Enzo will help Wendy. I know he will.

I'm just about finished with the laundry when a crash comes from down the hallway. I've heard a crash here like that before. The difference is, now I know that it's the sound of Wendy being hurt.

I come out of the master bedroom to see what's going on. As always, the door to the guestroom is closed tight, but I can hear Douglas's voice coming from inside:

"I just saw this charge on the credit card!" he booms from down the hall. "What is this? Eighty dollars for lunch at La Cipolla?"

I've never heard him speak to her this way. He must not realize I'm in the house. He told me to leave early, so he must think that I have already left and that he can say whatever he wants to her without me hearing.

"I... I'm sorry." Wendy sounds frantic. "I met my friend Gisele for lunch, and she's between jobs, so I offered to pay."

"Who told you that you could leave the house?"

"What?"

"Who told you that you could leave the house, Wendy?"

"I... I just... I'm sorry, it's just so hard to be inside all the time and..."

"Someone could have seen you!" he rants. "They could've seen your face, and then what would they think about me?"

"I... I'm sorry, I..."

"I'll just bet you're sorry. You don't think about anything, do you? You *want* people to think I'm a monster!"

"No. That's not true. I swear."

There's a long silence coming from the room. Is the fight over? Or do I need to barge in or call the police? But no, I can't call the police—Wendy told me that's off the table.

What I wouldn't give for a friend in the NYPD...

I tiptoe as close as I dare to the bedroom, straining to hear them. Just as I'm about to knock on the door, Douglas starts talking again, and this time he sounds even angrier.

"That restaurant is awfully romantic for you and a friend, isn't it?" he says.

"What? No! It's not... romantic..."

"I can always tell when you're lying, Wendy. Who were you really having that fancy lunch with?"

"I told you! It was Gisele."

"Right. Now tell me the *truth*. Was it the same guy who drove you upstate?"

I creep closer to the room. Wendy is sobbing.

"It was Gisele," she whimpers.

"This is bullshit," he hisses. "I'm not going to allow my

tramp wife to go all around town with some other man! It's humiliating."

That's when a sickening crash comes from inside the room. And Wendy screams.

I can't let him hurt her. I've got to do something. Except all of a sudden, the room has gone completely silent.

And then I hear a gurgling sound coming from inside the room.

Like a woman is being choked.

There is no messing around anymore. Whatever is happening in that room, I have got to stop it.

And then I remember the gun.

THIRTY-EIGHT

I remember exactly where the gun is.

I race over to the bookcase and pull out the dictionary. The gun is nestled in the same hollowed-out spot where it was two days ago when Wendy showed it to me. Just as I knew it would be. I pick up the gun with only slightly shaking hands.

As I stare at the revolver in my hand, I wonder if I am making a grave mistake. Even though there is something terrible going on in that room, I don't know if it will make things better to bring a gun into the mix. When there's a chance of somebody getting shot, things can quickly take a turn for the worse.

But I'm not going to shoot Douglas. That is off the table. My only intention is to scare him. After all, there's nothing scarier than a gun. I am counting on the element of surprise to end things.

With the revolver nestled in my hand, I hurry back down the dark hallway to the guestroom. The fighting has stopped and everything is silent within the room. And somehow that is the scariest thing of all.

I consider knocking, but then I decide to try the knob. It

turns easily in my hand. As I push the door open, a voice speaks to me in the back of my head:

Put down the gun, Millie. Handle this without it. You're making a terrible mistake.

But it's too late.

I push open the door to the guest bedroom. The sight before my eyes takes my breath away. It's Douglas and Wendy. He's got her pressed against the wall, his hands wrapped around her throat, and Wendy's face is starting to turn blue. She has her mouth open to scream, but no sound can come out.

Oh my God, he's trying to kill her.

I don't know if he's going to choke her or break her neck with his bare hands, but I've got to do something right now—I can't just stand here and allow this to happen. But I have learned from past mistakes. I may have a gun, but I have no intention of killing him. The threat should be enough. And then I will tell the police what I saw.

You can do this, Millie. Don't hurt him. Just make him let her go.

"Douglas!" I bark at him. "Let her go!"

I expect him to back away from her, full of phony apologies and explanations. But somehow, his fingers don't budge. Wendy manages another gurgling sound.

So I take the gun and point it at his chest.

"I mean it." My voice trembles. "Let her go or I'll shoot."

But Douglas somehow isn't hearing what I'm telling him. His eyes are wild, and he seems determined to end this—right here and now. Wendy has stopped clawing at him and her body has gone limp. The time for negotiating has passed. If I don't do something in the next few seconds, he is going to kill her.

And I will have let it happen.

"I swear to God," I croak, "I'm going to shoot if you don't let her go!"

But he doesn't. He just keeps squeezing.

I don't have a choice. There's only one thing I can do in this situation.

I pull the trigger.

THIRTY-NINE

Douglas goes slack seconds after the gunshot rings out through the apartment. It's louder than I expected, loud enough that the neighbors certainly will have heard. Well, maybe not. The walls and ceilings are likely soundproof in a place like this and we've got the floor below us as a buffer.

On the plus side, Douglas's fingers slide off Wendy's neck.

Wendy collapses to her knees, coughing and crying and clutching her throat, while her husband lies beside her on the floor, his body immobile. After a second, a pool of crimson spreads beneath him onto the plush carpeting.

Oh no.

Not again.

The gun falls from my fingers and lands on the floor beside me with a loud thump. I feel completely frozen. Douglas Garrick isn't moving at all, and the puddle beneath him keeps growing. I meant to shoot him in the shoulder, enough to wound him and force him to take his hands off Wendy, but not enough to kill him.

Looks like I missed.

Wendy rubs her watery eyes. Miraculously, she's still

conscious. She kneels beside her husband, placing a hand on his neck, over his carotid artery. She keeps her hand there for a moment, then looks up at me. "There's no pulse."

Oh God.

"He's dead," she whispers in a hoarse voice. "He's really dead."

"I didn't mean to kill him," I sputter. "I... I was just trying to get him to take his hands off of you. I never meant to—"

"Thank you," Wendy says. "Thank you for saving my life. I knew you would."

We just stare at each other for a moment. I did save her life. I have to remember that. I'll have to explain it to the police when they get here.

"You need to leave." Wendy rises to her feet, even though her legs look shaky. "We... we can wipe the fingerprints off the gun. That should work, shouldn't it? Yes, yes, I'm sure it will. I won't call the police for a couple of hours, and then I'll tell them... Oh! I can say I thought Douglas was an intruder and shot him by accident. It was all an accident, you know? They'll believe that. I'm sure they will."

She's talking fast—she's in a panic. As much as I would love to have the heat taken off of me, there's a huge hole in her story. "But the doorman saw when Douglas entered the building."

She shakes her head. "No, he didn't. Some of the residents have access to the back entrance, and he always comes in that way."

"Is there a camera there?"

"No. No camera."

"What about the cameras in the elevators?"

"Those?" She snorts. "Those are merely decorative. One of them broke five years ago, and the other has been out of commission for at least two years."

Could this really work? I just shot Douglas Garrick in cold

blood. Is there any chance I could get away with this without any consequences? Then again, it wouldn't be the first time.

"Leave now." She steps over Douglas's body, carefully side-stepping the pool of blood. "I will take responsibility for this. This is on me. I brought you into this, and I am not going to drag you down with me. Get out of here while you still can."

"Wendy..."

"Go!" Her eyes look almost as wild as Douglas's did when his hands were wrapped around her neck. "Please, Millie. This is the only way."

"Okay," I say quietly. "But... if you need me..."

She reaches out to squeeze my arm. "Believe me, you've done enough." She hesitates. "You should delete all our text messages. The ones from me, and also the ones from Douglas. Just in case."

That is an extremely good idea. Wendy and I have discussed some things that I wouldn't want the police to know about if they started investigating this murder. And it might be better if they don't see the texts between me and Douglas, noting today would be my last session. I grab my purse, and my hands are shaking almost too badly to do it, but I manage to delete the conversations with both the Garricks off my phone.

"Don't try to contact me," she says. "I will take care of this, Millie. Don't worry."

I start to argue, but then I shut my mouth. There's no point. Wendy has already decided that she wants to take the heat, and it's in my best interest to let her. I say goodbye to the penthouse, knowing I will never set foot in this place ever again. The last thing I see when I leave the bedroom is Wendy standing over Douglas's dead body.

And she's smiling.

FORTY

The entire subway ride back home, I can't stop shaking.

Everybody on the subway must think I am a crazy person, because even though it's crowded, nobody has sat down on either side of me by the time I get back to the Bronx. I basically spend the entire ride hugging myself and rocking back and forth.

I can't believe I killed him. I didn't mean to.

No, that's not fair. I shot the man in the chest. It would be a lie to say that I didn't want him dead. But this was the last way I wanted things to unfold when I saw that gun in the dictionary.

But it's going to be okay. I've been through this before. Wendy will stick to her story, and the police won't have any idea that I was involved.

Now I just have to deal with the fact that I killed a man. *Again.*

The second I get out of the subway station, my phone buzzes. A missed call. I pull it out of my purse, half expecting it to be Wendy, but instead, the screen is filled with missed calls and voicemails from Brock.

Oh no. We were supposed to have dinner tonight. This was

supposed to be the night we were going to have the big talk. Well, that isn't going to happen anymore.

I stare down at Brock's name on my phone for a moment, knowing that I have to call him, but not wanting to do it. Finally, I click on his name. He answers almost instantly.

"Millie?" He sounds some combination of angry and concerned. "Where are you?"

"I..." I wish I had taken a moment to think of a valid excuse before calling him. "I'm not feeling well."

"Oh really?" He sounds skeptical. "What's wrong, exactly?"

"I... I have a stomach bug." When he doesn't say anything, I decide to embellish a few more details. "It came on suddenly. I feel awful. I just keep, you know, throwing up. And also... well, it's coming out of both ends. I think I need to stay in tonight."

I brace myself for him to call me on my phony story, but instead, his voice softens. "You don't sound good."

"Yeah..."

"I could come by," he offers. "I could bring you some chicken soup? Rub your back?"

I have the sweetest boyfriend ever. He is just such a good guy. And as soon as this blows over, I am going to absolutely make it up to him. I really do love him. I think.

"No, but thank you," I breathe into the phone. "I just need to be alone and recover. Rain check?"

"Sure," he says. "Just get better."

When I hang up the phone, I feel guilty now for how I'm treating Brock on top of everything else. But I don't want to drag him into this mess. The only person I could talk to about this is Enzo, and that's a bad idea for so many reasons. I need to just go home and try not to think about any of it. Soon, this will all be behind me.

FORTY-ONE

I wake up feeling like I got hit by a truck, and my right temple is pounding.

I couldn't sleep last night. I tossed and turned, and every time I started to drift off, I would see Douglas's dead body lying on the floor of the penthouse. Finally, I stumbled to the bathroom and took one of the sleeping pills I've got stashed there. Then I drifted into a dream-filled sleep, haunted by my former boss's dead eyes staring at me.

I roll over in bed, touching my rat's nest of hair. The pounding in my temple intensifies, and it takes a moment to realize that there is also pounding coming from the front door.

Someone is at the front door.

I manage to crawl out of bed and wrap a housecoat around my body. "I'm coming!" I croak, hoping the pounding might stop. But whoever is at the door is persistent.

I peek through the peephole. A man is standing there, wearing a crisp white shirt and black tie under a trench coat. "Who is it?" I call out.

"This is Detective Ramirez of the NYPD," the man's muffled voice responds.

Oh no.

But okay, there's no reason to panic. My boss is dead, so obviously they're going to want to ask me a few questions. There's nothing to be worried about.

I unlock the door and crack it open. He can't come in here without my explicit permission, and I have no intention of giving it to him. Not that I have anything to hide, but you never know.

"Miss Calloway?" he asks in a surprisingly deep voice. I would judge him to be about in his early fifties based on the bags under his eyes and the gray-to-black ratio in his close-cropped hair.

"Hello," I say tentatively.

"I was wondering if I could ask you a few questions," he says.

I do my best to make my face blank. "About what?"

He hesitates, studying my face. "Do you know a man named Douglas Garrick?"

"Yes..." No harm in admitting that. It would be easy enough to prove that I worked for the Garricks.

"He was murdered last night."

"Oh!" I clasp a hand over my mouth, trying to look surprised. "That's awful."

"I was hoping you could come down to the station and answer a few questions for me."

Detective Ramirez's face is a mask. His lips are a straight line, revealing nothing. But coming down to the station? That sounds serious. Then again, he's not whipping out a pair of handcuffs and reading me my rights. I'm sure they're just taking the case extra seriously because Douglas was so rich and important.

"When do you want me to come?"

"Now," he says without hesitation. "I can give you a ride."

"Do... do I have to?"

I am under no obligation to come with him if I'm not under arrest—I know my rights all too well. But I'd like to hear what he says.

"You don't have to," he finally replies, "but I would highly recommend it. One way or another, we are going to be having a talk."

I get a sick feeling in my stomach. This sounds like something more than a few casual questions about my employer. "I'd like to call my lawyer," I say.

Ramirez keeps his eyes on mine. "I don't think that's necessary, but it's your right to do so."

I don't know what kind of questions they're going to be asking me, but I don't like the idea of being at the police station without a lawyer present, no matter what he says. Unfortunately, there's only one lawyer I know well enough to call right now. And this is going to be a difficult conversation.

Ramirez waits while I retrieve my cell phone and select Brock's number. He's got to already be at work by now, but he picks up after just a couple of rings. Brock spends most of the day at his desk and is rarely in the courtroom.

"Hey, Millie," he says. "Are you okay?"

"Um," I say. "Not exactly..."

"Has the stomach bug gotten worse?"

"What?"

Brock is quiet for a moment on the other line. "You told me last night you had a stomach bug."

Oh right. I almost forgot the lie I told him when I didn't come to his apartment last night. "Yes, that's better, but I need your help with something else. Something important."

"Of course. What do you need?"

"So, um..." I lower my voice so Ramirez can't hear me. "You know my old boss, Douglas Garrick? He was actually... he was murdered last night."

"Jesus," Brock gasps. "Millie, that's awful. Do they know who did it?"

"No, but..." I glance over at Ramirez, who is watching me. "They want to interview me at the police station."

"Oh wow. Do they think you know something important?"

"I guess so—even though I really don't. Anyway... I would feel better if I had a lawyer present with me." I clear my throat. "So, you know, that's you."

"Sure, of course." I want to reach through the phone and hug him. "I can meet you there as soon as I finish up a few things. I'm sure it will be fine, but I'm happy to be there for you."

As I take down the address of the police station where Detective Ramirez will be questioning me, I can't help but think to myself that Brock and I are soon going to end up having the conversation I meant to have with him last night, after all.

FORTY-TWO

By the time I get to the police station in Manhattan, I am thoroughly freaked out. Detective Ramirez tried to make some conversation during the car ride to the station, but I mostly answered in monosyllables and grunts. Even when he was talking about the weather, I got the feeling he was digging for information and I didn't want to give him anything.

But when I get to the station, Brock is waiting for me there. He's wearing his gray suit and that blue tie that makes his eyes look really blue. He smiles when he sees me come into the station with the detective, not looking the slightest bit worried. That's probably going to change very soon.

"That's my lawyer over there," I tell Ramirez. "I'd like to speak with him privately before I get questioned."

Ramirez nods curtly. "We'll put you in a room to talk, and when you're ready, I'd like to ask you my questions."

He takes me into a small, square room with a plastic table and a few plastic chairs surrounding it. I haven't been in an interrogation room in years, and the sight of it makes my chest tight. Especially when he sits me in one of the chairs and leaves me all alone in there with the door closed. I thought Brock would be coming in here with me, but he seems to be busy outside.

I wonder what they're saying to him.

I spend nearly another forty minutes alone in the room, my panic mounting. By the time Brock's familiar face appears at the door, I almost burst into tears.

"What took so long?" I cry.

Brock has a troubled expression on his face. He seems a little stiff as he settles down into the chair across from me. There's a crater between his eyebrows.

"Millie," he says, "I've been talking to the detective outside. They're reluctant to tell me too much, but this isn't a routine questioning. You are a serious suspect."

I stare at him. How could that be? Wendy told the police she was the one who shot Douglas. Are they doubting her story? It should be open and shut.

Unless...

"They have a warrant to search your apartment," he tells me. A *warrant*? "They have a team there right now."

They're searching my apartment? I can't imagine what they're looking for. I don't have anything there that's at all suspicious. Thankfully, I didn't get any blood on my clothing last night. I checked.

"Why would they think you killed him?" Brock shakes his head. "It doesn't make any sense to me."

This is it. I have to tell him about my past. If he's going to act as my lawyer, he needs to know. Otherwise, he's going to look like an idiot. "Listen," I tell him, "there's something you need to know about me."

He raises his eyebrows at me, waiting.

This is so hard. I'm cursing myself for not saying anything sooner, but now that I'm doing this, I remember why I put it off so long. "I sort of have a, you know, a prison record."

"You have a *what*?" His jaw looks like it's about to unhinge. "A *prison* record? Like you were in *prison*?"

"Yeah. That's kind of what a prison record means."

"For *what*?"

And now comes the hard part. "It was for murder."

Brock looks like he's about two seconds away from keeling over—I hope his heart is okay. "*Murder*?"

"It was self-defense," I say, which isn't entirely true. "This man was attacking my friend and I stopped him. I was a teenager at the time."

He gives me a look. "You don't go to prison for self-defense."

"Some people do."

He doesn't look like he believes me, but I'm not going to go into great detail about the boy who was trying to rape my friend. About how I did what I had to do to stop him, even if the prosecutors made it sound like I went too far.

"No wonder you never got your college degree," he mutters to himself. "I always just told myself you were a late bloomer."

"I'm sorry." I lower my eyes. "I should have told you."

"Gee, you think?"

"I'm sorry," I say again. "But I was scared if I did, you would look at me like... well, the way you're looking at me right now.

Brock rakes a hand through his hair. "Jesus, Millie. I just... I knew there was something you didn't want to tell me about, but I never imagined..."

"Yeah," I breathe.

"Okay." He loosens his blue tie a notch. "Okay, you have a prison record. That aside for a moment, why do they think you killed Douglas Garrick?"

I can't answer that question because I don't know what Wendy told the police. Even though everything I tell Brock is supposedly confidential, I can't bring myself to tell him what happened last night. "I have no idea."

He cocks his head thoughtfully. "You told me last night that you were sick. Did you leave their apartment early?"

"Well, I finished up my work," I say carefully, knowing the doorman can confirm when I left the apartment. "But since I wasn't feeling well, I went straight home after. I was already almost home when we talked on the phone. Douglas... he wasn't even there when I left the apartment."

"Okay." Brock rubs his chin. "They're just giving you a hard time because of your record. We're going to sort this out."

I wish I had his confidence.

FORTY-THREE

It turns out Ramirez isn't able to talk to me right away, which I suspect is some sort of tactic to break me down. Brock has to take a call from work, so he leaves me alone in the interrogation room, where I spend the next hour silently panicking.

I've been at the police station for over two hours when Ramirez finally comes in to talk to me, with Brock following close behind. Brock sits next to me, and he gives my hand a quick squeeze under the table. It's comforting to know he doesn't completely hate me, despite finding out about my prison record. Although the day is still young.

"Thank you for your patience, Miss Calloway," the detective says. His expression is still a complete blank. "I have some questions for you about Mr. Garrick."

"Okay," I say. We are being recorded, so I keep my tone calm and measured.

"Where were you last night?" Ramirez asks me.

"I went over to the Garricks' penthouse to do some light cleaning and laundry, then I went home."

"What time did you leave the penthouse?"

"About six-thirty," I say.

"And did you speak with Mr. Garrick while he was there?"

I shake my head, remembering what Wendy told me. The two of us just need to keep our stories straight, and we should be fine. "No."

Ramirez looks surprised by my answer. "So Mr. Garrick did not ask you to meet him at the apartment last night?"

I blink at him, confused. "No..."

"Miss Calloway." The detective's eyes seem to get darker as he stares at me. "What is your relationship with Douglas Garrick?"

"My relationship?" I look over at Brock, who is frowning. "He's my employer. Well, him and Wendy, his wife."

"Do you have a sexual relationship with him?"

I nearly choke. "No!"

"Not even once?"

I want to reach out and shake the detective, but thankfully, Brock cuts in. "Miss Calloway answered your question. She is not having a relationship of any kind with Mr. Garrick aside from purely professional."

Detective Ramirez picks up the folder he placed next to him on the table. He pulls out a sheet of papers stapled together. He slides it across the table to me. "We found a burner phone in Mr. Garrick's dresser drawer. These were the text messages exchanged between the burner phone and your phone."

I pick up the papers and start scanning them while Brock looks over my shoulder. I recognize the text messages. They are the same messages that Douglas has been sending me for the last couple of months to confirm my work days. But out of context, they seem to take on a different meaning.

Will you be over tonight?

I'll see you later tonight.

Come tonight.

Moreover, all my messages about groceries and laundry have vanished. Every single message seems to involve planning meetings together. Brock's eyes are popping out as he reads the text messages.

"Yes, these are our texts," I say, "but they're all about work."

"Mr. Garrick was texting you about work from a burner phone?"

I clench my teeth. "I didn't know it was a burner phone. I just thought it was his regular phone."

"I see," Ramirez says.

"Plus," I add, "there were other messages. Mostly about groceries and laundry. They're not here... they look like they've been deleted."

"Do you have the messages on your own phone?"

"No..." Because Wendy told me to delete them. "I got rid of all the messages."

"Why?"

"Why wouldn't I?" I let out a laugh that sounds way too high. "I mean, do *you* save every text message you get?"

He probably does. He probably has text messages on his phone going ten years back. Although to be fair, I would never have deleted those text messages if Wendy hadn't told me to.

"Also," he says, "there were outgoing calls made to you as late as midnight. Are you saying that your *employer* was calling you at *midnight*?"

"It just happened once," I say lamely.

I recognize how weak it all sounds. It doesn't make sense—why was Douglas texting me from a *burner* phone? It's not like he was setting me up to take the fall for his own murder. I look over at Brock, who has gone strangely silent at the worst possible time.

"Also..." Ramirez opens the folder again. Oh God, there's

more? How could there possibly be more? "Do you recognize this?"

It's a grainy printed photo of a bracelet. I recognize it as the same bracelet Douglas gave to Wendy after he gave her that black eye. "Yes," I say. "That's Wendy's bracelet."

Ramirez's eyebrows shoot up. "Then why did we find it in your jewelry box in your apartment?"

"She... she gave it to me."

His eyebrows creep closer to his hairline. "Wendy Garrick gave you a ten-thousand-dollar diamond bracelet?"

A *ten-thousand-dollar* bracelet? That's what this bracelet cost? I've had something worth ten thousand dollars in my crappy little jewelry box?

"She told me it was a gift from her husband," I say.

"What about the inscription?" He pulls yet another photograph out of the folder and passes it to me. "Does this look familiar?"

The inscription that I had read on Wendy's bracelet is now blown up on the screen so that both Brock and I can read it clearly.

To W, You are mine forever, Love D

"Right," I say. "To W. To *Wendy*."

Ramirez taps the photo. "Doesn't your name start with W? Wilhelmina?"

"I..." My mouth is suddenly dry. I wait for Brock to interject and protest the line of questioning, but he is still mute, also waiting to hear my answer. "I always go by Millie."

"But your name is Wilhelmina."

"Yes..."

"Also..." Oh no, there's *more*? How could there possibly be more? But once again, he's reaching for that stupid folder. He pulls out another printed photo. "Was this a gift from Mr. Garrick?"

I take the photograph out of his hands. It's that dress that Douglas asked me to return. But then he never gave me any receipt or told me where it came from. With everything going on, I'd completely forgotten about it. So it's just been sitting in a gift bag in my bedroom closet.

"No," I say weakly, even though I can already see where this is going. "Mr. Garrick asked me to return the dress."

"So why has it been sitting in your bedroom for over a month?"

"He... he never gave me the receipt."

I can't even look at Brock. God knows what thoughts are going through his head. I want to assure him that this is all a terrible misunderstanding, but I can't have that conversation with him with the detective in the room.

"Look," I say, "I was going to return it. I asked him about the receipt and he said he would get it for me but we just both forgot."

"Miss Calloway," Ramirez says, "did you know that the dress was purchased from Oscar de la Renta for six thousand dollars? Do you really think he would just forget to return it?"

Holy...

I hazard a quick look in Brock's direction. He has a glazed expression on his face, and he's shaking his head ever so slightly. I brought him here to be my lawyer, but he's proving to be completely useless.

"Also," Ramirez adds. Oh no. There cannot possibly be anything else. I definitely did not accept any other handouts from the Garricks. There is nothing more he can pull out of that folder. "Did you spend the night at a motel with Douglas Garrick last week?"

"No!" I cry.

He clears his throat. "So you didn't check into a motel in

Albany last Wednesday while Mr. Garrick had a business meeting there, and pay for the night in cash?"

I open my mouth but no sound comes out.

"Last Wednesday?" Brock bursts out. "That's the day that we were supposed to meet for dinner and you stood me up! Is *that* where you were?"

I can't lie. I gave the clerk at the motel my driver's license. "Yes, I did rent a motel room in Albany. But it's not what you think."

Ramirez folds his arms across his chest. "I'm listening."

I don't know what to say. I don't want to give away Wendy's secret. If they find out about the marital problems the Garricks were having, the murder could get pinned on her. Even though I don't want to get blamed for this, I don't want her to get blamed either.

"I just needed a night away," I say lamely.

"So you went to a random motel in Albany to spend the night?"

"I wasn't having an affair with Douglas Garrick." I look between Brock and Ramirez, and both seem incredibly skeptical. "I swear it. And even if I were—which I wasn't—that doesn't mean that I killed him, for God's sake!"

"He broke it off with you last night." Ramirez keeps his eyes pinned on me as he drops this revelation. "You were furious with him and you shot him in anger with his own gun."

"No..." My mouth feels horribly dry. "That's not even remotely true. You have no idea."

Ramirez nods down at the photographs on the desk. "You can see why it looks suspicious."

"But it's not the truth!" I cry. "I was never having an affair with Douglas Garrick. This is absolutely insane."

The detective doesn't say anything this time. He just stares at me.

"I never even touched him," I say. "I swear to you! Just ask Wendy Garrick. She'll confirm everything I'm saying. Ask her!"

"Miss Calloway," Detective Ramirez says, "Wendy Garrick is the one who told us about your affair with her husband."

What? "Excuse me?"

"She said that Mr. Garrick came clean with her yesterday, and he invited you over with the intention of ending things," he says. "But when she got home, she found him lying on the floor, shot to death."

No... She didn't... After all I did for her...

"And," he says, "your fingerprints are on the gun."

FORTY-FOUR

The interrogation goes downhill from there.

I try to patch together some version of the truth. A version that doesn't end in me shooting Douglas Garrick dead in his home. I explain about Douglas Garrick being abusive to Wendy, and my attempts to help her. I tell him that Wendy had shown me the gun and said she was using it for protection, and that's how my fingerprints must've gotten on it, although I'm having trouble explaining why Wendy's fingerprints *aren't* on the gun. I can tell from the look on Detective Ramirez's face that he doesn't believe a word I'm saying.

By the end of my rambling story, I'm certain Ramirez is going to read me my rights and take me to a jail cell. But instead, he shakes his head. "I'll be right back," he tells me. "Don't go anywhere."

He stands up and leaves the room, the door slamming behind him with a resounding echo, leaving me and Brock alone in the interrogation room.

Brock is staring down at the plastic table, his eyes glassy. He was supposed to be here as my attorney, but he hasn't said one word in twenty minutes. If I had known how this was going to unfold, I never would've asked him to come.

"Brock?" I say.

He slowly lifts his eyes.

"Are you okay?" I say gently.

"*No.*" He gives me a seething look. "What the fuck was that, Millie? Seriously?"

"Brock," I squeak, "you can't possibly believe—"

"Believe *what?*" he snaps at me. "Up until a few hours ago, I didn't even know you had been in prison for murder. And now I find out that you've been *cheating* on me with that rich asshole you've been working for—"

"I wasn't cheating!" I burst out. "I would never cheat on you!"

"Then what the hell were you doing last Wednesday night?" he says. "What were you doing *last* night? And all the other nights we were supposed to be having dinner but you blew me off? You must see how this all looks pretty damn suspicious. Especially since, you know, you apparently killed a guy once."

Well, not just once. But I feel like providing that information wouldn't help my case. "I told you, I was trying to help Wendy."

"You were trying to help the woman who is now accusing you of having an affair with her husband and then *murdering* him?"

Okay, when he says it that way... "I don't know why she's telling the detective that. Maybe she panicked. But trust me, he was abusive to her. I saw it with my own eyes."

"Millie." Brock looks at me with a pained expression on his handsome features. "I called you last night, and you sounded really upset over something. Obviously, you didn't have a stomach bug. That was a lie."

"Yes," I admit. "That was a lie."

"Millie." His voice cracks on my name. "Did you kill Douglas Garrick?"

Almost everything Detective Ramirez accused me of was untrue. But one thing was absolutely true. I shot Douglas Garrick. I *killed* him. And even if I deny everything else, that fact remains.

"Oh Christ," Brock mutters. "Millie, I can't believe you would..."

"It's not what you think though," I say.

Brock's plastic chair scrapes against the hard floor of the interrogation room as he gets to his feet. "I can't represent you, Millie. It's not appropriate, and... I can't."

Despite how useless my boyfriend was during the interrogation, the thought of him abandoning me scares me even more. "You know I don't have any money for a lawyer..."

"So you can use the public defender," he says. "Or borrow money, or... I don't know. But it can't be me. I'm sorry."

"So that's it." My chin wobbles as I look up at him. "You're breaking up with me."

"I guess?" He shakes his head. "Honestly, I don't even know who *you* are." He runs his hand through his hair, pulling obsessively at the strands. "I can't believe this is happening. I really can't. I wanted you to meet my parents. I really thought that you and I..."

He doesn't need to complete the thought. He imagined a future where the two of us would get married. Have children together. Grow old together. He didn't imagine that it would end in a police station, with me being interrogated for murder.

So really, I can't blame him for leaving. But I still burst into tears as soon as the door shuts behind him.

FORTY-FIVE

The real miracle is after all that, Detective Ramirez does not arrest me. When he gives me the news I'm free to go, I actually ask him, "Are you sure?" I was certain they were going to take me into custody, but he lets me go with the warning that I should not leave town. Given I have no money and no car, I'm not going anywhere any time soon.

After I get out of the station, I reach for my phone instinctively. Then I realize I have nobody to call. Ordinarily, I would have called Brock to let him know I've been released, but I get the feeling he doesn't care.

Of course, there is one person who would care.

Enzo.

Enzo would help me. If I called him, he would believe every word I said without question. But I don't know if I want to go down that road again. And I made that whole speech about not needing his help, so I'm not about to crawl back to him a week later begging for him to save me.

I can save myself. I'm not even under arrest. Maybe this whole thing will work out.

After debating my options for a moment, I select Wendy's

phone number from my list of contacts. I don't know if it's kosher to be calling her right now, but I need answers. We had an agreement last night, and what the detective is claiming goes completely against what we decided. Then again, he might have just been making things up to scare me into confessing or implicating Wendy. I wouldn't put anything past that detective.

Naturally, it goes straight to voicemail.

I may as well go home. After all, tomorrow they could arrest me and I won't be able to go home ever again. It's not like I could afford bail.

I take the train back out to my apartment in the Bronx. After everything that has happened today, I can barely put one foot in front of the other. I have to search inside my bag for a good five minutes, looking for my keys, until I'm certain I lost them. Just when I'm about to give up, I find them wedged in the bottom of the bag.

"Millie!"

Almost the second I step into the building, my landlady Mrs. Randall is rushing out of her first-floor apartment, wearing one of her oversized dresses that doesn't cinch at the waist. Her wrinkled face is all scrunched up, and her lower lip is jutting out.

"The police were here!" she cries. "They made me open your apartment and they did a search! They had a paper telling me I had to let them in!"

"I know," I groan. "I'm sorry about that."

Mrs. Randall narrows her eyes at me. "You hiding drugs up there?"

"No! Definitely not!" I just murdered somebody, that's all. Sheesh.

"I don't want any more trouble in my building," she says. "*You* are nothing but trouble. Two times the police are here because of you! I want you *out*. You got one week."

"One week!" I cry. "But Mrs. Randall—"

"One week and I change the locks," she hisses at me. "Don't want you around and whatever you do in that apartment of yours."

My heart sinks. How on earth am I ever going to find another apartment with everything going on with me? Maybe it would be better if I did get arrested. At least then, I'll have a place to stay. And free food.

I trek up the two flights of steps to my apartment. I'm expecting the apartment to be ransacked, and I'm not disappointed. The police officers who searched the place didn't even make an attempt to put everything back where it was supposed to go. It will take me the rest of the night to clean it all up.

I drop down to my sofa, exhausted. I can't tackle this mess tonight. Maybe tomorrow. Maybe never. What's the point if I'm going to jail anyway?

Instead, I grab the remote control and turn on my crappy television. I guess this is what I'm going to be doing on my last night of freedom.

Unfortunately, the television is tuned into a news station. The story of Douglas Garrick's murder is all over the news right now. The newscaster on the screen with that shiny blond hair reports that the police are talking to a "person of interest."

Hey, I made the news. I'm a "person of interest."

Then the program cuts to a video of Wendy. She's talking to a reporter, and her eyes are bloodshot and puffy. The bruising on her face looks completely gone, which I assume is because of makeup. She turns to address the camera.

"My husband Douglas was an incredible man," she says in a surprisingly strong voice that doesn't sound like her at all. "He was kind, brilliant, and we had been planning to start a family together soon. He did not deserve to have his life cut short this way. It's not fair that he..." She stops talking, choked up by emotion. "I... I'm sorry..."

What was *that*?

How could Wendy talk about Douglas that way after what he did to her? I understand not wanting to talk ill of the dead, but she's making him sound like some kind of a saint. The man was seconds away from choking her to death when I ended his life. Why doesn't she tell the reporter *that*?

The video cuts away to the blond newscaster. Her clear blue eyes lock with the screen. "If you're just joining us now, our top story is the brutal murder of multimillionaire CEO of Coinstock, Douglas Garrick. He was found dead in his Upper West Side apartment last night, with a fatal gunshot wound to the chest."

The screen flashes to a photograph of a man in his forties with the caption "Douglas Garrick, CEO of Coinstock." I stare at the screen, at the man's dark hair and soft brown eyes, at his double chin, and the creases around his eyes as he smiles for the camera. As I stare at the photo of Douglas Garrick, I realize something.

I have never seen this man before in my life.

The man whose photograph is on the screen is completely unfamiliar to me. He looks a *bit* like the man I have been inter-acting with in the penthouse, and from far away, you might not know the difference. But it's not him. It's *definitely* not him. This man is somebody completely different.

So if the man on the screen is Douglas Garrick...

Who the hell did I kill last night?

PART II

FORTY-SIX

WENDY

You must think I'm a terrible person.

Would it help if I said that while Douglas never laid a finger on me, he was a terrible husband? He humiliated me and made my life miserable. And I would have been happy to get a divorce.

This did not need to end in his murder. That's entirely on him.

And Millie? Well, she is an unfortunate casualty. But she's not quite as sweet as you might think. If she spends her life behind bars, it's for the greater good.

But even after you hear my side of the story, you might still think I'm a terrible person. You might think that Douglas didn't deserve to die. You might think that I am the one who deserves to go to prison for the rest of my life.

And the truth is, I don't really care.

* * *

How to Get Away With Murdering Your Husband – A Guide by Wendy Garrick

Step 1: Meet a Man who is Single, Clueless, and Filthy Rich

Four Years Earlier

I don't understand contemporary art.

My friend Alisa sent me an invitation to this gallery exhibit, but it's too strange for me. I'm used to admiring paintings as beautiful works of artistic skill. But this? I don't even know what *this* is.

The title of the exhibit is simply: Garments. And that is exactly what it is. Clothing, Hanging from the wall, cut to shreds, reconstructed into a patchwork of corduroy, satin, silk, and polyester. It's absolutely *preposterous*. When did art become something that looks like a child made it during the arts and crafts class at school?

The work I am looking at right now is titled *Socks*. It is aptly named. It is a giant frame, at least as tall as I am, and every inch of it is covered in socks of various shapes and sizes.

I just... I simply don't get it.

"I have a hole in one of my socks," a male voice says from behind me. "D'you think they would be okay if I borrowed one of these?"

I swivel my head to identify the owner of the voice. Immediately, I recognize Douglas Garrick. Before this event, I studied with great care a rare photo Alisa found me—I memorized his unkempt brown hair, the crinkling around his eyes with an almost smile, a crooked incisor on the left. He's wearing a cheap white dress shirt that looks like it could have been purchased at Walmart, and he's missed a button. No wait, he has missed *all* the buttons. Every single button is off by one. And he needs a shave—badly.

You would never guess this man is one of the wealthiest people in the entire country.

"I don't see how they could miss it," I reply, trying to sound cool although my heart is doing jumping jacks in my chest.

He grins at me and sticks out his hand. It was barely noticeable in the photo I saw, but in real life, he has a double chin, although it's nothing that some diet and exercise wouldn't take care of. "Doug Garrick."

I take his hand, which is warm, and swallows mine up like they were designed to fit together. "Wendy Palmer."

"Very nice to meet you, Wendy Palmer," he says, as his brown eyes meet mine.

"Likewise, Mr. Garrick."

"So..." He rolls back onto the heels of his worn loafers. "What do you think of Garments?"

I look around the room at the various clothing-centered artwork. I know a little bit about Douglas Garrick, and I believe him to be a man who appreciates the truth. "Actually," I say, "I don't quite understand it. I could create any of these pieces myself with a little bit of Elmer's glue and a box of clothing from Goodwill."

Douglas frowns. "But isn't that the point? The artist is trying to challenge the status quo and provide a critique to traditional art, and demonstrate that even the most ordinary objects can be turned into something that triggers emotions."

"Oh." Damn it, now I have to think of something intelligent to say. "Well, I do find that the interplay of texture and color—"

I stop short when I see the smirk on Douglas's lips. He holds it for a split second, then he bursts out laughing. "Did that nonsense sound like I knew what I was talking about?"

"A bit," I admit sheepishly.

"You know what I love about this gallery?" he says. "The

food. It is..." He kisses the tips of his fingers. "Spectacular. I'm willing to look at a few walls of socks for these hors d'oeuvres."

"Yes," I murmur. I haven't had a bite to eat since I've been here. This Donna Karan dress fits me like a glove, hugging my boobs and stomach and ass all equally well, but there could be an unsightly bulge if I start guzzling shrimp with cocktail sauce.

He looks down at my bare hands. "Let me grab a few of my favorites for you. Trust me."

I smile at him. "I'm intrigued."

"Don't move a muscle, Wendy Palmer."

Douglas winks at me before dashing over to the table of hors d'oeuvres. He picks up a plate and starts stacking a disturbing number of items. Oh Lord. Why is he putting *so much food* on that plate? I don't indulge in breakfast or lunch, and I already had a salad before I came here. What is this man doing to me?

I am nearly having a panic attack at all the food he is putting on that plate, but it is a tiny plate, so it will be all right. I'll just have a smaller dinner tomorrow night.

"Here you go." He hurries back to me, eager to show me the items he foraged for me. "These are my favorites. Try the mushroom tart first."

I pick it up and take a bite. It is heavenly. This one bite probably has around five hundred calories in it if I had to guess. No wonder Douglas has a double chin. And he doesn't care, because he's not a woman and also so incredibly rich.

"Now," he says, "there's a piece over there called *Pants*. Want to hazard any guesses about what we're going to be looking at?"

He grins at me, holding my gaze even though my dress is exhibiting an impressive amount of cleavage. When I came here tonight intending to seduce Douglas Garrick, I didn't anticipate this man.

This will be far easier than I expected.

FORTY-SEVEN

Step 2: Get Hitched to the Filthy Rich Man

Three Years Earlier

Douglas can be absolutely maddening.

He is tormenting me. He pretends to be a nice guy—even down to earth, considering his job and personal wealth—but he is *sadistic*. There is no other explanation for why he would behave this way.

"What do you think you're doing?" I snap at him.

He at least has the good grace to appear sheepish. He should! It's bad enough that the man sits in our living room wearing his boxer shorts—boxers!—but we are supposed to arrive in *less than an hour* at a party at Leland Jasper's house and he's not ready *at all*. I had timed this perfectly for us to be fashionably late, and yet now he is standing in the kitchen, dressed in sweatpants and a T-shirt, and *eating Nutella out of the jar using a butter knife*.

My heart cannot take this madness.

"I got hungry," he says. He puts down the knife on the kitchen counter, smearing the dark brown spread over the marble surface.

"Douglas," I say with rapidly dwindling patience, "we are supposed to go in ten minutes. You're not even *dressed*."

"Go where?"

He is tormenting me. He is doing this on purpose. I can't imagine that this behavior is not intentional—nobody could be this clueless. "Leland's house! The party is tonight!"

"Oh, right." He groans and rubs his temples. "Christ, do we have to go? We hate Leland and her husband. Didn't we say that? Also, what kind of name is *Leland*? She definitely made that name up."

He is correct on all accounts, but that doesn't mean we can skip this party. Everyone will be at this party. And I want them to see me wearing my new Prada dress, my auburn hair perfectly styled and highlighted, hanging off the arm of my handsome and impossibly wealthy fiancé, who will be wearing an Armani suit that hides the paunch in his abdomen. I picked it out for that explicit purpose. Before he had me, he used to walk around in cheap suits where you could see the outline of his gut.

"We have to go," I say through my teeth. "I don't want to hear another word about it. You need to get dressed—now."

"But Wendy." Douglas grabs my arm and tugs me close to him. His breath smells like hazelnut. "Come on, the party is going to be such a drag. Let's just... I don't know, let's go see a movie, just the two of us? Like we used to when we were first going out? The new Avengers movie maybe?"

Something I didn't realize about Douglas before I first met him is that he is a hopeless nerd. He doesn't even try to hide it. All he wants is to watch superhero movies and veg out on the sofa with his laptop perched on his legs, eating Nutella out of the jar. The only way he got to be the CEO of Coinstock is because he's a crazy genius who invented a piece of technology that ended up being used by every bank in the country.

"We are going to this party," I say for what feels like the hundredth time. I swear, the man does not listen to me *ever*. "Now get dressed. Chop, chop."

"Okay, *okay*."

He leans in to attempt to give me a Nutella kiss, but I am wearing Prada, so I take a step back and put up my hands to keep him away. "You can kiss me after you change," I tell him.

Douglas shoves the jar back in the cabinet and trudges out of the kitchen into our impossibly small living room. This whole apartment is a disgrace. We only have three bedrooms, and one of them is Douglas's office, so it's as if we only have *two* bedrooms. As soon as we get married, we are going to get a serious upgrade, as well as my dream house in the suburbs. Well, it's really Douglas's dream house, because my dream is certainly *not* to live in the suburbs.

I smile whenever I think about the house where we're going to live someday. Growing up, my father was a maintenance worker, and my mother made barely minimum wage working at a preschool. We had a tiny house, and I shared a bedroom with my younger sister, who used to wet the bed at night until she was eight years old. I studied hard enough in school to earn a scholarship to a snooty private high school, where all the other kids made fun of me for not dressing as well as they did.

All I wanted was a pair of designer jeans like my beautiful, cruel classmate Madeleine Edmundson. And maybe a winter coat that wasn't a hand-me-down with holes in it.

I thought I could turn things around for myself in college, but it didn't work out the way I had hoped. There was that awful incident where they accused me of cheating, and I wasn't allowed to return for my junior year. All my career prospects seemed to go out the window when I was escorted off campus.

I wish they could all see me now.

Maddeningly, the doorbell rings at that moment. Before I can tell Douglas that I'm going to take care of whoever is at the door, he says, "That's probably Joe. He's dropping off some papers I need. It'll just be a minute."

Joe Bendeck is Douglas's lawyer. Although he's probably part of the reason Douglas is so rich, he is not my favorite person in the world, and he has a barely concealed distaste for me as well. I'm glad for Douglas to be the one to get rid of him.

It is strange that he is stopping by so late in the evening though. Not unprecedented, but still unusual. I wonder what he wants...

While Douglas goes to talk to Joe, I linger nearby, listening in to their conversation. Douglas doesn't usually involve me in his business, but it's smart to know what's going on as much as I can.

"Is this everything?" Douglas's voice says.

"Yes," Joe replies, "and I also have something else for you..."

I hear the shuffling of paper. Douglas opening an envelope. "Aw, Joe. I told you, I can't ask her to do this..."

"Doug, you have to. Your wedding is in only a few weeks, and you can't marry that woman without a prenup."

"Why not? I trust her."

"Big mistake."

"Look, I can't... it's like starting a marriage on the wrong foot."

"Let me give you some free legal advice, Doug. If this falls apart on you, she is going to get half of everything you worked for. This document is the *only* thing protecting you. You would be a complete idiot to marry her without making her sign one."

"But—"

"No buts. You don't marry that woman unless she signs this. If she truly loves you and cares about staying married to you, then it shouldn't matter to her, right?"

I hold my breath, waiting to see what Douglas says. I wait for him to tell Joe to go to hell. But in addition to Joe being his lawyer, he's also his oldest and closest friend.

"Okay," Douglas says. "I'll get it done."

FORTY-EIGHT

"This is extremely generous," Joe Bendeck informs me.

Joe is standing over me and Douglas in our living room, taking me through the terms of the prenup. Douglas didn't give it to me that night. He waited a few more days, softening the blow with some flowers and a diamond necklace from Tiffany's. It didn't soften the blow very much.

"I don't feel comfortable with the idea of a prenup." I look over at Douglas, who is sitting next to me, dressed like a complete slob in jeans and a T-shirt. "Honey, must we go through this?"

"It's *very* generous," Joe says again. "Ten million dollars if you get divorced. But you can't go after any of his other assets."

"I don't want his assets." I put my hand on Douglas's knee. The fabric of his jeans feels worn beneath my hand. "I just want to get married in peace."

"So sign it," Joe says. "And I won't bug you about it ever again."

"I just..." I pull out an embroidered handkerchief from my pocket and dab at my eyes. "I thought you trusted me, Douglas."

"Oh, for Christ's sake," Joe mutters. "Doug, are you really falling for this crap?"

Douglas shoots his friend a look, and he throws his arm around my shoulders. He is a sucker for a woman crying. "Wendy, it's not like that at all. I do trust you. And I love you so much."

I lift my tear-stained face to look at him. "I love you too."

"But," he adds, "I can't marry you without a prenup. I'm sorry."

I see in Douglas's brown eyes that he means it. Joe has convinced him, and now he is drinking the Kool-Aid.

I sneak a look at the papers on the coffee table in front of me. It's a stack two inches thick. But Joe has highlighted the main points for me. It says in black and white that if we get divorced, I will get ten million dollars. That's nowhere near half of what Douglas is worth, but it's nothing to sneeze at. It will keep me comfortable for the rest of my life if things don't work out here.

Not that I expect us to get divorced. I expect Douglas and I to be together till death do us part, yadda yadda yadda. But you never know. Douglas is a fixer-upper, and I admit there's a chance I may not fix him up to my liking.

"Fine," I say. "I'll sign it."

FORTY-NINE

Step 3: Enjoy Married Life... For a Little While

Two Years Earlier

"Jesus Christ. This place is insane."

Douglas is reluctant to buy this penthouse apartment. He thinks we should live in that tiny three-bedroom apartment for the rest of our lives. Well, we do have the house we bought out on the island, but I don't know how much time I'm going to be spending there. Douglas likes the house though. It has five bedrooms, and he kept talking in an annoying way about all the children we were going to fill them with.

"This penthouse isn't any larger than what Orson Dennings has," I point out.

Tammy, our realtor, bobs her head enthusiastically. "This is only a *mid*-level penthouse."

Douglas blinks up at the skylights. "I don't understand why we need a penthouse at all! We have an entire house!"

I didn't realize how stingy my husband is until we went apartment hunting. Anything more than four bedrooms is "way too big." And he keeps bringing up the house on the island, as if anyone is going to spend all their time on *Long Island*. Please.

"I was keeping the apartment in case I needed to hang around the city for meetings," he reminds me. "But that isn't where we're going to be *living*. The house is where we're going to be living."

"Why do we only get to live in one place?"

"Because we're not *insane*?"

"A lot of people maintain a residence both in the suburbs and in the city," Tammy pipes up.

"We already have a residence in the city!" Douglas argues.

He's getting frustrated. Douglas grew up with a single mom in an apartment in Staten Island. He went to this special public high school downtown for super geeky kids and put himself through MIT by a combination of scholarships and work-study and loans. He's not used to having money. He doesn't know what to do with it.

He should take a lesson from me. My father never drove anything but used cars, and my mother clipped coupons. Every single item of clothing purchased for my older sister was not thrown away until the other three of us had a chance to wear it as well. Every piece of clothing was used until it was hanging together by a thread.

I hated living like that. I used to lie awake in bed and fantasize about what it would be like to be rich someday. And now that we are, why shouldn't we get everything we've ever dreamed of?

After spending our childhoods being poor, we both have money. And we're damn well going to act like it.

"Douglas." I run a finger down his arm. "I know it seems a little extravagant, but this is my dream apartment. I've already fallen in love with it."

"And," Tammy says, "the price has been slashed."

"Because nobody can afford this ridiculous place," Douglas

grumbles, although I can tell some of the fight has gone out of him.

"Please, honey." I bat my eyes at him. "It will be so great to have a place to stay for the night when we bring the children into the city."

That always works on him. Anytime I want to get my way, all I have to do is bring up our fictional potential children. Douglas wants four, but he's not the one that has to squeeze them out.

"All right." His eyes soften. "What the hell? I guess it could be, like, a tax write-off or something."

"Sure!" Tammy, who is completely full of it, chirps.

"Thank you, sweetie." I lean in to kiss my husband. As he encircles me in his arms, I can't help but notice he's gotten a little doughier than he was when we first met, which is the opposite direction of where he should be going. It's something he's going to have to work harder on, among other things. Douglas is still very much a work in progress.

FIFTY

I love having lunch with my friend Audrey. She always has the *best* gossip.

I always dreamed of having a life like this. Where I am free in the middle of the day to have lunch with a friend at one of the most expensive restaurants in the city. Sometimes I want to pinch myself to make sure it's not a dream.

And then there are other times when I am with Douglas and he is sapping every last bit of my strength. Sometimes I want to pinch *him*.

Audrey looks like she's busting with some great gossip. She's married to a man who is quite wealthy (and quite a bit older than she is) but he's not as rich as Douglas is. She could never afford a penthouse like the one we have.

"So guess what," Audrey tells me as she dabs at her raspberry-colored lips. That is always the start of some amazing gossip. I don't know how she hears all this stuff—I would *never* tell her any secrets about myself. "Ginger Howell's divorce went through."

"Ooh," I say. "That was a rough one."

Ginger's husband Carter is the opposite of Douglas. He is

this super possessive guy who never took his eyes off Ginger whenever we were at parties. Whenever she went out with us, she always had to tell him exactly when she was leaving, what she would be doing, and when she would be back. I'm sure it was exhausting for her, but there was also something about the way her husband commanded her that was sexy to me. Carter is also devastatingly handsome and keeps himself quite fit, unlike my husband.

"Well." Audrey nibbles on a lettuce leaf. "She had help from Millie."

"Millie? Who is that?"

Audrey looks at me in astonishment, and my cheeks flush. Is Millie somebody important in our social circle that I have somehow forgotten about? But then Audrey says, "She's a cleaning woman."

"Okay..."

"But she has a reputation..." Audrey lowers her voice a notch, which means she's about to tell me some *really* good gossip. "For women having issues with their husbands, she helps them out. Takes care of it for them."

"Issues?"

In my brain, I tick off the laundry list of Douglas's bad habits. When he uses the toilet, he always uses up half the toilet paper roll. He eats food directly out of the containers in the refrigerator, even though I have repeatedly asked him not to. When we go to a fancy restaurant, he can't be bothered to learn which fork to use at the proper time, and even when I point it out to him at the beginning of the meal, he still gets it wrong half the time, which makes me think he's just guessing.

I used to think I could change Douglas. That with my help, he could become a better person, like I did. But it seems like he's only getting worse.

"Bad issues," Audrey clarifies. "Like, Ginger's husband was abusive. He was smacking her around—even broke her arm."

"Oh!" I gasp. I can't claim that's an issue I have. Douglas would never lay a finger on me. He'd be horrified at the idea of it. "How awful."

She nods soberly. "So this Millie woman, she helps you out. Tells you what to say and do. Gets you the right resources. She found Ginger a great lawyer. And I've even heard that she's helped a few women disappear when that was the only option."

"Wow."

"That's not all." Audrey crunches on one of her lettuce leaves, then dabs her lips with her napkin. "I've heard in a couple of situations when there was no way out, Millie... you know, took the guy out."

I cover my mouth. "No..."

"Yes!" Audrey looks delighted to be sharing this revelation. "She's hardcore, believe me—she's dangerous. If she thinks a guy is hurting a woman, she will do pretty much anything to make it stop. She went to *prison* for wailing on some guy who was trying to rape her friend. She killed him."

"Goodness..."

Audrey takes another bite of her salad then pushes away. "I am just so full," she announces, even though she has barely eaten half of it, and it was a small garden salad to begin with. "Wendy, are you sure you don't want anything to eat?"

I take a sip of my mimosa. "I had a massive breakfast."

She narrows her eyes at me, possibly because I have not ordered any food during our last three lunches together. But I always have a drink.

"I guess you're not having any luck on the baby front," she says.

I curse the fact that a few months ago, I happened to mention that Douglas was excited to get pregnant soon. It just slipped out. We have been trying for a baby for about a year now. It hasn't been going well—meaning, I'm not pregnant.

"Not yet," I say.

"I know of a fabulous fertility specialist," Audrey says. "Laura went to him, and look at her now."

Our friend Laura now has twin baby boys, who wouldn't stop screaming the last time I ran into her on the street. I cringe. "That's okay. We prefer to try the old-fashioned way."

"Yes, but you're not getting any younger," she reminds me. "Tick-tock, Wendy."

"Fine. Give me the name of the fertility doctor."

I program the number into my phone, though I have no intention of calling. But if Douglas asks me about it, at least I can pretend I'm doing something.

FIFTY-ONE

Step 4: Realize You and Your Husband are Completely
Wrong For Each Other

One Year Earlier

Douglas steps into the dining room of our Long Island home
and stops short when he sees the two place settings.

"Where's the rest of our dinner?" he asks. "In the kitchen?"

"No." I am already seated at the table, a napkin on my lap.
"This is our dinner. Blanca made us a salad."

Douglas eyes the bowl of greens like he has been served a
bowl of poison. "That's it? That's the whole dinner?"

I sigh. I remember noticing Douglas's double chin the first
time I met him; I vowed that night to get him in shape so that it
would disappear. But if anything, he's even *more* out of shape
than he was that night. Honestly, it's like he doesn't even *care.*

"It's lettuce and tomato and cucumber and shredded
carrots," I point out. "Eating salad every day is what keeps me
from ballooning up. You should try it."

"Wendy, you're a stick figure," he points out. "You're terrified at the idea of eating anything that isn't a lettuce leaf or a celery stick."

I stiffen. "I'm just staying healthy."

"I'm *worried* about you." He frowns as he sits down in front of the offending salad. "You never eat anything. And you passed out after your run yesterday."

"I didn't pass out!"

"You did! You looked so pale and then you sat down on the couch and I couldn't wake you up. I was about to call for an ambulance."

"I was *tired*. I had just had a long run." I brighten. "Why don't you go with me on my run tomorrow?"

"Jesus, I don't think I could keep up with you."

I cock my head. "Hmm. So which of us is unhealthy then?"

Douglas scratches his dark hair. "Also, maybe being so skinny is what's keeping you from getting pregnant. I read that it's not good for fertility."

"Oh God," I groan. "It always has to come back to that, doesn't it? We can't have one conversation anymore where you don't blame me for not getting pregnant yet?"

Douglas opens his mouth to say something but then seems to change his mind. "Sorry, you're right."

He drops his eyes down to the salad in front of him. He crinkles his nose. "Is there dressing on it?"

"It's a fat-free vinaigrette."

"I can't see it."

"It's colorless."

He digs his fork into the crunchy lettuce and spears a few pieces. He shoves it into his mouth and chews. "Are you sure there's dressing on this? Because it feels like I'm eating the grass outside our house."

"I told Blanca just a splash. It's fat-free, but not calorie-free."

Douglas continues chewing. His Adam's apple bobs as he

swallows the mouthful of salad. After he's done, he scrapes his chair back on the floor and rises to his feet.

"Where are you going?" I ask him.

"KFC."

"What?" I rise to my feet. "Come on, Douglas. You can do this. We'll do it together."

"Why don't you come with me?" he says.

"You're joking."

"We sometimes used to eat fast food while we were dating," he reminds me. It's true, although I've tried to forget those awful memories. "Come on. We'll do the drive-through. It'll be fun. I heard they have a sandwich where the bun is made out of fried chicken. Don't you want to try that? Or at least, see what it looks like?"

My fast-food days were supposed to have ended when I married a tech millionaire. I shake my head.

Douglas gives me a sad look, but he doesn't stop. He leaves the house, gets in his car, and drives off, presumably to get a sandwich with a bun made out of fried chicken.

It's at that moment I know that I can no longer be faithful to my husband, because I no longer respect him.

FIFTY-TWO

In the face of my marriage falling apart, I decide some retail therapy is in order. Namely, we require new furniture.

I wait until I'm back in the city, because you can't possibly find anything decent on the island. Unbeknownst to me, Douglas arranged to have most of his furniture moved from his apartment to our penthouse, and all of it is dreadful. It looks like the sort of furniture you would purchase from a store with the word "discount" or "warehouse" in its name. I can barely stand to look at it.

I tried to explain to Douglas that the furniture in a home must fit together, and that classic, old pieces would fit not only with each other, but also with the décor of our gothic building. Douglas just looked at me blankly because I wasn't speaking in JavaScript or Klingon or whatever it is he understands best. Finally, he nodded and told me to get whatever I wanted.

So I'm on my way out to hunt for some beautiful antiques with which to decorate our penthouse when I run smack into Marybeth Simonds in the lobby of my building.

Marybeth is a receptionist at Douglas's company. I've met her a handful of times, and she's pleasant enough. Early forties, blond hair that's turning to gray, and a bland-looking face. She wears all these tacky skirts that are the absolute exact right length to make her calves look as wide as possible. The first time I laid eyes on her, I determined her not to be a threat to my husband's fidelity, and I never gave her a second thought.

"Wendy!" she exclaims. "Oh, I'm so glad I caught you."

She's clutching a manila envelope, likely some incredibly uninteresting documents meant for Douglas. She has to fetch them for him, because he rarely comes to the office. He prefers to work in any number of random coffee shops scattered throughout the city, or else in our Long Island home.

"Is Doug in?" she asks me.

"I'm afraid not." I glance down at my watch. "And I don't have time to take any random paperwork for him. You'll have to leave it with the doorman."

Marybeth's smile falters slightly, but she nods. Douglas likes her because of her good-natured quality, which I suspect means that she's a doormat. "Of course, sure thing, Wendy. Where are you headed?"

I am slightly taken aback by her familiarity, but I am reminded of how when I was poor, the daily lives of the incredibly wealthy used to fascinate me. I used to read articles about people like me. "I'm just buying some furniture," I tell her.

"Furniture?" Her eyes light up. "You know, my husband Russell is the manager of a furniture store. It's a small store, but the furniture there is incredible. And he would give you a great deal." She digs around in her purse, nearly dropping the manila envelope, and finally comes up with a white rectangular card with a small stain of lipstick on it. "This is his card. Just tell him I sent you over."

I take the card between the tips of my index finger and thumb, reluctant to touch it after it was in Marybeth's mystery bag. "Yes. Perhaps."

"Well..." She smiles brightly at me. "It was good seeing you, Wendy."

She starts to walk over to the doorman, but before she can, I call out her name. "Marybeth?"

She turns, that same pleasant smile plastered across her features. "Yes?"

"I would prefer if you refer to me as Mrs. Garrick," I tell her. "We aren't friends, after all. I'm your boss's wife."

Marybeth struggles to maintain the smile on her lips. "Of course. I'm so sorry, Mrs. Garrick."

I wonder if I'm being mean. But I didn't marry one of the richest men in the city just to be called *Wendy* by his receptionist.

FIFTY-THREE

Just to prove that I am not the most horrible woman on the face of the planet, I decide to buy a piece of furniture or two from Russell Simonds. May as well throw them a little of our business. And if it's truly too tacky to have in my home—which I suspect it will be—I can always donate it.

It's no surprise that the furniture store is compact. I expected boxy, stiff sofas, but instead when I walk in, I am confronted with a lovely chest of drawers. I stop for a moment to admire the stunning oak dresser that has been carefully sanded and stained, and it's ordained with a beautiful ornate mirror. I run my finger over one of the three dovetailed drawers, each of which contains a small keyhole.

This is exactly what I've been looking for. I need this for my home.

"It's a beautiful piece, isn't it?"

I pivot my head to identify the owner of the rich deep voice behind me. For a split second, I almost think that I'm looking at my husband. But no, this man is most definitely *not* Douglas Garrick. He is roughly the same height as Douglas, with a similar build—or the build Douglas might have if he went to the gym every once in a while—and his hair is about the same color, although trimmed neatly. Despite working in a furniture store, he is wearing a crisp white dress shirt and an expertly knotted tie. This man looks like the man that I had hoped to turn Douglas into when I first met him at that modern art exhibit. He is Douglas 2.0, while my husband is barely even the beta version.

"It's a vintage piece," he tells me, "but I restored it personally."

"You did an amazing job," I breathe. "I love it."

He smiles at me and my knees tremble slightly. "Now that's no way to bargain."

"I have no interest in bargaining," I say. "When I want something, I'll do whatever it takes to get it."

There's a flicker of amusement in his eyes at my comment. "I'm Russell." He holds out a hand to me, and when I take it, a delightful tingle goes up my arm. "This is my store, and I would *love* to sell you this dresser today. I bet it would look great in your apartment."

Russell Simonds. This must be Marybeth's husband. Somehow I expected a man with a potbelly and a large bald spot on the top of his gray hair. Not *this* man.

"I'm Wendy Garrick," I tell him. "Your wife Marybeth works for my husband. She suggested I come here."

That playful smile lingers on his lips. "I'm glad she did."

I end up buying about half the store before I'm done. Every time Russell tells me about another piece of restored vintage furniture, I simply have to have it. And then when I'm handing over my credit card with the shockingly high limit, he takes out his business card, this one impeccably crisp and white, and he scribbles ten digits on the back.

"Any problems with the furniture," he tells me, "you just let me know."

I slide the card into my purse. "I absolutely will."

And as Russell rings up my purchases, I can't help but think there is one other thing in the store that I would like to bring home with me. And when I want something, I'll do whatever it takes to get it.

FIFTY-FOUR

Step 5: Try to Find Happiness Elsewhere

Six Months Earlier

I may be falling in love.

I tried to fall in love with Douglas. I truly did. I thought that he would grow on me. I thought that he would change—the same way I changed when I picked myself up by my bootstraps. Douglas has no idea how amazing he could be if he bothered to take care of himself or got a little plastic surgery or fixed that crooked tooth. (For God's sake, what multimillionaire walks around with imperfect teeth? Does he think this is *England*?)

But Douglas has no interest in any of those things. He doesn't have any interest in being the man I want him to be. He only wants to be *himself*.

Russell, on the other hand...

Even though we've been sleeping together for six months now, I can't stop gazing at this man across the table. At his thick dark chocolate-colored hair cut short on the sides but long enough on the top to curl just slightly and his thick powerful eyebrows. I've never described a pair of eyebrows as "powerful" before, but the man could command a room with those eyebrows. It's my favorite of his features. But to be fair, I love everything about him.

Except his bank account.

The waitress approaches our table, an ear-to-ear smile plastered on her face. At a restaurant this expensive, the waiting staff is always unwaveringly nice. Douglas hates places like this. *I don't like it when they fuss over me so much.*

"Would you care for any dessert?" the waitress asks us. "We have an incredible flourless chocolate cake."

"No, thank you," Russell says.

I nod in agreement. We never get dessert. Like me, Russell takes good care of himself. He goes to the gym several times a week, and his body is all sculpted muscle, with only a tiny bit of unavoidable middle-aged paunch. Too bad Marybeth doesn't appreciate it. She doesn't even bother to dye her blond hair—in a few years, she'll be gray as a mule.

Russell reaches across the table for my hands. Given that we are in public and both married, it's completely inappropriate. Yet in the last few weeks of our torrid affair, we have thrown caution to the wind a bit. Part of me almost wants to get caught. Because for the first time in my life, I am in love.

If Douglas wants to divorce me, I'll take my ten million and be on my way.

"I wish I didn't have to get back to work," he murmurs.

"Maybe you could be late?" I suggest.

A smile plays on Russell's lips. I love his eagerness. Douglas hasn't been this way since soon after we got married, and even before that, he was never quite as skilled in the bedroom as Russell is. He just didn't have as much *stamina.*

For a while, we were reserving hotel rooms for our trysts, but lately, Douglas rarely goes to our penthouse apartment, so I've just been taking Russell there. There's the back entrance, where I know for a fact there are no cameras, so we don't have to deal with the doorman's judging eyes.

"I shouldn't," he says. "The store has been busy lately."

"Isn't that what salespeople are for?"

Russell usually has one other salesman working at the store, although he might be able to afford another since I have been practically financing the store with my purchases. To be fair, I have loved every single beautiful antique item I have purchased there. Russell has impeccable taste. If he had money, he would truly know how to spend it.

"How about tonight?" he suggests.

"What about Marybeth?"

His lips curl in disgust like they always do when the topic of his wife comes up. It's something that he and I have bonded over—our mutual distaste for our spouses. "I'll tell her I'm working late again."

The waitress returns with the check, and I hand over my platinum card. I always pay when we go to fancy restaurants, because although he doesn't like to admit it, Russell is a bit strapped for cash. But that doesn't bother me. I don't like him for his money—I've got plenty of my own right now.

"I'm going to be counting the seconds until I see you tonight," Russell murmurs. Under the table, his fingers move up my skirt until I start to feel a little breathless.

"Russell," I giggle softly. "Not here. There are *people* around."

"I can't help myself around you."

"Russell..."

My enjoyment of what my lover is doing under the table is interrupted by the waitress clearing her throat. She's got my platinum card in her hand. "I'm so sorry, but this did not go through. It was declined."

I roll my eyes. "It's an issue with your machines. Please run it again."

"I tried it three times."

I let out a sigh. My God, the people at these restaurants are nice, but sometimes painfully incompetent. There's a reason they are waiting tables for a living. I dig into my purse and pull out my Visa. "Try this one."

Except a minute later, the waitress comes back with the second card. "This one was declined too," she informs me. Her tone is not quite as gentle as it was while she was waiting on us. And the people at the table next to us have started to stare.

I don't know what is going on. I am married to Douglas freaking Garrick. My credit limit is infinite. Clearly, it has to be an issue on their end, but it doesn't look like anyone else is having a problem.

"Try my card," Russell speaks up. He takes his credit card out of his wallet and hands it over.

As the waitress dashes off to try the new card, I cast him an apologetic look. "I'm so sorry about that. I don't know what's going on."

"No problem," he says, even though he really can't afford a restaurant like this. It's not the sort of place we would have gone if we knew he would be paying. But there's not much we can do at this point.

Russell's credit card goes through without an issue. Something is happening with my cards. Are we having some sort of financial problems that I'm not aware of? People like us do not have credit card debt. But the truth is, I'm not up on the finances. I have my credit cards, and I use them without thinking about it.

I'll have to talk to Douglas about this tonight.

FIFTY-FIVE

I have called Douglas multiple times, and he's not picking up. I also have sent him numerous text messages that he has not responded to.

I don't know what's going on. I tried my credit cards at another store, and they were again declined. So it wasn't the fault of the restaurant.

I called the credit card company to try to get to the bottom of it. And they told me something shocking. My cards have been canceled. *All* of them.

I finally decide to drive out to our house on Long Island to talk to Douglas. Despite our gorgeous apartment in the city filled with antique furniture, he prefers the house. He says he likes the quiet. He sleeps better without the constant honking and sirens in the city, and he likes the fresh air. But Long Island is so painfully *dull*. There's absolutely nothing to do here and nowhere decent to shop.

When I get to the house, it's empty. I realize I haven't been here in over a week, even though Douglas sleeps here nearly every night. I suppose my husband and I have become more distant recently. The only time we ever have sex is once a month, when we're trying to conceive.

The house is clean, at least—when I walked in the door, I half expected to find dirty pizza boxes and used socks slung over the sofa, because Douglas can be a bit of a slob. The living room looks... cozy, I suppose would be the word. Douglas got rid of the white sofa I picked out, and he's replaced it with a dark blue one with beat-up-looking cushions. I sit down on the sofa to wait for him to come home, and I have to admit that it's comfortable, even though it is incredibly ugly.

It isn't until nearly nine o'clock that I hear the sound of the garage door opening. I sit up straighter on the sofa, then decide to stand. This is going to be the sort of conversation you need to stand up for. I can just tell.

Douglas enters through the back a minute later. His hair is more disheveled than usual, and he has circles under his eyes. His tie is hanging loose around his neck, and when he sees me in the living room, he stops short.

"You canceled my credit cards," I say through my gritted teeth.

"I was wondering what it would take to get you over here."

Does he think this is some sort of joke? "I was trying to have lunch and my card got *declined*. I had no way to pay. Do you realize that?"

Douglas steps into the living room, pulling his tie the rest of the way off. "What? Didn't Russell have his credit card?"

My mouth drops open. "I..."

He hurls his tie onto the sofa. "I don't understand why you're so surprised. Do you think you can go all over town making out with some other guy and I won't find out about it? Do you think you can pay for a hotel room on my credit card and I'll have no idea? How dumb do you think I am?"

"I... I'm sorry." My heart is pounding. I've never *ever* heard Douglas talk like this, but there's a part of me that's glad we're having this conversation. I'm tired of being married to Douglas Garrick. I'm glad we're getting it all out in the open. "I didn't mean for it to happen."

"Oh, please. Is that the best you can come up with?" He looks at me in disgust. "And Marybeth's *husband*? How could you, Wendy? Marybeth is practically like family."

Like family to *him*, perhaps. I never cared for the woman, even before sleeping with her husband. And now that I know what an inadequate partner she was to Russell, I dislike her even more. "Does she know?"

He shakes his head. "I couldn't do that to her. It would wreck her." He snorts. "Not that you would care about that."

"It's not like we have the perfect marriage, Douglas," I point out. "You know it as well as I do."

My comment takes some of the fight out of him. His brown eyes soften. Deep down, my husband is a bit of a pushover. That's why I married him in the first place. I knew he would give me everything I wanted.

"I think we should go to marriage counseling," he says. "I found a therapist who is highly recommended. I know I'm busy, but I'm going to make time for this. For *us*."

I imagine sitting with Douglas in a therapist's office, where we discuss our myriad of problems that add up to the fact that we want completely different things out of life. "I don't know…"

"Wendy." He comes close to me and takes my hand in his. I let him for a moment, knowing I'll take it back in a few seconds. "I don't want to give up on us. You're my wife. And even though we're having some struggles in that area, I want you to be the mother of my children."

I realize this is the moment I have to come clean with him. I have to rip off the Band-Aid, or else I might never be free of this man. And after all this time, he deserves the truth.

"Actually," I say, "I can't have children."

As it turns out, he is the one who yanks his hand away first. "*What?* What are you talking about?"

"Years ago, I had an infection that destroyed my fallopian tubes," I tell him. It happened when I was twenty-two years old. I had horrible pain in my pelvic area, and the doctors later explained that the infection was asymptomatic until it spread up into my tubes. The pain was so bad that I underwent a laparoscopic procedure to clean out some of the scarring, and that's when they told me that I would never be able to conceive a child naturally. *There's a small chance you could become pregnant with reproductive technology, but even that is extremely unlikely due to the extensive scarring.*

It was devastating to hear at the time. At the time, I cursed my luck. Even though I had grown up poor, I still dreamed of filling up my house with children someday, just like my parents did. I cried for twenty-four hours straight when I found out the news.

But over the years, I discovered it was a blessing. I saw so many of my friends tied down with children and observed how your offspring will bleed your bank accounts dry. I realized I was fortunate to be child-free. Really, that infection was the best thing that ever happened to me.

Douglas is shaking his head. "I don't understand. Are you saying all this time, you knew that you could never get pregnant?"

"That's right."

He falls onto the comfy sofa, a glazed look in his eyes. "We've been trying for *years.* You never even said a word. I can't believe you lied to me like that."

I've upset him, but it's for the best. Like I said, the Band-Aid needed to be pulled off. "I knew it wasn't what you wanted to hear."

He looks up at me, his eyes slightly moist. "Well, what about adoption? Or..."

Oh Lord, the *last* thing I want is to take care of somebody else's brats. "I don't *want* children, Douglas. I *never* wanted them. What I do want is to get out of this marriage."

"But..." His lower jaw trembles. He still has that double chin. In our entire marriage, I have not made any headway in helping him get rid of it. I had believed he was a work in progress, but I never made any real progress. "I love you, Wendy. Don't you love me?"

"Not anymore," I say. It's kinder than telling him that I never loved him. "I don't want to be with you anymore. I don't respect you, and we want different things. It's better to part ways."

When I have my ten million dollars, I won't have to worry about him canceling my stupid credit card again. I'll be independent. Russell can leave his wife, and we can do whatever we want.

"Fine." Douglas struggles to his feet. "You want out of this marriage? You got it. But you're not getting a penny of my money."

Unfortunately, it's not up to him. He wants to punish me, but I know my rights. "The prenup gives me ten million dollars. I won't ask for more than that."

"Right." The glazed look is gone from his brown eyes, and now they have become sharp and laser-beam focused on my face. "You get ten million dollars if we divorce. But the prenup says that if I have evidence of you cheating, you get *nothing*."

I think back to that thick document that Joe handed me before the wedding. I had considered giving it to a lawyer, but I could see in plain black and white that it said I get ten million in the instance of divorce. I didn't want to waste thousands of dollars I didn't have to hire an attorney.

"I'd be happy to show you the clause where it says that." A smile is playing on his lips. "It's right on page 178. I don't know how you could have missed it."

My hands clench into fists. "Joe tricked me. He was always so determined to make you mistrust me."

"No, the prenup was *my* idea. So was the clause about infidelity." Douglas undoes the top button on his collar. "I told him to act like it was his idea, so you wouldn't get mad at me. I wanted you to trust me. Even though I didn't trust *you*."

I stare at my husband, my fury growing. "You can't just throw something in without telling me. That's... that's deceiving me."

His eyebrows shoot up. "Oh, you mean like when you failed to tell me that you could never get pregnant?"

My chest feels tight. It's become a little hard to breathe. Douglas always talked about how much better the air is out here, but I don't notice it. "Fine. But good luck proving that I was unfaithful to you."

Even though it's going to kill me, I won't be able to see Russell for a while. I can't give Douglas any chance to prove my infidelity.

"Oh, don't worry. I've already got pictures, videos... you name it."

I gasp. "You hired a detective to spy on me?"

He glares at me with venom in his eyes. "All I had to do was put a few hidden cameras in our own apartment. Subtle much?"

Damn. We should never have been so careless. If only I had known...

"You might be able to get your old job back," Douglas says thoughtfully. "What did you do? Didn't you work at some counter at Macy's? That sounds like fun."

I hate this man. I have felt a lot of emotions for him over the last three years, but I have never felt this kind of hatred for anyone in my life. Yes, I wasn't entirely honest with him. But to leave me penniless? He is truly a sadistic person.

"I won't divorce you then," I say. "I won't sign the papers. You won't get me out of your life."

"Fine," he says with maddening calm. "But you're not getting your credit cards back. And all the bank accounts are in my name—I'm cutting off your access."

I didn't know Douglas had it in him. But I suppose you don't get to be the CEO of such a huge company without having a pair of balls.

"You can still stay at the penthouse," he adds. "For now. But in a few months, I'm putting it on the market. So you can decide what you want to do."

With those words, he turns around and heads out of the living room. His tie is still lying on the sofa, and there's part of me that's tempted to grab it, wrap it around his neck, and squeeze the life out of him.

I don't do it, of course, but the idea is incredibly appealing.

Because if Douglas divorces me with proof of my adultery, I get nothing. But if he is dead, according to his will, I get *everything*.

FIFTY-SIX

Step 6: Figure Out How to Turn Your Husband into a Man Who Deserves to Die

Four Months Earlier

"Douglas is threatening to put the penthouse on the market soon," I tell Russell. "I don't know what to do."

We are lying together in the gigantic king-sized bed in the master bedroom. I was panicked about coming back here after I found out about the cameras Douglas installed, so I hired an expert to find them all and dismantle them. Not staying at this apartment was not an option—after all, it's mine as much as it is Douglas's. I'm the one who picked out this bed, although I can probably count on my hands the number of times Douglas has slept in it. He never liked this apartment. Russell, on the other hand, is completely enamored with it. He likes it as much as I do.

But even if I got the ten million dollars, I wouldn't be able to stay here. And without that money, it's a ridiculous dream.

"He won't do it." Russell runs his fingers over my bare stomach. "If he sells the apartment, you'll have to go live with him. And he doesn't want that."

I want to throw up my hands. "Who knows what he wants? He's just trying to punish me." The whole lie about me trying to get pregnant clearly pushed him over the edge. He wants me to suffer for my sins. "But what can I do?"

"You could divorce him anyway," he says. "And you could be with me. I'll leave Marybeth."

"But we'll be destitute!"

"No, we won't." He looks offended by this suggestion. "I have my store. And you could find something as well. We won't be destitute."

Sometimes I feel like Russell and I are made for each other, but other times he says things like *that*.

For now, I'm waiting it out. Once Douglas and I get divorced, that's it—I have no claim to his money. So every day, I cross my fingers that while he's walking down the street, he gets hit by a bus. That happens all the time in the city. Why can't it happen to my husband for once?

"If only he would die," I say. "You'd think with the amount of greasy food he eats, he would have dropped dead of a heart attack."

"He's only forty-two."

"Men die from heart attacks all the time in their forties," I point out. "Douglas even takes medication for his heart. It could happen."

"Hoping Douglas has a heart attack isn't a solid plan for the future."

Russell doesn't seem to enjoy fantasizing about Douglas's death the way I do. That's only because he doesn't know him like I do.

"There must be a way out of this prenup situation," I say. "Douglas is being a sadistic asshole, and he needs to pay for the way he's been treating me. There should be some way to punish husbands who treat their wives this way. Cutting off my money and threatening to take my home away... That's basically, like, abuse."

As I say the words, something tugs at the back of my head. A story my friend Audrey was telling me ages ago. About some sort of housekeeper who advocates for women who are treated badly by their husbands.

She's hardcore, believe me... If she thinks a guy is hurting a woman, she will do pretty much anything to make it stop.

I close my eyes, trying to remember the woman's name. Then it comes to me:

Millie.

Douglas isn't terrible in the same way as Ginger's husband was—he's not physically abusive. But he's evil and manipulative nonetheless. Abuse isn't necessarily only physical—isn't my husband throwing me out of my own home and leaving me penniless just as abusive as breaking a bone?

Would this cleaning woman agree? I don't know. She might need a little persuading.

But... what if she saw a man treating me terribly, and she believed him to be my husband? Of course, it couldn't actually be Douglas because he's actively avoiding me. And Douglas would never physically lay a hand on me, even if I provoked him. But this Millie person doesn't know who my husband is. Douglas has meticulously swept the internet of photographs of himself. If Millie saw a man slapping me around, she would be motivated to help me. If what he does is bad enough, I won't even be able to stop her.

Slowly, a plan is forming in my head.

FIFTY-SEVEN

When I look at myself in the mirror, I almost scream.

My face looks like a nightmare of blossoming purple bruises, mixed with other bruises that are fading to yellow. It is painful to gaze upon. Russell watches me putting the final touches on my cheekbone, and he seems impressed.

"You're a magician, Wendy," he tells me. "It looks real."

I spent hours practicing. I watched several YouTube videos, and now I am one of the world's experts on creating realistic-looking bruises. It truly does look like somebody gave me a substantial beating.

I hope Millie appreciates the work that went into this masterpiece.

For the most part, Millie seems to be truly buying into our little act. And aside from that, she is an excellent cook and housekeeper. She's even managed to find me some cucamelons —my favorite. It's a shame what's going to happen to her.

But there's no other way.

"It's almost perfect," I say as I put away my canvas of makeup. "It's just missing one thing."

Russell raises an eyebrow. He has been playing the role of Douglas to perfection since Millie arrived. It's incredible—when you combine Russell's looks and personality with Douglas's wealth and power, you truly have the ideal man. "Really? Looks pretty perfect to me."

I inspect my face in the mirror one more time. Perfect isn't good enough. It has to be *better* than perfect. If Millie suspects for one second that this is makeup, it's game over. It has to be *impeccable*.

"You have to punch me," I say.

Russell throws back his head and lets out a laugh. "Right. Sounds good."

"I mean it. I need you to split my lip. It needs to look *real*."

The smile slides off Russell's face as he realizes I am 100 percent serious. "What?"

"She can't suspect this is makeup," I tell him. "And I can't fake a split lip with the supplies I've got. You need to punch me."

Russell shoots me a horrified look as he backs away from me. "I'm not punching you in the face."

"You don't have to feel bad about it. I'm telling you to do it."

"I've never hit a woman in my life." He looks slightly ill. It makes me wonder if he has the guts to go through with this plan. He's going to have to do a lot worse than punch me in the face before this is over. "I'm not going to hit you, Wendy."

"You have to."

"I won't. I *can't*."

I am so frustrated, I could scream. Does he think this is a *joke*? I have a small amount of savings that I tucked away for a rainy day in my own personal account, plus some money I made selling jewelry and clothing. But I've been using that to live on and to pay

Millie's—extremely generous, I might add—salary. I have now also spent a chunk of it purchasing a dress that the police will eventually suspect Douglas gave Millie, as well as an expensive engraved bracelet. And of course, I packed the closet with cleaning supplies that I purchased under the guise of having terrible allergies, but really bought so that the doorman wouldn't catch Millie lugging around bottles of floor cleaner and furniture polish.

In any case, the money isn't going to last much longer. I need to wrap this up—soon.

I need him to punch me.

"You're pathetic," I spit at him. "I can't believe you won't do this little thing for me. We have a chance to strike it rich, and here you are, screwing it up."

"Wendy..."

I sneer at him. "No wonder you're in your forties and you're nothing but a furniture salesman. *Pathetic.*"

"Enough, Wendy," Russell says through his teeth.

His right hand balls into a fist. He is sensitive about his career. I know he is. He always dreamed of being a successful businessman, and managing a floundering antique furniture store is very far from that dream. I could help him do so much more—I could turn him into the man he wants to be. The man he *deserves* to be.

He just needs to *hit* me.

"You're such a loser," I go on. "What are you going to do when the store goes belly up? Get a job at McDonald's, salting French fries?"

"Enough! Stop it!"

"You want me to stop? Then *hit me!*"

Before I even know what's happening, a burst of pain explodes on the left side of my face. I gasp and stumble backward, catching myself on the towel rack. For a second, I am seeing stars.

"Wendy!" Russell's anguished cry breaks me out of my haze. "Jesus Christ, I'm so sorry!"

He looks like he's about to burst into tears, but he doesn't feel as bad as my face feels. God, he hit me really hard. I wasn't sure he had it in him. I touch my face and I realize there's blood streaming out of my nose.

"You're bleeding," he gasps.

He grabbed me some paper towels, and I do my best to staunch the flow of blood out of my nose. After a couple of minutes, it seems to stop. Well, mostly.

When I look up at Russell, his powerful eyebrows are bunched together. "Are you okay? I'm so sorry."

The bathroom is a disaster. My blood has dripped all over the floor. And there is a bloody handprint on the edge of the bathroom sink, from where I was gripping it when I was desperately trying to get my nose to stop bleeding.

Oh my God, it's perfect.

FIFTY-EIGHT

Step 7: Kill the Bastard

The Night Douglas Was Murdered

The gears are grinding painfully in the elevator. Douglas is home.

This is the moment. This is what we have been working up to for the past several months. Millie left the apartment an hour ago, shaking and convinced that she just murdered my husband. The police will question her. She will break and confess to what she did. And I have planted careful evidence to convince them that she did it because she has been having an affair with Douglas. I cannot afford to be involved.

Now there is only one piece left of the puzzle. We must kill Douglas for real this time.

Russell is waiting in the kitchen, clutching the gun that Millie just used to shoot him with a blank—except this time filled with real bullets. He's ready.

The doors to the elevator swing open, and I head down the hallway to greet my husband one last time. I stop short, surprised by his appearance. He's lost weight since the last time I saw him, and there are dark purple circles embedded under his eyes. There's at least two days' growth of a beard on his chin.

"You look awful," I blurt out.

Douglas looks up sharply. "Nice to see you too, Wendy."

"I mean..." I brush a strand of hair away from my face. I carefully scrubbed off all the makeup from my fake bruises after Millie left. "I mean, you seem... tired."

He lets out a long, tortured sigh. "I've been working around the clock on this new update to the software. And then you call and beg me to come here practically in the middle of the night."

"Did you bring it?"

Douglas holds up that tattered leather briefcase he always carries around. "I've got the divorce papers right here. I hope you're ready to sign."

Not exactly. But he doesn't need to know that.

I lead Douglas into the living room. My body tenses, waiting for Russell to emerge from the kitchen and shoot my husband point-blank in the chest. He is supposed to do it right when we walk into the room. He's supposed to do it... right now.

Damn it.

Douglas manages to make it all the way to our sectional sofa without being murdered by my lover. I'm quite disappointed. He sinks into the cushion and puts the briefcase down on the coffee table.

"Let's get this over with," he mutters.

No, not yet. I didn't bring him here to sign divorce papers. That's the opposite of why I wanted him here. Except Russell is not coming out. I don't see him, and I can't hear him. What is going on?

"Can I get you something to drink?" I ask. He looks like he's about to refuse, so I quickly say, "I'll get you some water."

Before Douglas can protest, I dart off to the kitchen, leaving him behind on the sofa with the divorce papers. I am absolutely furious right now. Up until this moment, everything has gone exactly as I planned it. Only one more thing needs to happen. Russell needs to kill Douglas.

Except when I get into the kitchen, Russell is cowering in the corner. The gun is on the counter, and he looks like he's having a panic attack. He is clutching the counter with his leather gloves and breathing too quickly, his face like a sheet.

"Russell!" I hiss at him. "What the hell are you waiting for?"

He has been remarkably difficult tonight. Before Millie even came over, he was threatening to back out, stating a laundry list of concerns. *Are you sure it's safe to be shot with a blank? Isn't that how Brandon Lee died? What if she stabs me instead?*

Finally, I got him to go through with the scene where he pretended to strangle me. And after Millie shot him with the blank and he didn't die, I thought we were past it—the hardest part was over. Except now he seems to be having trouble sucking air into his lungs.

"I can't do it," he gulps. His brow is sweaty and his powerful eyebrows have merged together at the center of his forehead. "I can't shoot him, Wendy. Please don't make me do it."

Is he joking? We have spent months setting this up together. We have been so careful to always come in through the back entrance and to set the scene in exactly the right way. I barely leave the apartment because I can't chance running into Millie, and I've been dedicating all my energy to making it look like Douglas is still living here. I even purchased a bunch of men's clothing that she could wash. (Although the first day I stupidly forgot to unfold it all. I'm sure she thought we were a bunch of psychopaths who fold our dirty laundry.) I have spent so much time and energy setting all of this up.

And now here he is, about to ruin everything.

"You are absolutely ridiculous." I clench my teeth. "What is wrong with you? This was the plan from the beginning! This is how we're going to get everything we want."

"I don't want this!" His voice is an urgent whisper. "I just want to be with you. And we still can." He crosses the kitchen and tries to put his hands around my waist. "Listen to me, we don't have to do this. We can leave right now. You leave Douglas, I leave Marybeth, and we can be together. We don't have to kill him."

"Except then we'll have *nothing*." I shrug away his embrace, furious with him. I thought Russell wanted the same things I did, but now I'm not so sure. Because if he did, my husband would have a bullet in his chest right now. "This is the only way, Russell."

"I don't want to do this." He's whimpering now. "I don't want to kill him, Wendy. Please don't make me do this. *Please*."

Oh Lord.

I have been in this kitchen way too long. Douglas is going to start wondering what is taking me so long and come to investigate. Or he might even hear Russell panicking. I don't have time to give Russell a pep talk. I have to take care of this myself.

I grab a pair of disposable rubber gloves under the sink that Millie uses when she cleans the kitchen. I slide them onto my hands, then I pour my husband one last glass of water. I pick up the gun, but after hesitating a little, I slip it into the pocket of my cardigan. The pockets are large, and the gun fits perfectly—it's as if when I put it on, I knew I was going to have to do this because Russell was going to be a big baby about it and almost ruin everything.

When I get back into the living room, Douglas is sitting on the sofa, rifling through the stack of papers that is our divorce settlement. He has been asking me to sign this for a long time, and I have been refusing. I knew that agreeing to sign would get him to come over here.

With my free hand, I feel the gun in my cardigan pocket.

It's heavy, straining the fabric slightly. There's no reason to wait. I could pull it out right now and shoot him dead. But no. I need to do it right to his face. So it looks like Millie shot him head-on.

And also, part of me wants to see his face when I do it. So he understands the consequences of messing with me. He tried to take everything from me and leave me destitute, and now he will get what he deserves.

I quickly place the glass of water on the table before he can notice that I'm wearing rubber gloves, and then I shove my hands back into my pockets. Millie put away this set of dishes, so her fingerprints will be all over the glass. It's too perfect.

"I've got a pen in here somewhere," Douglas mutters as he rifles around inside the old briefcase. After a moment, he retrieves a ballpoint pen. "Here it is."

"Okay then." My fingers are wrapped around the revolver in my pocket. "Let's get this over with, like you said."

Douglas starts to hold out the papers to me, but then he stops. His shoulders sag. "I don't want it to be this way, Wendy."

I frown at him. "What does that mean?"

"I mean..." He tosses the divorce papers onto the coffee table. "I love you, Wendy. I don't want to get divorced—I've been sick over it. I don't care what happened in the past... I'd like to make a fresh start. Just the two of us."

There is a hopeful expression on his face. I have to admit, the idea is appealing. As much as we planned the events of tonight, there is no guarantee that Russell and I will get away with murder. My original plan was to spend my life with Douglas, and although I failed to mold him into what I wanted, he's not entirely objectionable. And most of all, we will have unspeakable amounts of money. You can be happy with anyone if you have enough money.

"Maybe..." I say.

A smile touches his lips, and the purple circles under his

eyes grow a bit lighter. "I'd really like that. I'd like to make a completely fresh start."

"In what way?"

"First, I want to get rid of all of this." He looks around our spacious apartment. "We don't need this gigantic place or even the huge house on Long Island if it's just the two of us. All this money got in the way of our marriage. We have too much." He smiles shyly. "I've spoken to Joe about starting a charity foundation with most of my money. Especially if we're not having children, there's so much good we can do with all this money—God knows, *we* don't need it. Maybe you can be part of the foundation? We could do it together."

Is he out of his everloving *mind*? How could he possibly think that's what I want? "Douglas, I don't want that. I want to go back to our lives the way it was before."

"But you weren't happy before." His face darkens. "You cheated on me. We were completely disconnected."

I grit my teeth. "So you think being poor will make us happy?"

"No, but..." He rubs his hands over his knees. "Look, we won't be poor. We just won't be zillionaires anymore. And I don't see anything wrong with that. Like I said, I don't even know why we need all this money. I don't even want it!"

And this is why Douglas and I will never be happy together. He just doesn't get it. He doesn't know what it's like to have the other girls laugh at you and ask if you found your coat in the garbage bin. He doesn't know what it's like for your father to hurt his back so he goes on disability, but the payments aren't quite enough to keep the lights on, so every so often you have to do everything in the dark, with flashlights. And even though your sisters act like it's an adventure, it's *not*. It's not an adventure. It's being dirt poor and having nothing.

Douglas doesn't understand that. He will *never* understand that. We finally have the money that I dreamed of when

I was doing my homework by the light of a flashlight, and he wants to just give it all away! It makes me so angry, I want to reach out with my bare hands and strangle him the way Russell pretended to strangle me earlier, except for real this time.

Except I don't need to strangle him.

I've got a gun in my pocket.

I pull out the gun, and my hand is surprisingly steady as I point it at my husband's chest. His slightly bloodshot eyes widen. He knew things were bad, but he didn't know it was this bad.

"Wendy," he croaks. "What are you doing?"

"I think you know."

Douglas stares down the barrel of the gun, and his body seems to shrink. He shakes his head almost imperceptibly. I would've thought he might beg for his life, but he doesn't do that. There is a look of resignation in his eyes.

"Did you *ever* actually love me?" he finally says.

The answer to that question would hurt his feelings. Despite everything, I don't want to destroy him in his last few moments of life. So I just say, "It's not about that."

I've never shot a gun before, but it always seemed self-explanatory. I had thought Russell would be the one to do it, but he is still cowering in the kitchen, so it's up to me.

The gunshot is much louder than I thought it would be—a powerful bang that seems to echo through the room long after the gun has fired. The force travels through my arms, into my shoulders, and whips back my neck and head. But I keep my hands steady.

The bullet hits Douglas square in the chest. It's a good shot, especially for my first time. There's a second or two before he dies when he looks down at the blood rapidly spreading across his white shirt and realizes what's about to happen. But then the color drains from his face, and he collapses against the couch.

His eyes are still cracked open, rolled up in their sockets, and his chest isn't moving.

"I'm sorry," I say softly. "I truly am. I wish we could have made it work."

My ears are still ringing when Russell comes running out. The first thing he does is clasp a hand over his mouth, and I'm just thinking to myself that I hope he doesn't vomit all over the floor. That will *really* mess things up when the police get here.

"You did it," he gasps. "I can't believe you did it."

"I did." I rise from the sofa and drop the gun on the coffee table. I peel the rubber gloves off my hands. "And if you don't want to go to jail, I would suggest you get out of here right this minute."

Russell looks like he's still trying to get his breathing under control. "You really think you can pin all this on Millie?"

"Watch me."

PART III

FIFTY-NINE

MILLIE

My head won't stop spinning.

I shut off the television and close my eyes for a minute. It's only been a day since I shot and killed a man in an Upper West Side penthouse, but what I've just seen has changed everything.

I try to picture Douglas Garrick. I can clearly see his slicked-back hair, his deep-set brown eyes, his prominent cheekbones. I've seen him countless times in the last couple of months. And that man on the television news report was not him.

I don't think so, anyway.

I dig out my phone and pull up the internet browser. I have searched for Douglas Garrick before, and there have always been articles about his CEO position at Coinstock, but never any photos. However, now dozens of links fill the screen, and I can click on any one of them to bring up that same headshot of Douglas Garrick.

I study the photo on the screen of my phone. This man has a passing resemblance to the man I know, but it's not him. The man in the photograph has at least twenty or thirty pounds on the man I met, and that crooked left incisor is different as well. And his features are all slightly different—his nose, his lips, his slight double chin. Although I suppose some people do look different in photographs than they do in real life. Maybe he's airbrushed a lot?

Maybe it *is* the same person. It has to be, doesn't it? Because otherwise none of this makes any sense.

Oh God, I feel like I'm losing my mind.

Maybe I really am going crazy. Maybe I *have* been having a secret affair with Douglas Garrick. I mean, that detective certainly seemed to have a lot of evidence. And apparently, Wendy Garrick said it was true.

But I didn't spend the night in that hotel with Douglas (or whoever the man I knew to be Douglas was). And I can prove it. Because I drove back to the city after dropping Wendy off. And I have a witness.

Enzo Accardi.

I've been reluctant to reach out to Enzo, but I don't have a choice. My boyfriend has abandoned me, which wasn't entirely surprising, but nevertheless heartbreaking. I've been terrible at getting close to people over the last four years because I've been so scared of what they'll think of me when they find out about my past. And I was right. The second Brock learned about my prison record he was gone. So here I am, with nobody in my corner. Nobody who believes in me.

Except Enzo. He will believe in me.

And if he doesn't, that's how I know I'm really in trouble.

I find Enzo's name in my contacts, waiting for me as always. I hesitate for a split second, then I click on his name.

The phone has barely rung when he picks it up. I almost burst into tears at the sound of his familiar voice. "Millie?"

"Enzo," I manage. "I'm in big trouble."

"Yes. I see the news. Your boss is dead."

"So, um..." I cough into my hand. "Is there any way you could come over?"

"Give me five minutes."

SIXTY

Four minutes later, I'm opening the door for Enzo.

"Thank you," I tell him as he steps inside my small apartment. "I... I didn't know who else to call."

"Broccoli is not here to help?" he sneers.

I drop my eyes. "No. That's over."

His face falls. "I'm sorry. I know you liked the Broccoli."

Did I? I liked him, but the truth was, every time he told me he loved me, it made my skin crawl. That's not how you're supposed to feel about your significant other. Brock was just about perfect, but I could never fall entirely in love with him—it always felt temporary. I'm sure he'll make some other woman extremely happy, but it was never going to be me.

"I'm okay," I finally say. "I've got bigger problems right now."

Enzo follows me into the apartment and we sit together on my ratty futon. When he and I used to live together, our sofa was only slightly better than this one. But I had to give up that apartment when he wasn't available anymore to pay his half of the rent, and I couldn't figure out a way to transport the sofa so I left it behind. I try not to think about it right now though. No point in getting pissed off at Enzo when he's trying to help me.

"The police are saying all kinds of crazy things about me," I tell him. "Wendy told them I was having an affair with Douglas. It makes no sense, but they twisted all these things that happened to make it look like I was going there to sleep with him."

Enzo nods slowly. "I told you they are dangerous."

"You said Douglas Garrick was dangerous."

"Same thing."

"Not the same thing," I say. "In fact, when I was watching the news just now, I realized something. The man who hired me, who called himself Douglas Garrick, he's not the same man on the news. He is somebody entirely different."

Now Enzo is looking at me like I've lost my mind.

"I know that sounds nuts," I admit. "I hear the words coming out of my mouth, and... Like I said, I know it's weird. But it was a different guy in that apartment. I'm sure of it."

The more I think about it, the more certain I feel. But if that wasn't Douglas, who was it? And where was the real Douglas while this guy was in his house?

Who is the man I murdered?

"So I will tell you something interesting," Enzo says slowly. "When you told me about the Garricks, I went to look them up. And you know what? That penthouse in Manhattan is not listed as their primary residence."

"*What?*"

"Yes, it is true. This apartment is just extra for them. Their primary residence is a house on Long Island. Well, they say it is a house. It is probably more like a mansion."

This is starting to make a little bit more sense. If the real Douglas Garrick actually lived out on Long Island, that means it would be easy for two other people to make it look like they were living in the Manhattan apartment. The real Douglas Garrick would never have to know.

"So," I say, "you believe me?"

Enzo looks affronted. "Of course I believe you!"

"But there's something you need to know." I wipe my sweaty hands on my jeans. "The night that Douglas was killed, I saw... Well, I *thought* I saw him trying to strangle Wendy. I saw *someone* trying to strangle her in the apartment. And he wouldn't stop. So I got their gun and I... I shot him. To make him stop."

I've never been much of a crier, but I feel the waterworks coming on for the second time today. Enzo reaches for me, and I sob into his shoulder. He holds me for a long time, letting me cry it out. When I finally pull away, there is a damp stain left behind on his T-shirt.

"Sorry I ruined your shirt," I say.

He waves a hand. "It is just a little snot. No big deal."

I drop my eyes. "I just don't know what I'm going to do. The police think that I killed Douglas Garrick, and even though I know I didn't, I shot *somebody* that night. Somebody is dead because of me."

"That is not certain."

"Of course it is!"

"You *think* you killed someone," he points out. "But after you shot him, you went home. Did you check and make sure he is dead? Not breathing? No pulse?"

"I... Wendy said he didn't have a pulse."

"And we believe Wendy?"

I blink at him. "There was *blood*, Enzo."

"Was it blood though? Is easy to fake blood."

I frown, thinking back to last night. It all happened so fast. The gun fired, Douglas went down, and then there was all that blood spreading under his body. But it's not like I went and checked him out. I'm not a paramedic. After I shot him, all I wanted to do was get out of there as fast as I could.

Is it possible none of that was real? And if it wasn't...

"She tricked me," I gasp. "She completely tricked me."

All that time, I was feeling sorry for her. I was trying to protect her. And meanwhile, she was telling anyone who would listen that I was having an affair with her husband—that was surely why Amber Degraw was grinning at me when she brought up Douglas Garrick that day I ran into her on the street. No wonder that doorman kept winking at me! And nobody knew that I was never alone with Douglas because he was coming in through the back entrance, where there is no doorman or camera.

No, not Douglas. I never even *met* Douglas Garrick. I have no idea who that other man was.

"Where is Wendy's house?" I ask him. "I need to talk to her."

"You think you can go over there?" He shakes his head. "There are one million reporters around her house. And she will not talk to you anyway. If you go there, it will just be more trouble."

I know he's right, but it's still super frustrating. After what she did to me, I just want to look her in the eyes and ask why. But he's right. Nothing good will come out of driving over there.

"This man who called himself Douglas Garrick..." Enzo rubs his chin. "Do you have any idea how we can find him? This man may be easier to access than Wendy Garrick."

"No." I clench my fists in frustration. "All I know is that his name isn't Douglas Garrick. I have no idea who he really is."

"Do you have a photo of him?"

"No, I don't."

"Think, Millie. There must be something. Maybe a detail about him that is distinctive?"

"No. He's just a generic middle-aged white guy."

"There must be something..."

I close my eyes, trying to conjure up an image of the man who called himself Douglas Garrick. There was absolutely nothing distinctive about him, and maybe that's why Wendy chose him. He looks just enough like the real Douglas Garrick.

But Enzo's right. There must be something...

"Wait," I say. "There *is* something!"

Enzo raises his eyebrows. "Yes?"

"I saw him go into a building once," I recall. "He was with another woman. A blond woman. I thought she was some woman he was having an affair with, and maybe he was. But... it was an apartment building. Either he lives there or the woman lives there or..."

"This is good." Enzo cracks his knuckles. "We will go there and find either him or the woman. Then we will get the truth."

For the first time since Detective Ramirez was interrogating me at the police station, I feel a spark of hope. Maybe there's a chance I'll come out of this with my freedom intact.

SIXTY-ONE

Enzo helps me clean up my apartment, since it looks like a hurricane hit after the police search. Thankfully, it's just two rooms, so despite the mess, it doesn't take that long. Mostly, I'm grateful for the company. It would be *so* depressing to clean all this up myself.

"Thank you for doing this," I tell Enzo for what feels like the hundredth time as we put back clothes from my dresser drawers that now seem to be flung all over the room.

"Is no problem," he says.

As I drop a shirt in the laundry hamper, I noticed that it isn't as full as it seemed yesterday. I sift through the clothing—something is missing.

They took the clothing I was wearing last night.

I chew on my thumbnail, trying to remember the shirt and jeans I stripped off last night before I fell into bed. There wasn't any blood on it—I'm sure of it.

Pretty sure, at least. But what if there were little microscopic particles that will be found on testing? That seems possible. Although if Enzo's theory is correct, there never was any blood while I was in that apartment. But I'm not absolutely *sure.*

Enzo is busy stuffing clothes into a drawer. I am grateful he's here, but part of me wants him to leave so I can panic more thoroughly.

I clear my throat. "If you need to leave, it's okay," I tell him.

"No, this is fun." He holds up a pair of lacy pink panties that are on the floor. "This is nice. New?"

I reach over and yank them out of his hands. He's a good distraction, at least. "I don't remember."

"I can see why the Broccoli liked you so much with such nice panties."

I shoot him a look. "Enzo..."

"Sorry." He ducks his head down. "I just... I do not get that one."

We have been cleaning for over an hour without discussing Brock. I guess I shouldn't be surprised he has mentioned it. "What's to get?"

"He does not seem like someone you would like."

"Yes, well..." I plop down on my bed, a bunched-up sweatshirt on my lap. "He's a good guy. I mean, he was nice. He was a successful lawyer. There's nothing not to like."

Enzo settles down beside me on the bed. "If he is a good guy, where is he now?"

It's not an unfair point, but Enzo doesn't know the entire situation. "I kept some things from him about my past. He was hurt. He said he felt like he didn't know who I am. It's understandable he felt that way."

"Who you are is not something you did when you were a teenager." His black eyes look intently into mine. "It is clear who you are. If he could not tell from spending time with you, then he is right—he does not deserve to be with you."

It wasn't like Enzo and I had the perfect relationship, but I never doubted that he understood me. Sometimes he seemed to understand me better than I understood myself. And I knew that if I were ever in trouble, he would do anything to help me.

"Sometimes I think..." I chew on my lower lip. "We never entirely connected. And it's probably my fault because I kept things from him. Anyway, it's over."

"Are you sure?"

I remember the look Brock gave me when he walked out of that interrogation room. "Yes. I'm sure."

"So," he says, "if I kissed you, he would not punch me in nose?"

"No, but *I* might."

A smile twitches on his lips. "I will take my chances."

He leans in to kiss me, and I feel like I've been waiting for this for nearly two years. I finally understand why I was hesitant to move in with Brock and tell him my secrets. It's because I never felt this way about him. Not even close.

And Enzo is right. I don't punch him in the nose.

SIXTY-TWO

We have been out in front of the brownstone building since six in the morning.

It was hard to drag myself out of bed so early, especially since Enzo and I had a late night together, if you know what I mean. And the night before, my sleep wasn't exactly stellar. But Enzo was adamant that we should be there first thing in the morning, to make sure we don't miss anyone going in or coming out.

We are wearing what Enzo calls "disguises." When he said it, I imagined big black glasses with fake mustaches, but really, it's just a couple of baseball caps and sunglasses. Enzo is wearing a Yankees cap, and he gave me one that says "I love New York." Except instead of "love" it's a big red heart. I look like a freaking tourist. It's humiliating for someone born and raised in Brooklyn.

"Tourist is best disguise," Enzo tells me.

Maybe he's right, but I hate it. Still, I'm willing to do anything to get to the bottom of whatever the hell is going on. Before I end up back in prison again.

We can't stay in one place all morning, so we move around,

all the while keeping our eyes on the entrance to the building. If there's a back entrance like the Garricks' penthouse, we are screwed. But lots of residents are coming and going, so I'm hopeful this is the only way in or out.

Right now, it's eight o'clock in the morning. We have been here for two hours and there has been no sign of the mystery man—if I really didn't murder him, like Enzo thinks—or the blond woman. About ten minutes ago, Enzo announced he was hungry, so he went into the Dunkin' Donuts across the street. He comes out carrying two cups of coffee and a brown paper bag.

"Take," he instructs me.

I take the coffee gratefully. "What's in the bag?"

"Is bagels."

"Ugh." My stomach turns at the thought of eating anything. I don't even know why I asked. "I'll pass."

"You must eat at some time."

"Not now." I peer through my sunglasses at the brownstone. "Not until we find him."

I'm afraid to take my eyes off the building. I could miss them, and then I will never find the mystery man. I am scared that I will get arrested today, and even though Enzo will keep trying to help me, he doesn't know what that man looks like. The only person who can find him is me.

"So," Enzo says. "Last night... it was good, yes?"

I take a long sip from my coffee. "I can't focus on anything right now, Enzo."

"Oh." He looks down at his own container filled with coffee. "Yes. I know."

"But yes, it *was* good."

One corner of his lips quirks up. "I missed you so much when I was gone, Millie. I am so sorry for that. I do not regret being back home in Italy for my mother, but I did not want to have to choose between the two most important people in my life. I wanted you to wait, but I could not ask that."

I hang my head. "I *should* have waited."

Enzo opens his mouth to say something more, but before he can get out any words, I grab his arm. "That's her! That's the woman!"

Enzo squints through his sunglasses across the street, at the woman with blond hair coming out of the brownstone, wearing a knee-length skirt and a blazer. "You are sure?"

"Pretty sure." I recognize her face and her hair color, but it is styled differently. It's possible that it isn't her. But I haven't seen anyone else who even comes close. "Now what?"

The woman adjusts her purse strap, then crosses the street. I get ready to start following her, but then she goes into the Dunkin' Donuts that Enzo just came out of. Judging by the line, she'll be in there for at least ten minutes.

Enzo cracks his knuckles. "I will go talk to her."

"You? What are you going to say?"

"I will think of something."

"So you think you're going to approach her in Dunkin' Donuts and she's just going to tell you everything?"

He places a hand on his chest. "Yes! I am very charming!"

I roll my eyes.

"You watch, Millie." He squeezes my arm, then hands me the paper bag with the bagels. "I will find out everything."

SIXTY-THREE

Enzo is taking forever in Dunkin' Donuts.

He told me to stay across the street, but after ten minutes pass, I start to get antsy. What is happening in there?

I wish I had gone with him. I don't think it would've cramped his style too much. Well, maybe it would have. But given it's my life at stake here, I'd like to know what's going on.

Finally, I cross the street to Dunkin' Donuts. The storefront is made of windows, so it's easy enough to look inside. I peer through the windows, and at first, I don't see them at all. But then I do. All the way at the other end of the store where people pick up their orders. The two of them are talking together intently. Enzo's black eyes seem completely focused on hers.

For a moment, I feel a twinge of misgivings. I have always trusted Enzo, but there are times when I'm not entirely sure he's trustworthy. After all, the reason he left Italy in the first place was because he beat a man half to death. He had a really good reason, at least according to him, but the fact remains. And then he took off to go overseas again, claiming the bad man who was after him met with an untimely demise, although he wouldn't provide any further information on that.

He told me his mother was sick. She had a stroke. But really, I only had his word to go on. It wasn't like I ever *saw* his alleged sick mother.

And then when he came back to the States, instead of giving me a call like any *normal* person would have, he followed me around for three freaking months, under the guise of protecting me. I told him all the details about the Garrick family. He's savvy enough to have guessed Wendy was scamming me, even if I didn't see it. Why didn't he say anything?

And oh my God, what on earth are they talking about in there for so long?

Now that we are closer, I notice the blond woman has puffy eyes, like she's been crying. But then she smiles at something Enzo says to her, and her face brightens slightly. It does look fairly innocent, I have to admit. He *is* very charming when he wants to be. Between his accent and the way he looks, he's very good at talking to women.

After what feels like another ten minutes, Enzo and the woman exit the Dunkin' Donuts. He waves to her and says, "*Ciao, bella!*" Which makes her blush.

When he sees me standing in front of the shop, he gives me a disapproving look. "I say stay across the street, yes?"

I fold my arms across my chest. "You were in there a long time."

"Yes, and I know everything now." He tilts his head. "You want I should tell you?"

I look into Enzo's dark eyes. This man doesn't always do everything by the book. Like me, he has done some bad things in his life, although it has always been for the right reasons. I have seen him risk his own life to help women in danger. If there's anyone in this world that I can trust, it's him. I should never have doubted him for even a second. "Yes. Tell me."

Enzo glances down the street at where the woman is ducking into a subway station. "That woman, she is the assistant to Douglas Garrick. And she is the wife of the man you are looking for."

I stare at him. "Seriously? Are you sure?"

"We will know in a second." He digs into his pocket for his phone, types something into the screen, scrolls for a moment, then hands the phone over to me. "Is this him?"

The picture on the screen is a headshot from LinkedIn, and I recognize the image immediately. It's the man who was choking Wendy to death last night. The same man that I shot in the chest. "It's him," I gasp.

I read the name of the LinkedIn profile: Russell Simonds.

"As of this morning..." Enzo tugs his phone back out of my hands. "He is alive."

He's alive. I didn't kill anyone after all. The relief I feel is somewhat tempered by the fact that even though I didn't kill anyone, the police definitely think I did.

"But this morning he went away on... well, his wife says it is a business trip. This man is very busy, she says. Always working late."

Maybe that's what they were arguing about that day on the street. Or maybe they were arguing because she suspected he was seeing another woman.

Wendy.

"So now what?" I say. "Do we wait until he returns from his alleged business trip?"

"No," Enzo says, "now I find out more about this Russell Simonds."

"How?"

"I know a guy."

Of course he does.

SIXTY-FOUR

We end up going back to Enzo's apartment.

It's only about ten blocks away from where I live, which I guess makes sense if he was taking on the role of my secret bodyguard. The apartment is even smaller than mine, just a studio with one room that serves as the kitchen, bedroom, living room, and dining area. Thankfully, there is a separate bathroom. It's a far cry from the Garricks' penthouse or even Brock's spacious two-bedroom apartment.

When we get inside, Enzo tosses his keys on a small table next to the door, then he goes to the kitchenette, where he turns on the water and splashes it on his face. I wonder if he's as tired as I am. I feel a strange combination of tired and wired. I didn't get enough sleep last night, but anxiety about the police coming for me has got my heart racing at all times.

"You sit down," he tells me. "You want beer?"

"It's barely eleven in the morning."

"It has been a long morning."

That's for sure.

I decide against the beer though. I plop down on a futon that looks like he probably got it from the curb—it's even slightly worse than mine. Most of his furniture looks like it might have been garbage in the recent past.

"What are you doing for work?" I ask him. He had a decent job before he left, but I'm sure they haven't been holding it for him.

"I get job at a landscaping company." He lifts a shoulder. "Is okay. Pays bills."

I look down at his phone, which he has put down on a coffee table. "What is your guy going to find out?"

"I am not sure. Maybe a prison record for Russell. Something we could bring to the police, and they could check the apartment for his fingerprints. I am sure they found unfamiliar prints at the penthouse, so it would help if we could match them—anything to take the heat off you."

"What if it's not enough?"

"I am sure we will find something."

"What if we don't?"

"Trust me," Enzo says, "there is a way. You will not go to jail for something that you did not do."

As if on cue, Enzo's phone starts ringing. He picks it up and leaps off the futon to take the call in the kitchenette. I crane my head to watch his expression, which gives away little. Neither do his responses, which mostly consist of "uh-huh" and "okay." At one point, he grabs a pen and scribbles something down on a paper towel.

"*Grazie*," he tells the person on the other line before he puts his phone down on the kitchen counter.

For a moment, he just stands there, looking down at the paper towel. "Well?" I finally say.

"No prison record," he says. "Record is clean."

My heart sinks. "Okay..."

"I got the address of a second residence," he says. "Is at a lake about two or three hours north of the city. Maybe... maybe this is where he is staying."

I jump off the futon and grab my purse. "So let's go there!"

"And we do what?"

I walk over to where he is standing in the kitchenette. I look down at the address on the napkin. I vaguely know where it is. Google Maps will lead me there. "Get the truth out of him."

"We *know* the truth." He tugs the paper towel out of my reach. "We need the police to know it."

"So what do you suggest?"

"I am not sure." He rubs his eyes with the balls of his hand. "Do not worry. We will come up with an answer. I just need to think."

Great. And while he is thinking, the police are busy building their case against me. "I think we should go out there."

"And I think it will make things worse."

I don't know what to think, but I am itching to *do* something right now. Because the police aren't sitting around in a kitchenette at the moment, mulling things over.

Before I can attempt to persuade Enzo, my phone rings inside my purse. I pull it out, and my breath catches in my throat when I see the name on the screen.

"It's Brock," I say.

SIXTY-FIVE

Enzo's already black eyes darken even further. He's not thrilled to hear that my ex-boyfriend is calling. But he's not the jealous type and he'd never tell me not to answer. And even if he did, I wouldn't listen.

"Just a minute," I say to Enzo.

He nods. "You do what you must."

I knew he'd be okay with it. Well, he doesn't look thrilled. But he doesn't protest, at least.

"Hello?" I say into the phone.

"Millie?" Brock's voice sounds distant, like we're two people who knew each other only briefly and in passing. We only broke up yesterday, and it already seems strange that we once dated. "Hey..."

"Hey," I say stiffly.

I can't imagine what he wants. He doesn't want to get back together, that's for sure. He's probably thanking his lucky stars that we didn't move in together. *You're welcome, Brock.*

"Look," he says, "I... I wanted to apologize for running out on you at the police station yesterday."

"Oh?"

He heaves a sigh. "I was upset, but it was incredibly unprofessional of me. Whatever you did wrong, you asked me to be there as your attorney, and I owed you that."

"Thank you. I appreciate your apology."

"And that's why I'm calling." He pauses. "I spoke to the detective again this morning, and I feel like I owe it to you to warn you that they tested some clothing they took from your laundry hamper."

I grip the phone tighter. "For blood?"

"No, for gunshot residue. And it was positive."

My mouth falls open. I just assumed they were looking for blood on my clothing. It didn't even occur to me that they would be searching for something else. "Oh..."

"I think they were waiting for that to come back for their case to be a slam dunk," he says. "I'm guessing they're obtaining an arrest warrant right now."

I freeze, my knees trembling. "Oh..."

"I'm sorry, Millie. I just wanted to give you a heads-up. I owe you that much."

"Yes..."

"And..." He coughs into the phone. "Good luck, you know, with all *that*."

I turn away from Enzo so he doesn't see my eyes fill with tears. "Thanks."

Thanks for nothing. Thanks for abandoning me when my life is in shambles.

Brock hangs up and I'm left holding the phone to my ear, struggling not to let the tears fall. I am totally screwed. Wendy has brilliantly set me up to take the fall for the murder of a man I never even met.

"Millie." Enzo's large hand drops onto my shoulder. "What happened? What did he say?"

I swipe at my eyes before I turn around. "He said the police found gunshot residue on my clothing that they took from the laundry hamper."

Enzo nods. "If you fire a blank, you still have the gunshot residue on your clothing."

I bury my face in my hands. "Brock says they've probably got a warrant for my arrest, or they will soon. What am I going to do?"

"I will not give up." He grabs me by the shoulders. "Do you understand me? No matter what happens, I will not give up. I will get you free."

I believe he means it. But I don't believe he's capable of getting me out of this mess. If they arrest me, that's it. They're going to stop looking for the real murderer. Everything will be pinned on me, and it sounds like they have a strong case. Gunshot residue on my clothing, my fingerprints on the murder weapon, and the doorman can testify I was in the building at the approximate time of the murder.

I am so screwed.

"I want to go to that cabin on the lake." I glance over at the address scribbled on the paper towel. "I want to find that bastard. I need to get to the bottom of this."

"It will not do any good."

"I don't care," I growl. "I want to see him. I want to look him in the eyes and ask him why he did this to me. And if Wendy is there too, I want to..."

My eyes meet Enzo's. His eyes widen for a moment, then he races over to the kitchen and grabs the paper towel with the address on it before I can get to it. He crumbles it in his hand and holds it under the sink until the ink bleeds.

"No," he says firmly. "I will not let you do something stupid."

"Too late," I say. "I already memorized the address."

"Millie!" His voice is sharp, his eyes wide. "Do *not* go to the cabin. You are not thinking clear right now. You have done nothing wrong and you will not go to prison unless you give them a reason to send you!"

"You're wrong." I lift my chin. "I'm going to prison no matter what. I may as well earn it."

"Millie." He grabs my wrist with his large hand. "I am not going to let you do something stupid. Promise me you will not go to that cabin."

I stare up at him.

"Promise me. You will not leave here unless you promise."

He's not holding me tight enough to hurt me, but enough that I can't get away. He's trying so hard to save me from myself. It's sweet. Brock couldn't get enough of saying it, but Enzo truly does love me. And I believe that even if I do get arrested, he will do everything he can to get me out. He'll do everything he can to expose the truth.

"Fine," I say. "I won't go."

"You promise?"

"I promise."

He releases my wrist. He takes a step back, looking miserable. "And I promise, I will make this right."

I nod. I left my purse on his futon, and I reach for it now. "I may as well go back to my apartment and face the music."

"You want me to go with you?"

"No." I sling my purse on my shoulder. "I don't want you to see it when they snap the cuffs on me."

Enzo reaches for me. He gives me one last kiss, which is honestly almost enough to get me through a couple of years of prison. Nobody can kiss like that man. Brock sure couldn't.

"I promise," he whispers in my ear. "I will not let you back to the prison."

I pull away from him, trembling slightly. "I'm going to go home now."

He squeezes my hand. "I will find you a good lawyer. I will figure out a way to pay for it."

His tiny studio apartment is filled with furniture from the garbage, and I bite my tongue to keep from saying something sarcastic. "I'll miss you."

"I'll miss you too," he says.

"And... I love you."

It didn't feel right when I said it to Brock, but it feels right now. I couldn't leave here without saying it to him.

"I love you too, Millie," he says. "So much."

I do love him. I have always loved him. And that's why I hate lying to him.

But I can't let him know that I've got his car keys stashed away in my purse.

He'll figure it out soon enough.

PART IV

SIXTY-SIX

WENDY

Russell and I are celebrating with a bottle of champagne.

Even though it was a bit of a risk, he drove me out to his cabin on the lake, to get away from the massive number of reporters camped out in front of both the penthouse and the house on Long Island. Technically, this is Marybeth's cabin, and when he leaves her, it will be hers again. That's fine, because I am now rich beyond my wildest dreams. I am rich beyond all human comprehension. I don't need this dinky two-bedroom cabin.

Although it does have an incredibly nice whirlpool setting in the extra-large bathtub. It's like being in a Jacuzzi.

During the drive, we kept an eye in the rearview mirror to make sure no reporters were following us. The last leg of the journey was fairly deserted, so anybody trailing us would have easily been spotted. Russell told Marybeth that he was going on some sort of business trip. Scouting furniture or whatever. I don't care what he told her. She doesn't matter anymore.

"I'm so happy," I murmur. "I don't think I've been this happy in a long time."

Russell smiles, although there's something tight in his

expression. He hasn't made a secret of the fact that he didn't want to kill Douglas. I still can't believe he made me do the dirty work while he cowered in the kitchen. He's lucky he's handsome because I lost a lot of respect for him that night. He should be grateful to me, not looking at me like I'm some sort of *monster*, for heaven's sake.

Well, if he isn't happy, he can go back to his shrew of a wife and I will find somebody new to enjoy my millions of dollars with.

I tip the last of the champagne into Russell's glass. "This is delicious," I say. "Where did you get it?"

"Marybeth likes it." It feels like he's been talking about his wife more often lately, and with less resentment than before. It's not a good sign.

"Do you have any more?" I ask.

"I don't think there's any more champagne. But there may be some wine in the kitchen."

I'm irritated that Russell doesn't offer to get it himself. Men are all the same—in the beginning, they trip over themselves to give you anything you want, but then eventually, they take you for granted. What sort of gentleman doesn't offer to grab a bottle of wine for a woman?

But I'm craving it and the champagne we've been drinking was only half full to begin with, so I grab a towel to wrap around my naked body and I step out of the bathroom and into the living room, my feet making wet prints on the wooden floor. The rain is coming down hard on the porch, dripping down the roof. It's a good thing in case somebody was trying to follow us. There will be no tire tracks to follow.

I step into the kitchen, and sure enough, there's a bottle on the counter. It's pinot noir, three-quarters full, and it looks a bit cheap but better than nothing. I grab it and start to head back to the bathroom, but then I stop short.

One of the windows in the cabin is wide open.

SIXTY-SEVEN

Was that window open when we got here?

I don't remember it being open. Then again, we were more focused on celebrating the fact that Detective Ramirez told me he was planning to arrest Millie Calloway. We got away with it —we really got away with it.

So was it open when we came in? I truly can't remember. It certainly could have been.

And the window is a lot more noticeable now that it's raining. Droplets are streaming inside, dampening the wood surrounding the window. That window should be closed.

I rest the bottle of wine on the end table next to the sofa, then I march over to the window. The raindrops are ice cold, smacking me in the face and peppering my bare arms. After a brief struggle, I manage to get the window closed.

There.

I grab the wine and bring it back to the bathroom, where Russell is still in the tub, his dark hair plastered to his skull. At first, I think his face is wet from the water in the bathtub, but then I realize what's going on.

"Are you *crying*?" I blurt out.

Russell self-consciously wipes his eyes. "I just... I can't believe we killed him. I've never done anything like that."

I don't understand why *Russell* is crying. *I'm* the one who killed Douglas. And I don't feel even the slightest bit sorry. As far as I'm concerned, Douglas deserved everything he got.

"Pull yourself together," I snap at him. "What's done is done. He was a terrible person anyway. He was tormenting me."

"Because you cheated on him."

And that's enough to leave me penniless? Although Russell doesn't know how I lied to Douglas about not being able to have children. Probably better I don't tell him. It will make him feel even worse.

"Look..." I peel off my towel and let it fall to the floor. Then I top off his glass with the maroon liquid as well as filling up my own. "Why don't you let me help you forget about it?"

As I climb back into the tub, immersing myself in the hot liquid, Russell guzzles the contents of the wine glass, leaving behind a red stain on his lips. I decide he has the right idea and I throw back my own glass of wine. It's cheap stuff, so it's not like I need to savor it. After another glass or two, we'll both be feeling a lot better.

SIXTY-EIGHT

I was absolutely right.

After two glasses of wine, Russell isn't crying anymore. And I've got a nice little buzz going. It's been a long time since things have worked out exactly how I wanted. After the last six months, I needed a win, and today was a big win. Douglas is dead, I'm getting a massive inheritance, and Millie is completely taking the fall for everything. She served her purpose quite well.

"I could stay in this tub forever," I sigh as I lean back, my bare skin sliding against Russell's. "This is nice, isn't it?"

"Mm-hmm," he says. "Except I'm kind of sleepy. I might be a little drunk."

I'm not drunk, but I'm definitely feeling slightly buzzed. It's nice. It's so peaceful in the tub, except for some music playing in the distance.

"Wendy," Russell says. "Isn't that your phone?"

He's right.

That must be Joe Bendeck. I asked him to give me a call regarding Douglas's considerable estate. I take a little bit of pleasure in the fact that Joe never liked me, and now I own Douglas's entire estate as well as his company, so I'm essentially

Joe's boss. He has no choice but to suck up to me. I'm going to enjoy being a rich bitch.

This time I reach for a bathrobe, which I wrap around my naked body before dashing out into the living room, where I left my phone on the coffee table. Sure enough, the name Joseph Bendeck is on the screen. I catch it just before the call goes to voicemail.

"Hello, Joe," I say.

"Hey, Wendy."

I take pleasure in how utterly miserable he sounds. It feels good to win.

"You were supposed to call me this afternoon," I remind him. "It's nearly ten o'clock."

"Sorry." There is a bitter edge to his voice. "My best friend was just murdered. I'm not exactly functioning at 100 percent right now."

"Well, that's a problem," I say stiffly as I wander into the kitchen. I look out the window—the rain is really coming down. "You are the executor of Douglas's estate, and if you can't do your job, perhaps somebody else should take your place."

"No. Doug wanted *me*. It's... it's the least I can do to follow his wishes."

"Fine." If he tries any funny business, I'll make sure he is removed from the company. Actually, I should probably remove him anyway. I don't trust him any more than I trusted Douglas at the end. "So when are his assets going to be transferred over to me? I need to be able to pay my bills."

Douglas's death doesn't mean the mortgage won't need to be paid. I don't even have a working credit card because he canceled them all. The penthouse alone has a six-figure mortgage, so I'm going to need some cash—fast.

"You want Doug's money transferred over to you?" Joe asks.

"Yes." I drum my fingers on the kitchen counter. "That's how this works, isn't it?"

"Not exactly..." Joe is silent for a moment. "Wendy, are you aware that Doug changed his will last month?"

What? "No. What are you talking about?"

"He changed his will. Left everything to charity."

A wave of dizziness washes over me. A few months after we got married, Douglas had a will drawn up that left everything to me. I went with him to the attorney to make sure he did it, especially since Douglas was a master procrastinator. It hadn't even occurred to me that he might have changed his will in the short time since we separated. He wouldn't have done that.

Unless...

"You're lying," I spit into the phone. "You're making this up just to keep me from getting any of his money."

"That would be tempting. But no, I'm not making it up. I have a notarized copy of his will right in front of me."

"But..." I sputter. "But how could he do that?"

"Well, when Doug explained it to me, he mentioned something about you being a lying, manipulative bitch, and he didn't want you to have any of his money."

My heart seems to skip in my chest, and for a moment, my vision blurs in and out. How could this be happening? Douglas mentioned giving all his money to charity, but I never imagined he had already put the wheels in motion.

"This is an outrage," I rant. "He can't cut me out of his will! I'm his wife, for God's sake! I will fight this, and believe me, I will win."

"Okay. Whatever you say, Wendy. But in the meantime, I'm going to need you to vacate both the penthouse and the house on the island, because we're putting them up for sale."

"Go to hell," I hiss into the phone.

I click the red button on my phone to end the call, but my hands are shaking. I have to believe that Douglas couldn't just sign a paper saying he's leaving me with nothing, and that's it. I can fight this. And with Douglas gone, he can't fight back. One way or another, I'm going to get my fair share.

Although I won't have quite the estate that I had imagined. But that's okay.

While I'm staring at my phone, trying to figure out my next move, it starts to ring again in my hand. I suck in a breath at the identity of the caller:

The New York Police Department.

SIXTY-NINE

It must be Detective Ramirez. He called me hours ago, back when I was in the city, to let me know they were going to arrest Millie. I'm hoping this is a follow-up call to let me know that she is safely behind bars.

Hopefully, this will not be as upsetting as the last call.

"Hello?" I say into the phone, trying to sound like a heart-broken widow. Those acting classes I took in college are paying off. I deserve an Academy award for my performance in front of Millie.

"Mrs. Garrick?" It's Ramirez's voice. "This is Detective Ramirez."

"Hello, Detective. I'm hoping you have that woman who killed my husband safely behind bars!"

"Actually..." Oh Lord, now what? "We have not been able to locate Wilhelmina Calloway. We came to her apartment with an arrest warrant, and she wasn't there."

"Well, where is she?"

"If we knew, we would have arrested her, wouldn't we?"

Again, I feel that skip in my chest. "What are you doing to find that woman? She's very dangerous, you know."

"Don't worry. We're going to track her down eventually. I promise."

"Good. I'm glad you have a handle on things."

"But there's one other thing I need to talk to you about, Mrs. Garrick."

What now? I glance in the direction of the bathroom. I don't know why Russell is still in there when he knows I've gotten out. He's going to get all pruny. "Of course, Detective."

"So here's the thing." Ramirez clears his throat. "The building manager for the penthouse has been out of town the last two days. Over in Europe, and we couldn't get a hold of him. Anyway, I finally talked to him this afternoon, and he told me something really interesting."

"Oh?"

"He said that there's a security camera at the back door of the building."

I think my heart stops for a good five seconds. "Excuse me?"

"Somehow we missed it," he says. "He says he puts it out of sight because the residents don't like to feel like they're getting spied on. And here's the funny part—*your husband* was the one who provided the security equipment from his company about a year ago, because he was worried about that back entrance."

"He... he did?" I choke out. There is a crash that seems to be coming from the bathroom, followed by a splash of water, but I ignore it. If Russell tried to get out of the bathroom and fell, he's just going to have to get up on his own.

"Yeah, and we just got done reviewing all the tapes. And it's crazy—according to those tapes, your husband hasn't been in that apartment in *months*. Like, the entire time Miss Calloway was working there. So I don't know how she was having an affair with him in the apartment if he was never even there. You know?"

My mouth feels almost too dry to get out any words, but I manage to say, "Maybe they were meeting somewhere else?"

"Maybe. Except I don't see any credit card bills for hotel rooms or anything like that."

"Of course he wouldn't pay with his credit card. Then I would see it. He probably paid cash."

"You might be right," Ramirez concedes. "But here's the *really* crazy part. The night that your husband was murdered, he didn't show up at the back entrance until *after* the time when the doorman saw Millie leaving the building."

"That... that's strange..."

If he saw that footage, he must also know I was in the building at the same time Douglas was murdered. And if he knows that, I'm in very deep trouble.

"Listen," he says, "I was wondering if you could come to the station to clear up some confusion on our parts. We're sending a squad car over to your house."

"I... I'm not at my house right now..."

"Oh yeah? Where are you then?"

I pull the phone away from my ear. Detective Ramirez's voice sounds suddenly distant: "Hello? Mrs. Garrick?"

I press the red button to end the call and drop the phone on the counter, like it might scald me. I lean over the kitchen sink, pushing away a wave of nausea and dizziness.

I can't believe there was a camera at the back door. I asked *specifically* about it, and I was told there wasn't one. But that was before Douglas so kindly provided one, because of course he would do something like that—that's the kind of concerned, generous, technology-loving geek my husband was. Or maybe it was yet another attempt to document me screwing around behind his back.

If there was a camera, it will be enough to exonerate Millie. And place a very big nail in my coffin.

I rub my temples, which have started to throb. I have to figure out a way to spin this, because I am *not* spending the rest of my life in prison. But I have some ideas. I already played the role of the abused wife so well for Millie. I'll just have to tell the story of my terrible, abusive husband. Maybe on that fateful night, he was coming at me, ready to beat me senseless, and I did what I had to do. Self-defense is legal—it was him or me.

This could work.

"Russell!" I call out. "We need to talk."

Russell is a huge complication. If the police went through the video feed of the back door, they would have seen him entering that night as well. But perhaps there's nothing to tie him to me directly. He and I have to get our stories straight. I hope he isn't a baby about this whole thing. I can imagine him breaking down and telling the police the entire sordid story.

I sprint over to the bathroom. Russell is not going to be happy to hear this—it was too much to expect entirely smooth sailing. We will get through this, one way or another. I've been in bad jams before and got out of them.

"Russell," I say again, "what—"

As I walk into the doorway of the bathroom, the first thing I see is all the red. So much red, swimming before my eyes. The water in the tub that used to be clear, bordering on foggy, is now a deep crimson color. I lift my eyes and locate the source of the blood, coming from a gaping wound on Russell's throat.

And then I look at his face. At his slack jaw. At his eyes, staring straight ahead, unblinking.

SEVENTY

Russell is dead.

Murdered.

And it happened between the time I left the bathroom and right now.

I think back to that open window I spotted when I came outside before to get the wine. Somebody got into this cabin. Somebody came into this cabin and did this to Russell.

I'm scared I know who that person is. There is one person who has a vendetta out for me right now, as well as a history of violent behavior. And the police were unable to find her.

"Millie?" I call out.

No answer.

And then the lights go out.

I'd like to say it was the storm, but I don't think the wind is strong enough to kill the power. Somebody cut the power.

I hug my arms to my chest as a chill goes through me. The cabin has gone pitch black now that the power is out. I've got my phone and was getting some reception, but I left it all the way in the kitchen. If she's smart, she has probably taken it by now. Which means I have no way to call for help.

"Millie?" I call out again.

There's no answer. She's toying with me—she must hate me right now. And she has every right to hate me. She was trying to help me, and I pinned everything on her. She made it way too easy.

And now my friend Audrey's words ring out in my head: *She's hardcore, believe me—she's dangerous.*

Millie is extremely dangerous. That much is clear.

And I have made an enemy of her.

"Millie," I squeak out. "Please listen to me. I... I'm sorry. I shouldn't have done what I did. But you have to know, Douglas *was* abusive. I was telling you the truth."

Glass shatters somewhere on the other side of the room. I jerk my head in the direction of the sound. Unless Millie has night vision goggles, she has got to be as blind as I am in the dark. Maybe I can somehow use that to my advantage.

"Douglas did all these terrible things to me. He was horrific as a husband. I needed to get out of that marriage. You have to understand..."

Millie is still not answering. But I can feel her seething rage. I have messed with the wrong woman.

"Millie," I continue, "you have to know, I wasn't faking it. And your kindness to me... It meant everything. I had to do what I did."

There's a flash of lightning, and it's just bright enough to show that I've got a clean shot at the kitchen. The kitchen, which is filled with knives and other things that I could theoretically use as a weapon, even if she's taken my phone.

To hell with reasoning with that psychopath. If she wants a fight, she's going to get one.

I sprint in the direction of the kitchen. Millie's footsteps are behind me, but I don't stop. I keep my arms out in front of me, hoping I don't run straight into a wall. By the grace of God, I make it into the kitchen. I move past the small kitchen table, trying not to trip over it. I make it past that hurdle, and then my feet slip out from under me.

There's blood all over the floor.

It must be Russell's blood, tracked in here by the soles of her shoes. When I close my eyes, I can still see him lying in the bathroom, his throat slit, his eyes staring at nothing. Millie did that to him, and he's not even the one she truly hates. I can't even imagine what she must have in store for me.

I'm not going to give her a chance to do it. I'm going to go down swinging. She may be tough, but so am I.

I scramble to my feet, even though my right hip is throbbing from the fall. I feel my way to the kitchen counter, and I blindly grope around for the block of knives. I definitely saw a block of knives on the counter. I'm not imagining it.

Please be here. Please.

But my hands come up empty. I can't feel anything that resembles a weapon on the kitchen counter. Of course, Millie is too smart for that. I was only able to fool her before because she trusted me, but now that she knows my game, she has anticipated all my moves. She has already murdered one person tonight, and she has every intention of making me her next victim.

I feel around for the stove. I'm certain I saw a frying pan on it. If I could grab that and somehow swing it at her hard enough, I might be able to take her down. It's my only chance.

But then I hear the footsteps behind me, growing closer. Too close.

Oh God. She's in the kitchen with me.

SEVENTY-ONE

I grope around blindly. Millie is right behind me. Probably less than six feet away. If only there were another bolt of lightning. Then I might be able to find something that I could use against her. But it's too dark. I can't see what's right in front of me.

"Wendy," she says.

I turn around, backing up against the stove. My heart feels like it's going to explode out of my chest, and for a moment, the room starts to spin. I take a deep breath, trying to calm myself down. It won't do me any good if I pass out. I'd probably wake up with my hands and feet bound together.

My eyes have managed to adjust to the dark. I can clearly make out Millie's silhouette across the room. And then something glints in her right hand.

It's a knife. It must be the same one she used to kill Russell, probably still wet with his blood.

Oh God.

"Please," I beg her. "I can give you whatever you want. I'm going to be filthy rich."

Millie takes a step closer.

"I know you've been struggling financially," I babble on. "I can pay for your entire education. Your rent. And then a bonus on top of that. You'll never have to worry about money again."

I can just barely see it in the dark kitchen, but Millie's silhouette shakes her head.

"I'll tell the police I got it wrong." My voice has taken on a hysterical quality. "I'll tell them you weren't there at all. I was mistaken about everything."

I may as well promise that, considering the police have the videotapes that show Millie wasn't ever in the apartment at the same time as the real Douglas. But Millie doesn't know that. When I get out of here, there's a good chance that the police will take me into custody, but I accept that. I'll go to jail if I have to, but I don't want to die.

Millie doesn't seem to be moved by my offer. She takes another step forward while I try to back away, but there is nowhere for me to go.

"Please," I beg her. "*Please* don't do this."

A bolt of lightning illuminates the room at that moment—too late to help me find a weapon on the counter. My eyes strain to take in the tiny bit of light, and for a moment, I can clearly see the face of the woman moving toward me with a knife in her right hand.

Oh, Jesus Christ.

It's not Millie.

SEVENTY-TWO

"Marybeth?" I whisper.

My husband's secretary—who also happens to be Russell's wife—is standing only a few feet away from me now, her eyes boring into me. I've never been frightened of Marybeth before. Even when I was sleeping with her husband, I never gave her a second thought. She seemed nice enough, and Russell never told me otherwise.

I have underestimated her. Russell's slashed throat is proof of that.

I am more attractive than Marybeth—objectively. She's about ten years older than I am, and she looks it. Her blond hair is stringy, she has fine lines around her eyes and around her mouth, and the skin under her chin hangs too loose. But then the kitchen is plunged back into darkness, and she becomes a silhouette once again.

"Sit down," Marybeth says.

"I... I can't see anything," I stutter.

For a second, I am blinded by another flash of light—she has turned on the flashlight on her cell phone. She shines it in the direction of the kitchen table: a small wooden square with two folding chairs on either side. I stumble toward the table and collapse into one of the two seats seconds before my legs give out.

Marybeth sits in the other chair. Now that we have the light from the phone, I can make out the features on her face again. Her lips are a straight line, and her usually mild blue eyes are like daggers. She's wearing a trench coat that is stained in Russell's blood. She looks absolutely terrifying.

But I take some solace in the fact that she has not yet killed me. She wants me alive for some reason, and that buys me some time to figure out how to get out of here.

"What do you want?" I ask her.

She blinks at me. The whites of her eyes are glowing, set in dark hollow sockets. "How long have you been sleeping with my husband?"

I open my mouth, debating if I should lie. But then I look into her eyes and realize it's better not to mess around with this woman. "Ten months."

"Ten *months*." She spits out the words. "Right under my nose. You know, we were *happy* before you came along. For twenty *years*. He wasn't perfect, but he loved me." Her voice breaks. "And then as soon as he met you..."

"I'm so sorry. It's not like we planned it."

"But you did have plans. Big plans. He was planning to leave me for you..."

She doesn't say it like it's a question, so I keep my mouth shut. Russell claimed he was planning to leave Marybeth for me, but at the very end, I wasn't so sure anymore. He ended up not being the man I thought he was. "He loved you very much," I finally say, hoping to placate her.

"Then why was he sleeping with *you?*" she bursts out.

"Look," I say, trying to stay calm even though my heart is still racing, "he wanted to go back to you. He was having doubts. If you hadn't..."

She stares at me. I can't forget that this woman just murdered her husband. She isn't looking to get back together with him. The only thing on her mind is vengeance.

"And Doug..." Her eyes are like ice as they stare into mine. "You killed him, didn't you? You and Russell."

I open my mouth, ready to deny it. But then I see the look in her eyes, and I realize it wasn't a question. "Yes, I did."

For a split second, her eyes soften as they fill with tears. "Doug Garrick was a really good man—the best. He was like a brother to me."

"I know. And... I'm sorry."

"Sorry!" she bursts out. "You didn't cut in front of him in line at the movie theater. You murdered him! He's dead because of you!"

I press my lips together, afraid to say another word because nothing I say will make it right. Marybeth is furious with me—I slept with her husband and I killed her beloved boss. But that doesn't mean I deserve to die here, at her hands.

I've got to find a way out of this.

My eyes fall on the knife in her right hand. She has it on her lap, and it's still wet with Russell's blood—his blood is absolutely everywhere. Is there any chance I could get the knife from her? Marybeth isn't exactly in peak physical condition.

"What do you want from me?" I ask her.

She reaches into the pocket of her trench coat and pulls out a piece of white paper. Then she rifles around until she finds a pen. She slides both items across the kitchen table to me.

"I want you to write a confession," she says.

Bile rises in my throat, and I have to push it back down again. "What?"

"You heard me." Her eyes flash. "I want you to write down everything you did. How you seduced Russell. How the two of you conspired to kill your husband. I want a full confession."

"Okay..." I don't want to do this, but I saw what she did to

Russell. The thought of her slitting my throat like she did to him...

"Do it!"

My hands won't stop shaking as I write my confession on the white piece of paper, which is now stained with crimson fingerprints. I don't know exactly what she wants me to say, so I try to keep it simple. I'm not too worried about it, because nothing that I write while held at knifepoint is going to stand up in court.

> *To whom it may concern,*
>
> *I have been having an affair with Russell Simonds for the last ten months. Together, the two of us killed my husband, Douglas Garrick.*

I study her facial features. Her face gives nothing away. "Is this what you want?" I ask.

"Yes, but you're not finished."

"What more do you want me to say?"

"Here's what you need to write." She taps the paper with her long fingernail. "*I can no longer live with the guilt.*"

I scribble down the sentence, which is almost illegible because my hands are trembling so much. For a second, the page blurs and I can't even keep writing, but then it comes back into focus.

"*So tonight,*" she continues, "*I have decided to take both our lives.*"

I stop writing, the pen falling from my numb fingertips. "Marybeth..."

"Write it!"

She raises the knife, bringing it close to my face. I close my eyes for a second, remembering the gaping wound on Russell's throat. Oh God. This woman means business. I write down the final sentence of my confession.

"Now sign your name," Marybeth says.

I do it. I'm not in a position to refuse.

She takes my signed confession and reads it over, although she still has one eye on me. "Good," she says.

I realize what has to be next. The confession ends with me saying that I am taking my own life. Which means that by the end of the night, she is going to kill me. The thought makes me extremely dizzy, and even though this woman is threatening me with a knife, I race over to the kitchen sink to throw up. She lets me go.

I lean over at the sink, dry heaving even after I have emptied my stomach. I have stained the sink red with my vomit, because of the pinot noir. The kitchen chair creaks behind me, and a second later, Marybeth is standing next to me at the sink.

"Please don't do this," I beg her.

She tilts her head. "Isn't this what you did to Doug? Don't you think you deserve it?"

It was different with Douglas. He treated me so horribly, I had no choice. And even in death, he continues to torment me with his will. God, how am I going to fight that stupid will? But I'll worry about that when I get out of here. First, I have to talk this woman down from the ledge.

"Everyone makes mistakes," I say. "I feel terrible for the things I've done. And now I have to live with it."

"That's not enough," she says.

My chest feels tight, like a corset is squeezing me. "It's not enough to send me to jail for the rest of my life?"

"No. You deserve worse. You are a truly despicable person. And you deserve to die in a painful and horrible way."

The corset tightens further. "So what do you think is going to happen? You think the police will believe that I stabbed myself to death? People don't really do that. They're going to know that somebody did this to me."

Marybeth is quiet for a moment. "You're right," she says

thoughtfully. "They would realize it wasn't a suicide if you were stabbed."

Oh, thank God. I finally got this woman to listen to reason. "Exactly."

"That's why you're not going to die that way."

I get another wave of dizziness that nearly knocks me off my feet. "What? What are you talking about?"

Does she have another weapon in here? A gun? A nunchuck? What is this woman going to do to me?

"Have you ever heard of a medication called digoxin?" she asks.

Digoxin? Why does that sound familiar?

Then it hits me. Douglas used to take that medication. For his heart. And Marybeth has a copy of the keys to the house in Long Island where he keeps his medicine.

"Digoxin toxicity is extremely serious," she continues. "First, you get nausea, dizziness, terrible abdominal cramps, and blurred vision. It's quite agonizing. But the way it kills you is that your heart goes into a deadly arrhythmia."

"So," I say slowly, "you expect me to swallow a bunch of digoxin?"

If she asks me to swallow pills, I'll have to find a way out of it. I can put them under my tongue and spit them out when I have a chance. She can't force me.

But then her lips curl into a smile. "You already have, Wendy."

Oh my God, *the wine.*

I heave into the sink once again, and nothing comes up. Simultaneously, my stomach is seized by an eye-watering cramp. Despite my growing dizziness, I have done a good job staying on my feet, but now I sink to the floor, clutching my stomach.

Marybeth crouches down beside me. "I'm not sure how

long this will take. Another hour? Two hours? There's no rush. Nobody's looking for us here."

I look up at her. Her face blurs in and out. "Please take me to the hospital."

"I don't think so."

"Please," I gasp. "Have mercy..."

"Like you had mercy for Doug?"

I reach out, my fingers barely grazing against the leg of her jeans. I try to hold on to her, but it's like my hand won't obey my commands anymore. "I'll do anything you want. I'll give you anything you want. I promise."

"And I promise," Marybeth says, "that your death will be slow and painful. And unlike you, I never break my promises."

SEVENTY-THREE

MILLIE

It's time to face the music.

I slept in Enzo's car last night. I knew the police had a warrant for my arrest, and I just wasn't ready to be locked up again. So I hid out, parked in a dark alley, sleeping in the backseat. There was a time when I used to live in my car, so sleeping in the backseat gave me some serious déjà vu.

It also made me realize that I can't sleep in the backseat of Enzo's car forever. I have to turn myself in and hope that the truth comes out.

When I pull up in front of my apartment building, I expect to see half the police force out there, camped out and waiting for me. But instead, there's just a single patrol car. Still, I know it's there for me.

Sure enough, as soon as I step out of Enzo's Mazda, a young police officer leaps out of the patrol car. "Wilhelmina Calloway?" he asks.

"Yes," I confirm.

Wilhelmina Calloway, you are under arrest. I brace myself for him to say the words, but he doesn't. "Would you come down with me to the police station?"

"Am I under arrest?"

He shakes his head. "Not as far as I know. Detective Ramirez would very much like to talk to you, but you're not under obligation to go."

Okay then. That's a good start.

I climb into the back of the police car. I've had my phone off the entire night, and I turn it on now. There are a few missed calls from the NYPD, and twenty missed calls from Enzo. He must've figured out I took his car. I don't listen to the voicemails, but I scroll through the long string of text messages he sent me.

Where are you?

Do you have my car?

You took my car!

Please come back with my car. We will talk.

Don't go to that cabin!

Where are you? Very worried.

Please come back. Don't go to the cabin. I love you.

I will fix this. Come back.

And it just goes on like that.

The text messages continue through the night. He has been up half the night worried about me. I owe him an explanation, or at least to tell him I'm okay. So I sent him a text:

I'm OK. In the back of a police car right now. Not under arrest. Your car is in front of my building.

Enzo's reply comes almost instantly, like he was staring at his phone, waiting for me to text him:

Where were you???????

I write back:

I slept in the car. Everything is fine.

Three bubbles appear on the screen as he types. I expect him to say something like he loves me or he was worried, or perhaps scold me for stealing his car. But instead, he says something extremely unexpected:

Wendy Garrick is dead. I saw on the news.

What? How???

She killed herself.

SEVENTY-FOUR

The interrogation room doesn't seem quite as scary this time.

While I was in the patrol car, I was gobbling up every story I could find about Wendy Garrick's suicide. Apparently, she slashed her boyfriend's throat, then swallowed a bunch of pills. She even left a suicide note.

This adds an entirely new dimension to what happened to Douglas Garrick.

I've been in the room for about half an hour when Detective Ramirez finally strides in. He still has that serious expression on his face, but it doesn't seem quite as ominous anymore. He just looks... perplexed.

"Hello, Miss Calloway," he says as he slides into the seat across from me.

"Hello, Detective," I say.

His brows knit together. "Did you hear what happened to Wendy Garrick?"

"I did. It was on the news."

"You should know," he says, "that in her suicide note, she also confessed to Mr. Garrick's murder."

I allow myself a teeny, tiny smile. "So I'm no longer a suspect?"

"Actually..." He leans back in his plastic chair, which creaks under his weight. "You already were no longer a suspect. It turns out there was a camera at the back entrance that nobody knew about. We reviewed the video feed, and it looks like you were never even in the apartment building at the same time as Mr. Garrick."

"Right. Wendy set me up."

This whole time there was a camera. All the panic and stress of the last two days... and all along, the proof of my innocence was right there.

He nods. "That's what it looks like. So I want to apologize. You can see how we might have thought that you were responsible for the murder."

"Of course. I have a prison record, so if a crime is committed, I must be the one who did it."

Ramirez has the good grace to appear embarrassed. "I did jump to some conclusions, but you have to admit, it didn't look good for you. And Wendy Garrick was so insistent that you had to be responsible."

He's right. She did a good job setting me up. But if she'd just been a little bit smarter, she wouldn't have had to set me up at all. In the end, Wendy Garrick made things a lot harder for herself than she needed to. She could've learned a lot from me.

The whole experience has soured me though. I helped a lot of women over the years, and although it didn't always go according to plan, I always felt like I was fighting the good fight. When women came to me for help, I never felt any hesitation to do the right thing.

But now I've started to wonder. Wendy legitimately seemed like a victim. It's going to be hard to trust the next person who comes to me for help after this experience. And that's one of the things I resent about her the most.

"So I'm no longer a suspect?" I ask Ramirez.

"That's right. As far as I'm concerned, the case is closed."

Douglas is dead. They know Wendy is responsible. And she's dead too. No need for an investigation, or any more arrests, or a trial. I'm free.

"Then I don't understand. Why am I here?"

"Well..." Ramirez smiles sheepishly. "It turns out you have a bit of a reputation."

"A reputation?" My stomach churns slightly—this doesn't sound good. "As what?"

"As a hero."

"A... excuse me?"

"I recognize you thought you were trying to help Mrs. Garrick," he says, "because you've helped other women before. And I want you to know, it's appreciated. We see some bad stuff in here, and sometimes we get to the victims too late."

His comment hits home. I have done everything possible to keep it from ever being "too late." And no matter where the future takes me—as a housemaid or a social worker—I'm going to keep right on doing it. "I... I do the best I can with the resources I have."

"I understand that." He smiles at me. "And I just want you to know that you can consider me one more resource. I want you to have my card, and if you ever see any situation where a woman is in danger, I want you to give me a call right away—I wrote my cell number on the back. This time, I promise I'll believe you."

He slides his card across the table. I pick it up, staring down at his name. Benito Ramirez. Finally—a friend on the police force. I can hardly believe it. "Just to be clear, you're not hitting on me, right?"

He throws his head back and laughs. "No—I'm too old for you. And I assumed you're with that Italian guy who came to the police station yesterday, making a fuss about you, about how we had the wrong person and he wasn't leaving until we listened to what he had to say. I thought we were going to have to arrest the guy."

I smile to myself. "Really?"

"Oh yeah. In fact, he's out there right now. He won't leave the waiting room until he gets to see you."

"Well then," I say, still unable to wipe that smile off my face (although I'm not really trying), "I guess I'll be heading out."

When I stand up, Ramirez stands too. He holds out his hand to me, and I shake it. Then I head out to meet Enzo and finally go home.

EPILOGUE

MILLIE

Three months later

I don't understand how Enzo had so much stuff in that little studio apartment of his.

He walks into my apartment, carrying what feels like the ten millionth box filled with his belongings, and sets it down on top of another box. Okay, it isn't torture watching Enzo carry boxes, the muscles in his arms bulging under his T-shirt, but for God's sake, what is in all these boxes? The man seems to rotate through like seven or eight T-shirts and two pairs of blue jeans. What else could he possibly have?

"Is that all of it?" I ask him, as he wipes sweat off his brow.

"No. Is two more."

"Two more!"

I am sort of starting to regret this. Well, not really. After breaking up with Brock, Enzo and I continued right where we left off before he went to Italy. Except this time we both knew we couldn't live without each other. So when he eventually pointed out that he was throwing away rent money every month when he was already spending all his nights at my apartment, I was quick to suggest that he move in with me.

It's funny. When it's right, you just know it's right.

"Two small boxes," Enzo says. "Is nothing."

"Hmm," I say. I don't believe him. His definition of "small box" is something that weighs less than I do.

He grins at me. "Sorry I am so annoying."

He is not annoying at all. In fact, he is the only reason I was allowed to stay in this apartment at all. Mrs. Randall was still ready to give me the boot, even after I was completely exonerated, but Enzo went to talk to her, and she was suddenly happy to let me stay. He *is* quite charming.

Enzo crosses the room to put his arms around me. Even though he's a little sweaty from carrying boxes back and forth between our apartments, I don't care. I still let him kiss me. Always.

"Okay," he says when he finally pulls away. "I go get other boxes."

I groan. The two of us are going to have to go through these boxes together and get rid of a *lot* of stuff. Also, I have a plan to clear out some drawer space today.

A few minutes after Enzo takes off, the buzzer rings for the door downstairs. Enzo mentioned ordering some pizza for dinner, but I don't think he put in the order yet. So that means there's only one person who could be down there.

I hit the buzzer to let him up.

A minute later, I hear the pounding on my door. I grab the box that's been sitting on top of my bed and carry it out to the living room. I keep it balanced in one arm while I unlock the door with the other.

Brock is standing at my door. As always, he is dressed in one of his expensive suits, his hair perfectly styled, his teeth gleaming white. It's the first time I've seen him in three months, and it's like I forgot how flawlessly handsome he is. I'm sure he is going to make some woman a wonderful husband someday. But it was never going to be me.

"Hey," he says. "You got my stuff?"

"It's all right here."

I heft the box into Brock's waiting arms. When I was trying to clear space for Enzo, I noticed I still had a drawer filled with Brock's clothing and random belongings he left behind. I considered just tossing it all, but I remembered the way he gave me a heads-up when the police had a warrant for my arrest, and I decided to call him and ask if he wanted his stuff back. He told me he would come by the next day.

"Thanks, Millie," he says.

"No problem."

He hesitates at the door. "You look good."

Oh God, are we playing *that* game? "Thanks. You too," I say. And then because I can't help myself, I ask, "Are you seeing anyone?"

He shakes his head. "No one special."

He doesn't ask me the same question, which I'm grateful for. After all the times I turned him down when he asked me to live with him, it would be hurtful to tell him that I'm moving in with Enzo. And despite the way things ended with Brock, when he walked out on me at the police station, I know he loved me. Much more than I loved him.

"Well..." He shifts the box between his arms. "Good luck with... everything."

"You too. I guess I'll see you around." I don't know why I added that last part. I'll probably never see him again.

I'm about to close the door when Brock puts out his hand to stop me. "Oh, hey. Millie?"

"Yes?"

He shakes the box, looks down at the contents, then looks back up at me. "Is my extra bottle of pills in here?"

I dig my fingernails into my palm. "What?"

"My extra bottle of digoxin," he clarifies. "The one I used to keep in your medicine cabinet for when I spent the night. Do you still have it? I take the extra bottle when I go on trips."

"Um..." I dig my nails deeper into the skin. "No, I.... I haven't seen it in the medicine cabinet. I must've tossed it. Sorry."

He waves a hand. "No worries. I'm just glad you didn't throw out my Yale hoodie."

Brock waves goodbye to me one last time, and instead of shutting the door, I watch him walk down the stairs, holding my breath the entire time. I don't let out the breath until he's disappeared from sight.

I didn't think he would remember that bottle of pills he left in the medicine cabinet. But I certainly remembered it. When I first found it in there back when we were dating, I looked up the medication, just to learn more about my boyfriend. That's how I found out that digoxin in large doses can cause fatal arrhythmias. It was a fact I filed away in the back of my head at the time.

Digoxin, despite its dangers, is a commonly used heart medication. So common that even Douglas Garrick was on it for his atrial fibrillation. But the pills that Wendy Garrick overdosed on did not come from Douglas's stash, as the police assumed.

After I took Enzo's car keys, right after I heard there was likely a warrant for my arrest, I didn't drive out to that cabin after all—I kept my promise to Enzo. Instead, I drove into Manhattan. I went to the apartment of Russell Simonds's wife Marybeth, who happened to be an employee of the real Douglas Garrick, and I introduced myself.

Marybeth turned out to be a lovely woman. She was quite broken up over the death of her boss, and I felt terrible having to explain what I knew about her husband. But she felt a lot better after we had a nice long chat. And after recalling a hefty life insurance policy Russell took out a few years ago, Marybeth decided to take a little therapeutic drive out to that cabin in the woods.

And as for me, I went on my way, minus one bottle of digoxin.

The ironic part is that if Wendy had instead slipped her husband a little bit extra of his own medication, it probably would have killed him, and it might have been hard to prove that the dose wasn't accidental. She could have saved herself a lot of trouble.

Instead, she made an incredibly bad judgment call. She underestimated an extremely dangerous person.

Me.

And she paid the ultimate price.

A LETTER FROM FREIDA

Dear readers,

I want to say a huge thank you for choosing to read *The Housemaid's Secret*. If you did enjoy it, and want to keep up to date with all my latest releases from Bookouture, just sign up at the following link. Your email address will never be shared and you can unsubscribe at any time.

www.bookouture.com/freida-mcfadden

I hope you loved *The Housemaid's Secret* and if you did, I would be very grateful if you could write a review. I'd love to hear what you think, and it makes such a difference helping new readers to discover one of my books for the first time.

Also, I love hearing from readers! Send me an email at freida@freidamcfadden.com. And don't be shocked when I answer! You can also get in touch with me through my Facebook group, Freida McFans.

Check out my website at:
www.freidamcfadden.com

For more information about my books, please follow me on Amazon! You can also follow me on BookBub!

Thanks!

Freida

KEEP IN TOUCH WITH FREIDA

facebook.com/freidamcfaddenauthor

twitter.com/Freida_McFadden

instagram.com/fizzziatrist

goodreads.com/7244758.Freida_McFadden

amazon.com/Freida-McFadden/e/BooELQLN2I

bookbub.com/authors/freida-mcfadden

ACKNOWLEDGMENTS

I want to thank Bookouture for helping make the first Housemaid book such a spectacular success and supporting me in this sequel. Thank you to my editor, Ellen Gleeson, who has an amazing insight into my books and boundless enthusiasm! Thank you to my mother for your early feedback, as well as to Kate. And as always, thank you to my incredibly supportive readers—you make it worthwhile!

Made in the USA
Middletown, DE
15 April 2023

28918099R00187